Eighteenth-Century Novels by Women

Isobel Grundy, Editor

Advisory Board

Paula R. Backscheider
David L. Blewett
Margaret A. Doody
Jan Fergus
J. Paul Hunter
John Richetti
Betty Rizzo

THE EXCURSION

Frances Brooke

PAULA R. BACKSCHEIDER
& HOPE D. COTTON,
EDITORS

THE UNIVERSITY PRESS OF KENTUCKY

Copyright © 1997 by The University Press of Kentucky
Scholarly publisher for the Commonwealth, serving Bellarmine College,
Berea College, Centre College of Kentucky, Eastern Kentucky University,
The Filson Club, Georgetown College, Kentucky Historical Society,
Kentucky State University, Morehead State University, Murray State
University, Northern Kentucky University, Transylvania University,
University of Kentucky, University of Louisville,
and Western Kentucky University.

Editorial and Sales Offices: The University Press of Kentucky
663 South Limestone Street, Lexington, Kentucky 40508-4008

96 97 98 99 00   5 4 3 2 1

Library of Congress Cataloging-in-Publication Data

Brooke, Frances, 1724?-1789
    The excursion / Frances Brooke ; Paula R. Backscheider and Hope D.
Cotton, editors.
        p. cm. — (Eighteenth-century novels by women)
    ISBN 0-8131-1979-0 (cloth : alk. paper). — ISBN 0-8131-1979-0
(pbk.: alk. paper) —ISBN 0-8131-0881-0
    I. Backscheider, Paula R.   II. Cotton, Hope D.   III. Title.
IV. Series.
PR3326.B37B33   1997
823'.6—dc20   96-26708

Contents

~

Acknowledgments   vii

Introduction   ix

Chronology   xlvii

Note on the Text   li

The Excursion

Preface to the Second Edition   1

First Edition   3

Notes to the Novel   155

Revisions Made in the Second Edition   171

Selected Bibliography   179

Acknowledgments

~

Much of the work on this edition was done during the summer of 1994, while I directed an NEH Summer Seminar for College Teachers. I would like to thank the students in the seminar for their intellectual stimulation and practical contributions, especially those of Elizabeth Larsen, Carol Wilson, and Susan Westbury. Antonia Forster, a friend from my 1992 NEH Seminar, generously shared the Brooke entries from her forthcoming *Index to Book Reviews in England, 1749-1774*, volume 2.

Hope and I are indebted to Linda Thornton, Glenn Anderson, Cassidy Chestnut, Boyd Childress, and many other members of the efficient, friendly Auburn University Library staff. We appreciate the help of Mary Kuntz, Samia Spencer, and John Richetti with foreign language annotations and thank Daniel Ennis, Elizabeth Russell, and Randall Smith for their help with the copy text. Support for the work has come from the West Point Pepperell–H.M. Philpott Fund, Auburn University.

Paula Backscheider

INTRODUCTION

~

The heroine of Frances Brooke's *The Excursion* (1777) comes to London with a novel, an epic poem, and a tragedy, which she believes the guarantee of her fame and economic security. Brooke herself may not have arrived in London in 1748 with her luggage stuffed with manuscripts, but before she died at age sixty-five she had published almost every kind of economically profitable literary type—and succeeded notably at each. At the midpoint of her career, a reviewer for the *Critical Review* wrote that Brooke was so well known "it would be superfluous . . . to say anything of her literary abilities." In the year *The Excursion* came out, a poem in the *Monthly Review* praised her and her generation of gifted women writers:

> To Greece no more the tuneful maids belong,
> Nor the high honours of immortal song;
> To Moore, Brooke, Lenox, Aikin, Carter due,
> . . . .
> Theirs the strong genius, theirs the voice divine.

At the beginning of the nineteenth century, Laetitia Barbauld wrote that Brooke was "an elegant and accomplished woman" and "perhaps the first female novel-writer who attained a perfect purity and polish of style."[1]

EARLY LIFE

Frances Moore Brooke was the daughter of Thomas and Mary Knowles Moore; she was christened on 24 January 1724 in the parish of Claypole, Lincolnshire. Her father was curate there, and both her parents' families had produced generations of Lincolnshire clergymen.[2] She and her two younger sisters were left fatherless in 1727, the year the youngest was born. Mary and her daughters moved in with Sarah Knowles, Mary's widowed mother in Peterborough, where they lived for ten years. Mary Moore died in 1737, the year after her mother; thirteen year-old Frances and her sisters were taken in by the Reverend Roger Steevens and his wife, Sarah, who was Mary's sister. In that same year, Frances's sister Catherine died, and the Steevens had a baby girl.

Brooke's biographer Lorraine McMullen concludes that Frances and her youngest sister were happy in their new home and that both received a good education. Brooke's published works and translations demonstrate wide reading and knowledge of French and Italian. A contemporary biographer says that her mother gave her "a most excellent education,"[3] but, brought up in homes with genteelly educated women and the libraries of generations of clergymen educated at Oxford and Cambridge, she was surrounded by extraordinary opportunities for cultivating her mind. When her surviving, younger sister reached age twenty-one, Brooke received the £500 her father had left her in trust[4] and perhaps more from her mother, and by 1748 she was living in London.

Numerous contemporaries describe Brooke as witty, intellectually engaging, widely read, "agreeable," and with a "literary turn." A notice of her death praises her for her "gentleness and suavity of manners."[5] Several of her works are collaborative, and she seems to have had a gift for making and taking suggestions with grace and good judgment. The popular provincial theatre manager, playwright, and stage historian Tate Wilkinson, for instance, notes that her observations on his work were "given with affability, and proved to me of great advantage."[6] In her early years in London, which was then still a small place with tight-knit literary communities, she made a number of friends who were firmly in such circles. The introduction to her first published play, *Virginia,* and other scattered allusions in letters and publications indicate that she was circulating manuscripts and discussing her writing with friends, a common practice among writers in the seventeenth and eighteenth centuries that approximated a form of publishing.[7]

The early 1750s was a good time to be a woman with literary aspirations. Women were well established and accepted as translators and poets, were increasingly writing and being commissioned to write essays, poems, and reviews for the numerous periodicals, and had made strides in establishing novel writing as respectable. Eliza Haywood's long novels, *The History of*

Miss Betsy Thoughtless (1751) and *The History of Jemmy and Jenny Jessamy* (1753), had improved her reputation considerably;[8] Charlotte Lennox's *The Female Quixote* (1752) had been a resounding critical and popular success, and novels such as Mary Collyer's *Felicia to Charlotte* (1744; vol. 2 in 1749) and Lennox's *The Life of Harriot Stuart* (1751) promised a line of Richardsonian, moral, epistolary novels.[9] No publisher now ignored female readers; indeed, these publications and others showed that the public would tolerate considerable originality from women writers.

Encouraged and befriended by men like Samuel Richardson and Samuel Johnson, women writers of these decades lived in what might be called a window of unusual tolerance. Before them, women writers often had scandalous reputations that discouraged other women from publishing;[10] after them, women often felt restricted to a limited number of themes, settings, plots, and even characters. The playwright Hannah Cowley described vividly in 1786 the pressure her generation felt: "They will allow me, indeed, to draw strong character, but it must be without speaking its language. I may give vulgar or low bred persons, but they must converse in a stile of elegance. . . . [T]he point to be considered, is . . . whether Mrs. Cowley ought to have so expressed herself."[11]

The century abounds with jokes about young people arriving in London with tragedies in their hand luggage, and Brooke's *Virginia. A Tragedy* comes close to belonging to that category. Tragedy, after all, was still the prestige genre and the theatre the most lucrative literary marketplace. Authors of novels, collections, and books of poetry sold their manuscripts outright, but only the proven, best, and most entrepreneurial got either large sums or what we might call royalties at that time. In 1759, for example, Samuel Johnson received only £100 for *Rasselas* and an additional £25 when the second edition was issued. Goldsmith received £60 for *The Vicar of Wakefield* in 1762.[12] The author of a successful play, however, got every third night's profits and some held contracts obligating them to deliver a new play regularly, an arrangement that all but guaranteed production. Playwrights often received over £100 for *each* benefit night. That the play would be produced by the company for which it was written was also an advantage because the parts would "fit" and provide attractive vehicles for stars who could help assure a hit. Brooke's *Virginia* was not produced, however, because two other plays based on Livy's story of the tyrant Appius's desire for Virginia were on the stage at that time.

In the preface to *Virginia. A Tragedy, with Odes, Pastorals, and Translations* (1756), Brooke wrote that "many Persons, of very distinguished Rank, and unquestionable Veracity" had seen the manuscript of her play before the productions of *Virginia* by Samuel Crisp in 1754 and of *Appius* by John Moncrief in 1755.[13] She had submitted her play to David Garrick, who had, she believed, simply held it until after the first performances of Crisp's play at his Drury Lane theatre.[14] As she said in the preface, she was then "precluded from all Hopes of ever seeing the Tragedy brought upon the Stage, by there having been two so lately on the same Subject." A sign of her determination to make her work known and her outrage over her experience is the fact that the title page reads "Printed for the Author and sold by A. Millar in the Strand." At the time Brooke published with Andrew Millar, only Robert Dodsley was as prominent and successful. Involved from early in his career in such culturally beneficial projects as the Society for the Encouragement of Learning, Samuel Johnson's *Dictionary*, and the establishment of a library in Mansion House, Millar earned a reputation for recognizing and investing in excellent literature.[15] Brooke was willing, then, not only to publish but to pay to get her play before the public and was capable of persuading Millar to help her. Her experience with *Virginia*, however, led to years of hard feeling between Brooke and Garrick.

The Chaos of Competition

On 15 November 1755, Millar published the first number of Brooke's weekly periodical, *The Old Maid*. Brooke wrote that her paper "had never gone to press, but for the generous approbation and favor which some essays of mine in manuscript, met with from some persons whom it is an honor to please."[16] Styling herself "Mary Singleton," she entered a healthy literary economy and a path well broken by women. The number of printing presses in London had risen from approximately 70 in 1724 to more than 124 by 1785;[17] London was supporting some eighteen essay periodicals, and more appeared in the 1760s. Competition was so intense that many papers lasted but a few numbers. Ralph Griffiths remarked on "the Chaos of Publication" when he launched the *Monthly Review* in December 1755.[18]

From at least the time of John Dunton's *Athenian Mercury* (begun 1691), newspapers and periodicals had included features for women or even regular female "contributors" such as the *Tatler*'s Jenny Distaff. Dunton and others quickly recognized women readers as a profitable market, and his *Ladies' Mercury* began a nearly unbroken stream of periodicals created primarily for women's consumption. In the generation before Brooke's, both

Delarivière Manley and Eliza Haywood had written successful periodicals;[19] Lady Mary Wortley Montagu had written an essay for the *Spectator* and had initiated and written most of her *Nonsense of Common Sense*. A series of papers called *The Ladies' Magazine* or *The Lady's Magazine* had been moderately successful; one by that title had run from 18 November 1749 to 10 November 1753, a long run in the very competitive market. *The Ladies' Curiosity* (1752) offered lively tales and anecdotes, short essays, poetry, and items of topical interest.[20] It was notable for its use of dialogues and inclusion of music and illustrated fables. Unusually well planned, numbers had considerable thematic unity, and often chose themes of serious interest to women, such as the causes of unhappy marriages (no. 2) and fashionable lifestyles (no. 20).[21]

The woman's point of view contrasts with that of papers such as *The Ladies' Curiosity,* however, which were written by men for women. Brooke's writing in *The Old Maid* about marriage and courtship gives steady insight into women's experiences, and she often points out ways women are equal to men. For instance, she writes that she knows many women "who are as good judges of polite literature at least, as most men" (17). Immediately after Brooke's paper, there were several notable periodical efforts directed at women. Charlotte Lennox's *Lady's Museum* was a true literary magazine with translations of French literature and poems, essays, songs, and serialized novels.[22] From March 1760 until February 1761, she published in it her *History of Harriot and Sophia* (later published as *Sophia*). The *Royal Female Magazine* set itself up as a moral watchdog and condemned Ranelagh, Vauxhall, and Sadler's Wells but took an enlightened stand on modern literature and the stage. Many of these periodicals were solid successes.

The Old Maid is an intriguing, stimulating publication, and Brooke obviously knew the market she was entering. The first number begins,

> Amidst the present glut of essay papers, it may seem an odd attempt in a woman, to think of adding to the number; but as most of them, like summer insects, just make their appearance, and are gone; I see no reason why I may not buz amongst them a little; tho' it is possible I may join the short liv'd generation; and this day month be as much forgot as if I had never existed. . . . everybody knows an English woman has a natural right to expose herself as much as she pleases . . . and since I feel a violent inclination to show my prodigious wisdom to my cotemporaries [*sic*], I should think it giving up the privileges of the sex to desist from my purpose.[23]

This mixture of savvy realism and cheeky irony is consistent through the weekly's thirty-seven numbers. Brooke remarks, for example, that she will declare to which political party she belongs "as soon as I see how the [Seven Years] war will end, and who will be the Ministry[24]. . . but till that time shall beg leave, in imitation of many very shrew'd Politicians, and pretty good Patriots, to observe a profound silence on this subject" (220). Her paper, she declares, would be governed by the goddess of Great Britain, Caprice, and she shall follow her whims in selecting subjects (2, 9). Like most of the periodicals for women, hers features short essays and includes play reviews, topical commentary, and some poetry.

Brooke creates an amusing, slightly eccentric "author," a spinster nearing fifty who has reared her dead sister's child and who is a keen observer of society, manners, and the state of the nation. The range of topics in *The Old Maid* is impressive; Brooke fearlessly writes about self-righteous reactions to the Lisbon earthquake, ridicules contradictory reports about the war with France, and stridently calls on members of Parliament to support foundling hospitals. Her family background informs her judicious, detailed Holy Week 1756 essays on Catholicism and especially on "enthusiasm" and the evangelical movement. When a reader says clergy are starving and ill provided for, she disagrees, disputes that poverty is as widespread as her reader says, notes that the government generally supports the clergy well, and argues that some men won't work or have behaved badly (145-50). This kind of specificity contrasts markedly with the more common "fashionable commitment to the Establishment, popular opposition to Popery, conventional disdain for enthusiasm, or satirical denunciation of decadence."[25] Topics and attitudes that will appear in her novels are well handled. Among the letters she publishes, for instance, are the two reciprocal ones that ended "Mary Singleton's" engagement; his is a satire of hundreds of letters from fortune-hunting, jilting lovers in novels and hers is a witty, biting version of what women might wish to say in such a situation. The skeptical view of fashionable society that is also evident in her novels adds a dimension to the periodical. In an essay that prefigures the plot of *The Excursion*, she writes the story of Sylvia, who "lays snares for men of superior condition," marries one Philander, and is soon miserable (40-42).

In a few numbers, Brooke's engagement with belles lettres and literary London rises to genuine literary criticism that challenges her contemporaries and shows unusual historical and aesthetic perspective. She praises individual passages in Beaumont and Fletcher (a somewhat old-fashioned taste), knows Pope well, and breaks with many critics to single out and praise her nation's literary heritage. Her essays on *King Lear* are fairly well-known examples; in one she chides David Garrick and other managers for their preference for Nahum Tate's adaptation.[26] At the beginning Brooke had promised extensive coverage of the theatre, but what she produces is as sporadic and unsystematic as that in periodicals produced by others, including the playwrights Arthur Murphy (*Gray's Inn Journal*), George Colman the Elder (*The Connoisseur*), Hugh Kelly (*Lady's Museum*), and Henry Fielding (*Covent Garden Journal*). Designing a "little court of female criticism, consisting of myself, and six virgins of my own age, to take into consideration all stage offenses against sense and decency," she proposes to "take the theatres under inspection" (24). Only rarely does she use this group, although she puts in their mouths the famous comments on Spranger Barry's interpretation of King Lear.[27] She is a consistently alert critic to acting styles and effects, censuring overacting that approaches "burlesque," as in Edward Berry's Henry VIII, and reporting on Kitty Clive's delicious parody of the Italian singer Regina Mingotti (no. 26).

Brooke never lost her engagement with the periodical and news press. *The Excursion* includes a sarcastic snipe at the *Morning Post,* a trendy paper begun in 1772, and an extended section on scandal sheets such as *Town and Country Magazine,* which accepted contributions for its gossip column, called "Tete-à-Tete." One of the characters in *The Excursion,* Lady Blast, writes a "malevolent history of Maria" that is not only false but extravagantly fictional. Still concerned with the intersections of public well-being, art, politics, and the press, Brooke interrupts the narrative to reflect with outrage: "Amongst the evils of the present hour, there is not one which more loudly demands redress . . . than the licentious malignity of that press, the liberty of which is at once the glory and the strength of our constitution."[28]

CITIZEN OF THE WORLD

In 1756, Brooke published the collection that included *Virginia,* two pastorals, nine odes, and "imitations" of Battista Guarini.[29] She made no excuses for publishing. Rather, she wrote that the favorable reception to three of her odes printed in *The Old Maid* encouraged her to do so. Following the preface was an advertisement: "By this Author Speedily will be published Proposals for Printing by Subscription, A Poetical Translation with notes of *Il Pastor Fido* and other poems." The translations of Guarini's poems in her collection printed the Italian beside the English and may have been intended to demonstrate her competence and encourage subscriptions for her translation of his major work and other poems.

The proposal and translation never appeared. By this time, Frances was married to the Reverend John Brooke, vicar of St. Augustine's, Norwich, rector of Colney, Norfolk, sequestrator at St. Peter's at Southgate, Norwich, and permanent curate at St. Ethelred's, Norwich.[30] In that year, she began work on a pastoral, *The Shepherd's Wedding,* and a farce, which might have been produced in Dublin had the theatre not gone bankrupt.[31] On 10 June 1757 their only surviving child, John Moore Brooke ("Jack") was born. Her husband was appointed acting chaplain to the British army, which meant that he was often away during the first years of their marriage. He spent three months as chaplain on a hospital ship in 1757 and moved to Louisbourg, Cape Breton Island, where he was chaplain of the garrison from August 1758 to July 1760 when he moved to Quebec (McMullen, 49). On 28 October 1761, he was formally commissioned chaplain to the garrison at Quebec.

Thus, the Brookes' history was interwoven with the Seven Years War, which was declared in 1756. In September 1759 the British took Quebec, and the next year Montreal fell.[32] Essays and sharp comments in *The Old Maid* show that Frances was closely following the war and its press coverage. One of her characters, Julia, is engaged to a soldier whose opinions are reported and discussed. In March 1756, the group applauds "our spirited behavior against the insults, depredations, and perfidy of France" and laughs at the periodicals' contradictory accounts of events. Shortly thereafter, her papers reflect the pessimism and fear of invasion that swept the nation.[33] On 12 June 1756, Brooke reflects: "There never was a time in which it was so necessary to revive the dying embers of this noble flame: I grieve to say, that our ancient military spirit is lost, that we are become a nation of traders" (184). In July, she is still reacting to Britain's loss of Minorca and heaping scorn on Admiral John Byng, whom she called "the degenerate son of Lord Tor[ring]ton" for whom "death is too mild a punishment" (206-7). Byng was executed at Portsmouth on 14 March 1757 for failing to relieve Minorca. In other numbers, Brooke considers both seriously and humorously the ways women could contribute to the war effort.

The British saw victory after victory, and the foundation for their empire was laid. It has been said that Frances's happiness at the appointment of her husband to Quebec suggests financial difficulties, but her excitement over British success and its new territory may also explain her mood.[34] In her first novel, *The History of Lady Julia Mandeville,* she wrote, "Canada, considered merely as the possession of it gives security to our colonies, is of more national consequence to us than all the Sugar-islands on the globe . . . if population is encouraged; the waste lands settled; and a whale fishery set on foot, we shall find it . . . an acquisition beyond our most sanguine hopes!"[35]

For economic or personal reasons, Brooke decided at this point to translate Marie Jeanne Riccoboni's *Lettres de Milady Juliette Catesby à Milady Henriette Campley* (1759) rather than the Guarini poem. Riccoboni was being called "the new Madame de Lafayette" and compared to Choderlos de Laclos.[36] This novel, her third in three years, became the most popular of her wildly popular novels. There were twenty editions of it by 1800, and Dutch and German translations appeared in the year of its publication. Danish, Swedish, Russian, and Brooke's English translations quickly followed.[37]

Brooke had made or been assigned a harmonious choice, but it opened the second chapter of her problems with David Garrick. Riccoboni was a solid second-rank actress, and her dramatic experience contributed to her novels' energy and movement. Praised as a writer for her style, grace, and telling use of detail, Riccoboni contributed significantly to the mid-century reshaping of the epistolary novel.[38] Her best biographer, Emily Crosby, gives Brooke credit for introducing Riccoboni to English readers. From the time of the publication of *Letters from Juliet, Lady Catesby, to Her Friend, Lady Henrietta Campley* (1760), Crosby writes, the circle of Riccoboni's admirers in England grew rapidly, and she merited and received from the English the same honors and approbation that the French were giving Fielding.[39] In *The Theory of Moral Sentiments* (1759), Adam Smith ranked her with Voltaire, Racine, Richardson, and Marivaux as "one of the poets and romance writers who best paint the refinements of . . . private and domestic affections."[40] Riccoboni's critics agree that her other novels were poorly translated by "mediocre writers devoid of style" (Crosby, 142); "ponderous," "awkward," and "inexact" are favorite adjectives applied to the translations, but Brooke's was the exception. Her translation required a second edition in the year of its publication. Crosby writes,

> It is to be regretted that Mme. Riccoboni let herself be persuaded to refuse to accept Mrs. Brooke as the designated translator of her work. For, of all the English translations of her works, that of *Lettres de Juliette Catesby* by Mrs. Brooke is the best. The English novelist has a style of her own which, while being less elegant and pleasing than that of Mme. Riccoboni, is, however, clear and energetic. Also a dramatic author her-

self, she preserved in her version the dramatic movement that Mme. Riccoboni communicated in the original. It is evident that she loved her work and endeavored to do as well as she could. (143)

Garrick was the person who persuaded Riccoboni to leave her novels in the hands of Becket and DeHondt, who specialized in importing and translating contemporary French and continental books. Thomas Becket was one of Garrick's publishers, a subservient friend who kept Garrick informed of everything written about him in newspapers, periodicals, and even fiction.[41] On 15 May 1765, Riccoboni had written to Garrick to ask his advice. She had received a letter from Brooke explaining that her translation of *Catesby* was in the fourth edition and asking for permission to receive and translate Riccoboni's other novels. Garrick wrote back promptly: "I am not acquainted with Mrs. Brooke: she once wrote a play, which I did not like, & would not act, for which heinous offence she vented her female Spite upon Me, in a paper she publish'd call'd the *Old Maid,* but I forgive her as thoroughly as her Work is forgot." After these belittling and dismissive remarks, he advises her, "You will be civil to her & no more, all this is Entre nous."[42] Although she had pointed out problems with Becket and the other translations to Garrick, Riccoboni, who would show respect for Garrick's opinion and considerable loyalty to him whenever he was criticized, complied. Dodsley published four more editions of Brooke's translation, in 1763, 1764, 1769, and 1780; modern opinion holds that no other translation of any of Riccoboni's eight novels is as good as Brooke's.

Career as a Novelist

The third edition of Brooke's translation came in the year of the publication of her own first novel, the highly successful *History of Lady Julia Mandeville*. Published by Dodsley, as her translation had been, the novel went through three editions in its first year and six by 1773. The influence of Riccoboni's style, which Denis Diderot described as "like an angel," "natural," "pure," and elegant,"[43] and Brooke's continuation of the French novel's extended attention to emotions and subtle differences in emotions contributed to Brooke's lively analysis of fashionable London and her tendency to judge it and "manners" by centrist English moral standards; this complex blend animates all of Brooke's novels. Immediately compared favorably to Samuel Richardson's works, *The History of Lady Julia* received generous coverage and favorable reviews from the *Monthly Review,* the *Critical Review,* and the *London Magazine.* The *Monthly Review* began, "This performance is distinguished from the common productions of the novel tribe, by ease and elegance of style, variety and truth of character, delicacy and purity of sentiment." It continued, "A tender love-tale is the basis of the work, which is carried on in a series of letters, less tedious, because less laboured, than those of the celebrated Richardson" (29 {August 1763}: 159). Quickly translated into French, the novel was also well reviewed in a thirty-page essay in the *Année littéraire* (17 April 1764) and by Voltaire in the *Gazette littéraire de l'Europe* (30 May 1764). Voltaire put *The History of Lady Julia* in the context of the new popularity of epistolary novels, a form he praised highly, and ranked it the best of its kind since Richardson's *Clarissa* and *Sir Charles Grandison.*

The *History of Lady Julia* is a well constructed, original novel. Julia and Harry's sentimental, doomed romance is juxtaposed with Anne Wilmot's determined, pragmatic reactions to her widowhood, to her memories of an unhappy marriage, to the will her dead husband had crafted to discourage a second marriage, and to her developing romance with Colonel Bellville.[44] The novel form has always absorbed diverse modes and influences, and Brooke's *Lady Julia* can be related to the French *nouvelle* or *histoire galante,*[45] the amorous epistolary novel, the English sentimental novel, and—with its descriptions of activities and people on the country estate—the form we recognize as using the conventions of "literary realism."

Shortly after her return to London in the fall of 1768, Brooke delivered *The History of Emily Montague* to Dodsley. Her dedication to Sir Guy Carleton, lieutenant-governor and then governor of Quebec, 1766-78 and 1786-96, is dated 22 March 1769. This novel, too, received favorable reviews and, in eulogies published at the time of her death, was singled out for special praise. The *Edinburgh Weekly Magazine* captured the novel's special interest for the time: "[it] exhibits so faithful a picture of the manners of the Indians, as well as of the Canadian inhabitants, and so just and pleasing a description of that at present doubly important country" (13 November 1783, 194). With the establishment of the United States, Canada assumed greater value in the minds of the defeated British, and emigration was encouraged. Perhaps Brooke's best-known novel today, *The History of Emily Montague* has been reprinted five times since 1960, once in a bilingual edition published in Quebec, and is often described as the first Canadian novel.

Rich descriptions of the Canadian landscape, lively love stories, and strong characters give *Emily Montague* lasting appeal. Brooke's descriptions of

French, Indian, Canadian, and English politics, desires, and social customs explore and contest many of the issues and ideologies of the period and make the novel highly original.[46] Continuing her acute and often acerbic commentary on marriage in this novel, she has characters observe that the Hurons believe marriage for life "contrary to the laws of nature and reason" (1:67); one character makes a telling comparison between marriage and parents committing their daughters to a nunnery. A French woman reminds the company that nuns have a year of probation, while wives have no trial period and no reprieve. Brooke continues to explore the rules of polite courtship, to demonstrate how honest feelings are smothered, and to portray masculine behavior with obvious concern for defining conduct most conducive to lasting happiness. Brooke, thus, participates in women writers' longstanding critique of rituals of courtship and fashionable "propriety."

Within the epistolary structure, Brooke is able to continue the essay form of *The Old Maid;* individual letters have long passages that assess Canada's future, comment on international or British politics, or compare the customs of Indians, French, Canadians, and British. The quality of Brooke's mind and her ability to see complex relationships between social institutions can be discerned in many passages. Fermor, father of the heroine, concludes, "It seems consonant to reason, that the religion of every country should have a relation to, and coherence with, the civil constitution: the Romish religion is best adapted to a despotic government, the presbyterian to a republican, and that of the church of England to a limited monarchy like ours" (2:207).

Brooke, whose French must have been kept current if not improved in Quebec,[47] returned to translating. Dodsley published her rendering of Nicolas Etienne Framery's *Memoirs of the Marquis de St. Forlaix* in 1770, the year of its French publication, and of Claude Millot's *Elements of the History of England, from the Invasion of the Romans to the Reign of George the Second* (1769) in 1771. Brooke's edition of Framery was described as "elegantly translated" and "proof that Mrs. Brooke is mistress of the French as well as of her native language" and was complimented as preserving "the ease, the vivacity, and the spirit of the original." Even the *Monthly Review,* often highly negative about her work, remarked that it was "well executed, and discovers her taste and sensibility."[48]

Brooke's translation of the Millot work was compared unfavorably, however, to William Kenrick's translation, which appeared the same year.[49] The *Monthly Review,* edited by Kenrick's friend, Ralph Griffiths, carried a long comparison of the two translations with the original French and condemned Brooke in terms later applied to histories by Hester Piozzi and other women: Kenrick's had "ease and freedom, and the dignity of historical narration"; Brooke's "is faithful, but feeble, and too much in the style of conversation" (*Monthly Review* 45 {1771}, 269). A brief flurry of defenses and attacks on the two translations broke out in the press, but Brooke's hope that her translation would become a school text was destroyed. Another novel, *All's Right at Last* (1774) is sometimes attributed to Brooke, though her authorship was doubted even in her own time.[50]

THE EXCURSION AND ITS SIGNIFICANCE

Thomas Cadell—an apprentice of Millar who had become his partner and then in 1767 his successor, the publisher of David Hume's *History of England,* Hannah More's *Percy* and *Fatal Falsehood,* and Samuel Foote's last four plays—brought out Brooke's *The Excursion* in early summer 1777. Her earlier novels had featured a witty, strong-minded heroine and a sentimental, romantic one. Anne Wilmot in *Lady Julia Mandeville* had been called "the true woman of fashion" by *The Edinburgh Weekly Magazine* (13 November 1783), and the heroine of *The Excursion* is a woman of fashion wanna-be. Maria Villiers, lively, spontaneous, restless, and naive, schemes and cajoles until she is allowed to take a £200 inheritance to London, where she intends to marry a "ducal coronet"—that is, to marry into the nobility. Her guardian, Colonel Dormer, the uncle who loves his country retirement and nurtures his gardens with more discernment than his nieces, warns her against "worthless acquaintance, unmerited calumny, and ruinous expense." Ann Messenger notes that in the earlier novels "we see only the fringe" of the "heartlessness—the triviality and narcissism—of the fashionable world";[51] in *The Excursion,* Brooke makes it her subject.

The admonition from Maria's uncle locates Brooke's novel in a rapidly growing type. As in her earlier works, she draws heavily on the English courtship novel, which was by then a highly moral form, closely linked with the beginning of the female *bildungsroman.*[52] Unlike the heroines of English novels between 1680 and 1750, including Richardson's, these heroines are not threatened by rape, seduction, or being "swept away" by their own passions. Rather they are introduced into the way of the world and face loss of reputation because of social mistakes. Eliza Haywood's *The History of Miss Betsy Thoughtless* and Henry Fielding's *Amelia* (both 1751) are landmarks in this tradition.[53] Confronted not only by schemers, cheats, and rakes but also by scenes of misery, misfortune, and need, the heroine must learn to protect her reputation while acting benevolently as well as when under active siege. As critics since the 1930s have pointed out, the topics and admired virtues in these novels are those of contemporary "conduct books," books that prescribed behavior in relationships between husbands and wives, parents and children, and employers and servants.[54] Katharine Rogers, has found *The Excursion* a "convincing education of a young woman—more convincing even than that of Fanny Burney's *Evelina*."[55]

In *The History of Lady Julia,* Anne Wilmot often comments upon the simplicity and innocence of Julia and other characters. In *The Excursion,* that perspective is supplied by the narrator, whose tone combined with the London setting creates a "realistic" story of a young girl's initiation into society. Like Burney's *Evelina,* which was published the following year, *The Excursion* uses its heroine to depict an endangered, attractive adolescent in a fallen, glittering world. In a typical moment, Maria pauses to reflect on her uncle's categories of danger, and her naiveté is underscored in lines at which any worldling would smile—or sigh sadly: "As to calumny, such was her knowledge of the world, that she thought herself secure from its attacks, only by resolving not to merit them" (1:1:8). While Maria is struggling in the city and falling in love with a libertine, her stay-at-home sister Louisa has a nearly uneventful courtship with an exemplary young man. The novel includes most of the conventional characters and many of the familiar plots and episodes of the English courtship novel as written by Jane Barker, Eliza Haywood, Henry Fielding, and Oliver Goldsmith.

Brooke's literary and historical significance rests in part on her experimentation and development of the form of the English novel, and nothing Brooke does with traditional elements is conventional. Although many women novelists depict their heroines in the variety and sprawl of London, Brooke captures women's confinement even within the great, impersonal city. Tied to the few people she believes respectable, Maria must wait for introductions and invitations. She must be concerned about securing a companion for trips to the theatre and opera. As her money dwindles and her acquaintances drop her, she is imprisoned in Mrs. Merrick's house, and Brooke depicts her pacing and discomfited. Conventionally, rakes in novels tend to be heartless seducers and, as the narrator notes, even kidnappers. Brooke's Lord Melvile is an original, intriguing, individual character and another break with the expected. Attractive, polished, and skeptical to the last degree, he still has the "traces" of his "virtues" on his face. He makes the rounds of theatre, garden, cards, and mistress each night, but he can still blush and leave the sight of his mistress sitting at the head of his dead mother's table and beneath her portrait. His desires are elemental, yet streaked with romantic, domestic ones. He appears the dissolute, predatory social animal and also the apathetic worldling who expects little of life and, therefore, obeys his father without effort or resistance. Yet he can suddenly reveal conflicting impulses, including dreaming of an "affair of the heart" (1:4:10).

Brooke is one of the first novelists to create a wise, admirable older woman character who combines the roles of model, friend, and confidante: Lady Sophia, the foil to Mrs. Merrick and Lady Hardy. Here we see Brooke's observant eye and class consciousness. Mrs. Merrick is genteel, good-natured and well-intentioned, but she is unaware of the social forms and pastimes Maria needs to understand and is unable to cope with situations arising in London society. Lady Hardy, in contrast, has mastered these forms and pastimes but lacks the moral principles and "sensibility" that novelists of the period use to distinguish true aristocrats and persons of worth. Lady Sophia has some resemblances to Brooke's friend, Lady Elizabeth Cecil, who lived at the Manor House, Tinwell, and who in the mid-1750s had given her "a general invitation to while away an irksome hour with them; when I feel myself too much alone" (quoted in McMullen, 33).

Brooke's fictions have been called, not quite accurately, novels of sensibility, and the concept is central to the understanding of her novel. "Sensibility" is a difficult idea for the modern mind to comprehend.[56] Related to sense perceptions, it captured the connection and rapid transmission of feelings, such as sympathy or moral outrage, to physical feelings and signs of those feelings, such as tears or even violence. Sometimes simply defined as "fine feeling," it was not something the eighteenth-century thinker believed all people possessed in the same measure or even had at all. "Fine," then, took on implications for "taste" and "cultured" and, in turn, had links to both class and education. Unlike "mere" sentimentality, sensibility was the union of judgment with a conscious openness to feelings. By the 1770s and with increasing strength through the Romantic period, sensibility came to be associated with the qualities of mind that produce aesthetic objects, values, and judgments.

The possession and expression of sensibility was a test of human worth, and a hierarchy of characters within literary works could be established by their degree of true sensibility. The most discerning and virtuous displayed ideal sensibility, while some characters were callous and brutish and others mawkish and sentimental. Practices of conduct, such as scheming for social advantage, were condemned because they violated principles of sensibility. Elements of this system of making judgments can be found in *The Excursion.* Maria consistently displays sensibility, especially in her letters to her sister and in scenes composed to expose her heart. Louisa's idealized suitor, Mr. Montague, has some natural sensibility, while Lord Melvile's is undeveloped and surprises him when it dictates his responses. It is described as a "warm susceptibility of soul," which his corrupted reason often suppresses. Colonel Herbert, perhaps the most admirable man in the book, has both natural and cultivated sensibility, combining feeling and reason. Brooke emphasizes that shared sensibility is the foundation for the happiest marriages. She illustrates the working of the quality in different kinds of people with different temperaments and educations. Mr. Hammond, for instance, combines sensibility with the wit and literary acumen associated with the London gentleman intellectual. True to the form, characters expound extensively upon such matters as the relationship between happiness and various life choices, as in the discussion between the senior Mr. Montague and Colonel Dormer in volume 2, book 8, chapter 3.

The novel also continues and adapts a much older strain of fiction and draws upon several identifiable kinds of novels. Seventeenth and eighteenth-century English readers were raised almost as much on French novels as on English, and more on French before at least 1740. Within this French tradition was the very popular *histoire galante,* probably the major kind of fiction written by English women writers and a form perhaps written primarily for women readers.[57] This fiction explored and analyzed the emotions of love, what Du Plaisir called the "anatomy of the amorous heart."[58] It sought to identify and make fine discriminations among all the "tones" of love—each of the feelings of awakening love, of maturing affection, of rejection, and so on. The tradition that began with Madeleine de Scudéry, Marie-Catherine d'Aulnoy, Louise-Marie de Conti, Marie-Madeleine de Lafayette, and other "romance" writers was transferred to England and continued by writers such as Manley, Haywood, and Mary Collyer. This tradition, one that English women joined, has been obscured and nearly lost in the modern his-story of the English novel. So familiar was it that Brooke felt free to invoke it; in *The History of Lady Julia,* for example, she makes an unglossed reference to Celadon and Urania, major characters in Honoré D'Urfé's early seventeenth-century *L'Astrée* (164–65). Correspondence among women of the time shows continued careful reading of these and other French romances.[59] Twentieth-century critics have demonstrated, as Ellen Moers wrote in 1963, that "to be a woman writer long meant, may still mean, belonging to a literary movement apart from but hardly subordinate to the mainstream."[60] Indeed, many men belonged to alternate traditions as well, but women writers outweighed them exponentially in creativity and numbers.

Another characteristic of this French tradition was the commitment to the inseparability of what have come to be seen as "public" and "private" spheres. This idea was worked out through the lineage of the lovers, in the roles and information obtained in one sphere and used in the other, and in illustrations of how private conduct reveals the temperament, moral character, and opinions that determine public actions. In such novels the representations of individual characters often become critiques of whole classes as their education, ideology, and sense of privilege and responsibility construct them. Rightly or wrongly, critics have identified Lord Claremont, Melvile's father, with Lord Chesterfield. Reviews of Brooke's novel made strongly negative judgments of him and his book, *Letters Written by the Late Right Honourable Philip Dormer Stanhope, Earl of Chesterfield, to His Son, Philip Stanhope, Esq.,* which had been published three years earlier, in 1774, by Chesterfield's daughter-in-law. The *Gentleman's Magazine* said that the reader "will easily see" that Claremont is "formed on the detestable plan of Lord Chesterfield" (47 {August 1777}: 387), and *Town and Country* objected: "Mrs. Brooke seems to have had in her eye the precepts given by lord Chesterfield to his son upon gallantry, we can never suppose that nobleman, or any other man . . . would be the pimp and pander of his son" (9 {August 1777}: 433).

THE EXCURSION AND THE FASHIONABLE WORLD

In context and content Brooke's novel is part of the fashionable world of the late 1770s. By that time, owning and reading certain kinds of novels was part of the social scene. Some novels, probably including this one, were marketed as fashionable commodities and touted as offering cultured entertainment as well as instruction in worldly behavior and timeless morality. Brooke's publisher, Cadell, made considerable profit from this kind of book and eventually published the six-volume *Historical Pocket Library,* which he advertised as "useful, moral, elegant."[61] Such books represent the *ton,* but they help readers distinguish between cultured conduct and decadence. The "right" people read Brooke's book, and they discussed it in polite gatherings. In addition to gendered virtues, such books taught manners. As Mary Granville wrote, "There is nothing I wish so much for Mary, *next* to right religious principles, as proper *knowledge* of the polite world. It is *the only means* of keeping her safe from an immoderate love of its vanities and follies, and of giving her that sensible kind of reserve" (3:227). *The Excursion* delivered these kinds of instruction, and readers and reviewers acknowledged it.

In some ways, the novel reflects Brooke's participation in fashionable society. It carefully follows the theatrical season of 1774-75 and exhibits firsthand knowledge of distinctive social behavior, popular opinions, and affectations in language. The *au courant* narrator uses both Italian and French to comment on events and people; the characters who are aspiring social climbers reveal themselves in part through their affected use of foreign terms and fashionable phrases. Brooke's languages contribute richly to the elevated, wryly ironic tone of the novel.

The moral judgments the novel makes were also fashionable. Even the creation and condemnation of a Chesterfield character was a fad, for he had come to signify "all that was most cynical and depraved in an outmoded concept of gentility."[62] In addition to being a good, modest "psychological" initiation and courtship novel, *The Excursion* is a sustained critique of the *ton* and fashionable London. Novels, plays, books, and sermons were all expressing concern about the pursuits, the idleness, and especially the gambling of the upper and even middle classes. Seen by many as threats to domestic harmony and the most important values of the society, the scenes and pastimes portrayed in Brooke's novel offer an intriguing representation of fashionable London and an idle, rather dissolute part of society, as well as insight into some widely held anxieties and opinions. Many believed that their era was one of unprecedented and dangerous idleness, luxury, hedonism, and extravagance. Londoners saw social gatherings and especially such public places as Ranelagh, Vauxhall, and the theatres becoming marriage markets where social climbing, attempts to repair fortunes, and seductions seemed common. In his mid-century poem *The Demi-Rep,* Edward Thompson captured the common opinion: "Have ye not Wives and Mistress[es]?—yet still / Go we to Ranelagh, or where we will / We find you there; for ye like jackalls prowl / About for prey, and smell at ev'ry hole" (33-34).

They—and Brooke's novel—were particularly concerned about gambling. Newspapers and periodicals repeated and made up scandalous gossip about those in society, and reports of gambling debts in the tens of thousands of pounds were common.[63] In the year before the publication of *The Excursion,* John Damer, son of a lord, committed suicide over his £70,000 debt, and the renowned Theresa Cornelys tried to reopen Carlisle House, a site for cards, balls, masquerades, and private concerts. Lady Hardy's house resembles Cornelys's in many ways. That women played cards and gambled seemed especially pernicious. Objections to this behavior ranged from a recognition that it was an addiction and, therefore, took women away from home and domestic duties, to fears that women in debt would be tempted or urged to pay off their creditors with sexual favors. Such fears had been expressed consistently and prominently at least since the time of Vanbrugh's *Provoked Husband* (1728). Even private correspondence reinforces this point. Mary Granville, for instance, wrote that she had read and wept over Edward Moore's *The Gamester* and commented that "it is a very proper play at this time to be represented." Speaking of her own gambling, she wrote in 1771 to a friend: "gaming, a vice of such a deep dye at present, that nothing within my memory comes up to it! the bite is more malignant than that of a mad dog, and has all the effects of it" (*The Autobiography,* 3:214, 4:335).

Brooke's novel might thus be seen as part of the "outburst of hostility to feminine extravagance."[64] It should be placed, however, with such witty attacks on fashionable behavior as Richard B. Sheridan's play *School for Scandal,* produced almost simultaneously with the publication of *The Excursion,* rather than with the host of pamphlets, sermons, and conduct books aimed primarily at women.[65] It is, in fact, entertaining to read this play in conjunction with Brooke's novel, since they share many satirical targets.

Brooke's narrative point of view—a "Bel Esprit," wise, worldly, wry, judgmental, and witty—is one of the most notable elements of this novel and bridges the fashionable context and content. Brooke saw this pose as offering women freedom. Anne Wilmot in *Lady Julia* says, "I early in life discovered, by the mere force of genius, that there were two characters only in which one might take a thousand little innocent freedoms, without being censured—those of a *Bel Esprit* and a *Methodist*" (74). Strong elements of the freedom, power, and wit of the "Bel Esprit" characterize the narrator in *The Excursion.* "Wit" in the eighteenth century was considered one of the higher kinds of intelligence and signified quick perceptiveness, particularly the ability to associate ideas and express them brilliantly. All the arts and especially the theatre relied on wit as John Locke explicated it: "For Wit lying most in the assemblage of Ideas, and putting those together with quickness and variety, wherein can be found any resemblance . . . , thereby to make up pleasant Pictures, and agreeable Visions in the Fancy."[66]

Distanced from the heroine, the narrator is both sympathetic and ironic, a difficult balance to achieve and maintain. Later Jane Austen would manage it more famously in *Pride and Prejudice* and *Emma*. *The Excursion* opens with the sisters watching a sunset and the passing of Lady H——'s "superb carriage, with a numerous train of attendants." The narrator comments that at that moment Maria felt "the poison of ambition." The juxtaposition of a glorious sunset and beautiful rural scene with the display of wealth introduces a value system, which is immediately juxtaposed with the thought of ordinary human beings. Not only Maria is self-absorbed; soon the reader finds out that Louisa, who turns quickly back to the sunset, is not concentrating on its beauty either.

The narrator judges behavior quickly and categorizes it bluntly; Maria at one point, for instance, looks like a crass "adventurer" (1:3:9) and at another behaves "like a miss educated in shades" (2:8:6), a pastoral Never-Never land. Of the girls' father, the narrator observes that he was a squire, "a race happily almost extinct," who died young, "happily for his daughters" (1:1:2). The reader, as in many eighteenth-century novels, is told what to expect and led to study how it comes about and, when engaged with the character, to dread and then regret it. As early as the ninth chapter, when Maria is leaving her uncle's estate, we are told that she almost changes her mind about going to London, but "the fond Deceiver, Hope, painted to her lively imagination the gaudy scene which had originally misled her. . . . [E]very whisper of discretion . . . the pictures drawn by Truth and Nature, faded away before the dazzling blaze of a coronet" (1:1:9).

The narrator maintains a relationship with the reader, often sharing worldly smiles, regrets over the evil in humankind, and nods of agreement over commonplace opinions. Some sections slant into lectures: "Let their own experience, for they will never grow wise from yours, break the gay bubble" (1:2:1). The narrator may even, in the light of the reader's imagined desires, lament the responsibility for truth and candor (1:2:9). The influence of Henry Fielding's *Tom Jones* is evident in this novel, as it is in Haywood's *Miss Betsy Thoughtless*. Everywhere the awareness of the reader and of language contributes to the tone and the reader's enjoyment. Brooke juxtaposes classical and conventional poetic language with mundane situations: "How give wings to the lazy-footed time? How pass the tedious hours of Lord Melvile's absence?" (1:4:1) Sometimes the language unmasks social hypocrisy, as when the narrator says that Lady Hardy is what "every body knew to be what nobody chose to call her" (1:2:6). Brooke uses the same kinds of suspenseful, delayed gratification strategies that Fielding uses as she moves from one character to another, one location to another. The narrator assumes firm control of the story and the reader's interpretation by, for instance, stating motives in unequivocal terms. Of Mrs. Herbert it is said, "nothing but [Maria's] being fifty times handsomer than herself, could have prevented her giving her an invitation to her house in town" (1:1:6). Romantic illusions that Melvile would change because of Maria are brushed aside: he "forgot, before he reached Grosvenor Street, that there existed such a being as Miss Villiers" (1:2:9).

The narrator also provides thematic unity. Opposing the "bonds that hold society together"—community values—to the "individual"—of which the cardplayer is the most extreme example—Brooke takes a stand on a major intellectual issue in the period.[67] Also opposed are England and English education to the Grand Tour and French principles. Surprisingly strong in a novel of this date is sustained attention to good taste and the pleasures and benefits of the arts. The narrator sounds this theme first in a discussion of how the uncorrupted young will naturally prefer the theatre and good music to routs and card parties. The pleasures of tragedy are compared to those of comedy, and, in another place, the function of the theatre as a treasury of "national virtue" as well as of taste is asserted.

REVIEWS AND REVISION

The Excursion was reviewed in all the best periodicals, but one episode became news. The *London Review* began by titillating its readers: "with a masterly pencil, the author has pourtrayed the features of some distinguished personages." It then professed that it would "not refuse our readers . . . the opportunity of perusing the seventh chapter of the fifth book" (6 {August 1777}: 113). In the first edition, Brooke had chosen to introduce David Garrick into a major episode in the novel. She has the stage-struck Maria, through the intercession of Mr. Hammond, offer a play written as a vehicle for Garrick as actor-manager of Drury Lane. Garrick turns Maria's play down without reading it, and he cannot even recall whether it is a tragedy or comedy. Brooke satirizes Garrick, one of the two or three greatest theatrical geniuses of the century, as surrounded by servile petitioners and glorying pretentiously in his power to select among the hundreds of manuscripts offered him. She has him brag to Hammond about the "six-and twenty new tragedies on my promise-list" and the seven-year wait for production even after acceptance. Brooke captures his well-known stammer and identifies him in other unmistakable ways. In 1777 Garrick was retired and in ill health. The

1775-76 season had been his last; as he played one famous, signature role after another that year, the public sought tickets with frenzied urgency. These facts made Brooke's attack especially unwise.

Because of this episode, all but a few of the reviews were thinly disguised editorials with partisan literary comments. *Town and Country* called the attack on Garrick in *The Excursion* "the most scandalous chronicle we ever met with" and said that Mrs. Brooke was filled with "malignancy" (9 {August 1777}: 434). This hostile review also criticized her "incessantly boring" scraps of Italian and French. The *London Review* printed the Garrick scene, calling it an "admirable likeness" and "just" (6 {August 1777}: 113-17), and the *Critical Review* described it as "a humorous representation of the illiberal maxims of government, adopted by his theatrical majesty" (44 {July 1777}: 63). Even those who found the depiction accurate complained that it was not original and traced such satires back to James Quin and, more recently, to Tobias Smollett.[68] The perennial complaint was, in Oliver Goldsmith's words, that the stage, "instead of serving the people, is made subservient to the interests of an avaricious few."[69] Nearly all the reviews were mixed at best, but most acknowledged Brooke's characteristic "liveliness," solid creation of characters, and pleasant, clear style; they found the novel "instructive" and recommended it for such lessons as deterring "young ladies from launching out into the world, and affecting the *ton*, without discretion" (*Critical Review*, 44 {July 1777}: 63).

The longest, most severe review was in the *Monthly Review*, and it was an artful, anonymous attack by David Garrick himself.[70] Aimed at discrediting the novel and its author, the four-page review denied *The Excursion* the status of a novel by calling it "an heterogeneous mass" and levied charges of "venal" hypocrisy against Brooke. Garrick quotes from her own attack on the press in the novel ("Among the evils of the present hour . . . ") and observes self-righteously: "How will the reader be startled to find that this very rigid censor exhibits . . . the most flagrant and unjustifiable instance of the licentiousness she . . . condemns!"[71] He ridicules the plot as "lame" and improbable and observes, "It happens a little unluckily for Mrs. Brooke's credit" that he can oppose "public and uncontrovertible facts" to her "imaginary" ones. He then quotes grateful letters to himself from Richard Cumberland, Elizabeth Griffith, and Hannah Cowley. Artfully including two women, he says that "instances are endless" of his discerning, supportive conduct toward aspiring playwrights.

Garrick then makes a bitterly sarcastic, frontal assault on the episode involving himself. He raises the issue that must have occurred to others:

"Mrs. Brooke cannot surely have kept this stock of malice by her above twenty years." The reviewer continues, "Nothing can be more ungenerous than to attack a man, after he has quitted the field, and has retired, not only crowned with the laurel of genius, as Mrs. Brooke herself allows, but with the palm of virtue also, and . . . with the good wishes, and warm esteem of an admiring public" (144). Garrick, however, does not mention his part in thwarting Brooke far more recently than in the *Virginia* and Riccoboni incidents. She had tried to persuade him to read and stage a musical play of hers, perhaps *Rosina,* probably in the summer of 1776. Indicative of her distrust of him, she asked that he give her a prompt refusal if he could not stage it (McMullen, 133).

During this time, Brooke had become associated with another theatre. By 1771 she and the great actress Mary Ann Yates were intimate friends. When Yates and her husband Richard bought the King's Theatre in the Haymarket in May 1773 with James Brooke, Frances's brother-in-law, Frances became co-manager. The plan seems to have been to mount operas, musical performances, and plays there, but the Lord Chamberlain refused to license the theatre. King's, commonly known as the Opera House, then had to depend on music. In the first season the company mounted nine operas for a total of sixty-five performances and the next year added ballet with a star, Baccelli, from Italy. Brooke used her knowledge of languages to handle all of the foreign correspondence necessary to identify and engage talent from abroad. What Garrick had to do, if anything, with their inability to obtain a license can only be suspected.

In the spring of 1777, when the Yateses tried to get a license for a theatre in Birmingham, Garrick apparently tried to help. When Edmund Burke withdrew his support in late April, however, Garrick wrote, "God forbid that all the Patents in the World should injure Your Interest."[72] Brooke, so much a part of theatrical and literary London, could hardly have been unaware of Garrick's potential for mischievous, behind-the-scenes influence. In turn, Garrick suspected Brooke of delaying publication of her novel until after the vote on the license.[73]

Garrick's *Monthly Review* essay continued in its design to discredit by challenging the veracity of the incident. He demanded aggressively that Brooke produce "the *sublime genius* who carried the play, the title of the *excellent tragedy,* and the name of the great *beauty* who wrote it" and ridiculed the "story of the *genius,* the *beauty,* the *tragedy,* the *manager,* and the *levee*" (144). As many feminist critics have demonstrated, women writers' bodies are almost always on the minds of reviewers. In a veiled *ad hominem* attack, Garrick notes that *The Excursion* presents "a great beauty" as the author of the play and demands she be named. What makes this such a mean-spirited thrust is that Brooke was a physically unattractive woman, and Garrick knew it. In 1774 Frances Burney, who became a good friend of Brooke, described her as "very short & fat, & squints, but has the art of shewing Agreeable Ugliness."[74]

In fact, Brooke might have chosen to generalize the experience or produce a composite. By the time she wrote *The Excursion,* she had also tried to persuade John Rich to produce *Virginia* and George Colman the Elder and Samuel Foote to produce *Rosina.* In a letter to her friend Richard Gifford in 1772, she wrote, "There is nothing to me so astonishing as that Colman should be another Garrick." In another letter, she observed that her only hope was that either Drury Lane or Covent Garden would have a play fail so that "one of them will have a vacancy & take it for their own sakes. I know neither will for mine."[75]

Brooke published a revision of *The Excursion* in 1785. Her alterations fall into two categories: (1) modifications aimed at changing the tone and the relationship between the narrator and the protagonist and (2) substantive rethinking of some incidents. Generally, the narrative point of view is sharpened. The narrator becomes slightly acerbic, faintly more judgmental, and a little more superior to Maria. Mrs. Merrick, for example, is established more firmly as a figure of doting naiveté, by, among other things, predicting acceptance of Maria's tragedy and calling it "a *sweet pretty* tragedy." In the new ending for volume 1, book 4, chapter 7, Maria congratulates herself on having "a perfect knowledge" of the world, and the narrator observes that hers is an error "into which people are very apt to fall at the age of eighteen." Many of the changes are simple additions of words; "sanguine as she naturally was," for instance, becomes "sanguine and romantic as she naturally was" (2:5:9).

The Garrick section is the part of the novel that Brooke revised most extensively. In the first edition, she had used a Fielding-style introduction for emphasis: "But [Mr. Hammond's] narrative, which we recommend to the perusal of all young votaries of the Dramatic Muse, will appear to most advantage in a separate Chapter." The second edition prefigures disappointment from the entrance of Hammond, which is blended into the chapter smoothly and emphasizes theatrical protocol: "There is, it seems, an etiquette in respect to the reception of theatrical pieces . . . which, however plausible . . ." With words such as "etiquette" and "plausible," Brooke makes Garrick's behavior seem standard and even fair. "From friendship to me," Hammond says, Garrick offered to read the play "before its due course"; even that would be a wait of twenty months. This version places Maria's youthful, ignorant imaginings at odds with both "etiquette" and practicality: "She had expected, with the impetuosity of her time of life, and perfect inexperience of the world, to hear it was going into immediate rehearsal . . . and had even regarded the profits as a bank on which she might have depended in . . . a few revolving weeks." Her thoughts are those of an impatient child, and her new fantasies—giving the profits to a charity as opposed to making the play a gift to the company— those of, in the narrator's words, "a romantic girl." She concludes, "the manager . . . had only pursued a regular system of business."

The narration of the play's reception shrinks from nine dramatic pages to three told in the third person in the revised version; the scene concludes with Mr. Hammond's essay-speech on the importance of the theatre to national culture and the unsuitability of women for theatrical pursuits. Originally it had included several paragraphs lamenting that "a man . . . of the most distinguished talents, the idol of the public" could behave in such a manner and imagining what an honest Garrick would say—he would confess the theatre's reluctance to expand or experiment and the public's unwillingness to support theatre. As Garrick brought Brooke's appearance into play in his review, she had brought his manhood under scrutiny. Had Garrick been honest, Brooke wrote in the first version, he would have used "the language of a man" with "sufficient courage to avow his principles of action." Though many lines are preserved in the second edition and theatrical practice criticized, the condemnation is general. Hammond's reflections are made idealistic, and his maxims described as not yet "known to exist" anywhere.

This revised section is important for another reason: Brooke strengthens Maria's aspirations as a playwright. A remarkable new passage portrays Maria listening to a speech intended "to dissuade her from a pursuit in which her whole soul was irresistibly engaged." This pursuit is one of the novel's groundbreaking aspects; alterations to such passages, then, have heightened significance. *The Excursion* develops themes of perpetual interest to Brooke: women's self-fashioning and the forces that construct personality. For all her self-confidence, Maria is experimenting with identities and finding them tested and obstructed. Confident of her charms and the basic benevolence of the world and the people in it, she believes that she can attract a man like Lord Melvile and that he will marry her. She imagines herself as his wife with the accompanying power and pleasure of that role. The conclusion of the story of her romances is as much the story of coming to terms with identity as it is a plot resolution.

To an even greater extent, Maria believes in herself as a writer. With a satisfaction that is both amusing and ominous, she values her epic poem at £100, her novel at £200, and her tragedy at £500. Perhaps only a few of her readers would have known how wildly inflated these prices were, but they would have recognized her naiveté and the fact that these were large sums of money. A middle-class family could live in London for £125 a year. *Paradise Lost* had been sold for £20, of which Milton received only £5, and Alexander Pope, the greatest poet of his generation, received £15 for *The Rape of the Lock,* his mock-epic. In Brooke's generation, Frances Burney was paid £20 for *Evelina* and John Cleland the same for *Fanny Hill.* To make anything approximating £500 from a play, there would have to be a long run and successful publication. *School for Scandal,* for instance, earned Sheridan £1,430.61.4 in the 1776-77 season and *She Stoops to Conquer* earned £501.38.6 for Goldsmith in seventeen (not all consecutive) performances during the 1772-73 season. Some extraordinarily successful playwrights sold publication rights to plays for £150. In *The Old Maid,* among numerous comments about the life and work of writers, Brooke wrote that "as to profit, [the writer] must be very successful indeed, if after neglecting every other means of raising a fortune, and devoting his days to the most painful of all labour, that of the mind, he gets a support equal to that which recompenses the toil of the meanest artisan" (14). *The Excursion* puts Maria in contact with the literary marketplace at most of its key moments; we see its petitioners, its "hurries," its network, and its prejudices.

Maria's satisfaction, however, lies in far more than her works' cash value, and her art has special interest for that reason. In one of the few representations of a woman writer by an early woman writer,[76] *The Excursion* captures an author's psychological relationship to her manuscripts. They are physical objects—objects to be touched, packed, stored with pride, touched again as possessions that combine memories of happy hours spent writing them and as finished works of art. We have access to an author's intimate as well as her economic thoughts and aspirations. Her manuscripts are to be reread, shared with those willing to read them, and with confidence and trepidation submitted to the commercial arena. Maria is proud of them; although she finds her judgment of her play confirmed by her friends, her high opinion of her work does not depend on others' evaluations. Brooke makes her a writer, not a person posturing as a writer.

In both editions of *The Excursion,* after her disappointments with her manuscript and with Melvile, Maria decides to save for her next novel the letter that she had so carefully composed for Melvile but had not sent. Preserving one of her well-written texts takes precedence with Maria over disappointment in love or any attempts to rescue the relationship. Although saving the letter for later use is funny, it also captures the necessarily opportunistic way writers draw upon experiences. In both editions, the reader as the narrator's interlocutor asks, "Is she not then cured of the disease of writing?" The narrator answers, "Alas! my friend, it is plain you have never been an author" (2:8:6).

In harmony with these sections on the experiences of a woman writer and the novel's brief discussions of "genius" and the "household gods" as women's "guardians," the preface to the second edition begins with a demand to be evaluated in the public, political sphere. "'I APPEAL TO THE PEOPLE' was the celebrated form in which a citizen of ancient Rome refused his acquiescence in any sentence of which he felt the injustice. On giving a new edition . . . I find myself irresistibly impelled to use the same form of appeal." Confronting her own bad health and the resultant scaling down of her writing plans, Brooke writes in a deeply reflective and yet combative tone, moving rather uneasily between the public sphere, the arena in which she worked, and the private, which she now claims as that most suitable for women, even women in whom the "animating fire" of genius glows. Her desire seems to be to reconcile the two spheres, for she argues that women should be allowed "public" approval and the right to "intermix such studies" as are appropriate to their abilities but will not "interrupt" their domestic duties.

Keying "appropriate" to level of ability, which in her case she implies is high, she asserts what eighteenth-century writers of both sexes often explained: the combination of ability, irresistible inclination, and duty demands publication.[77] From her early publication in *The Old Maid,* she had recognized her fertile brain; at one point she wrote that she felt "distress" over having to choose among a "superfluity" of subjects (85). Maria is given these traits. Hammond, who throughout both editions is held up to be thoroughly admirable and discerning, describes Maria as having a "muse of fire," and the essay-like discussions of the high purposes of the theatre and Maria's art imply her duty to persevere as a writer. Like so many women writers, Brooke shows considerable ambivalence toward "genius" and the urge to write.[78] In *The Excursion,* she describes Maria as having genius, "that emanation of the Divinity, that fatal gift of heaven, pleasing to others, *ruinous to its possessor*" (italics mine, 1:1:14). Brooke's preface outlines the "task," the duty of women of genius; among the responsibilities is to "impress the gentler, social, duties, on the hearts of the rising generation." Her novel, with its concern for the conduct and opinions that hold society together and form community, is to a considerable degree the practice of this theory.

THEATRICAL SUCCESS AND RETIREMENT FROM LONDON

From 1779 until her death in January 1789, Brooke was never entirely healthy. In these years, however, she enjoyed the success as a playwright she had sought since her young womanhood. She also wrote a novel and worked on a brief, commissioned life of Samuel Richardson.[79] Her tragedy, *The Siege of Sinope,* was performed ten times in January and February 1781, enough to make it a moderate success. Thomas Harris, manager of Covent Garden, did what he could to contribute to the play's success. As the *Universal Magazine* noted, the scenes and props were elaborate and the costumes "new and elegant,"[80] both of which entailed more than customary expense. Loosely based on an Italian opera, the tragedy featured an excellent part for Mary Ann Yates. The reactions to it reveal the pettiness and carping of the competitive world in which Brooke worked. She was accused of expanding the part of Thamyris for her friend Yates, and the defense (that hers was true to the Italian, not the more familiar English version of the operatic story from Roman history) was ignored or greeted with skepticism. George Colman belittled the play in the *Monthly Review,* the periodical that consistently picked Brooke's work apart and characterized her achievements as mediocre. "From the acknowledged talents of the Writer of this tragedy," Colman wrote snidely, "we expected something of more importance than a meagre imitation of an Italian opera" (64 {February 1781}: 153).

Acknowledging the partisan nature of literary loyalties and reviewing, the *Critical Review,* which was consistently favorable toward Brooke, noted that "fastidious or splenetic readers" were taking "malignant pleasure" in "placing [the tragedy] in a gloomy and disadvantageous view" (51 {January 1781}: 158). She and Yates were attacked for allegedly parodying the mannerisms of the M.P. Charles James Fox and for inappropriately exposing his love of gambling in Arthur Murphy's epilogue.[81] A tribute published in the *European Magazine and London Review* at the time of her death notes that Brooke paid a price repeatedly for her theatrical efforts: "She certainly had some share of the libellous abuse which the management of that theatre . . . gave birth to" (15 {February 1789}: 100).

Brooke's revised *Excursion* (1785) appeared at a peak in the public's awareness of her literary achievement. *Rosina,* the comic opera she had tried so hard to get produced in the early 1770s, was finally mounted at Covent Garden on 31 December 1782. After *Rosina,* Brooke's reputation was as high as it had been after the publication of *Lady Julia;* the press regularly mentioned her and the *British Magazine and Review* published a short biography (February 1783). The influence of Brooke's years with the Opera House seems to have strengthened the play, and from the opening night it was a solid hit; it was performed more than two hundred times before 1800.[82] *Rosina* was admirably designed for the taste of the time. Drawn somewhat from the Book of Ruth, it took a familiar, lovely episode from James Thomson's "Autumn" in *The Seasons* and borrowed from a popular opera, *Les Moissonneurs,* by Charles Favart. The beautiful opening trio, "When the Rosy Morn Appearing," became a favorite in concert programs into the twentieth century.[83] William Shield's music contributed significantly to its popularity. In addition to his own compositions, he included popular French and Scottish tunes and carefully imitated the Highland bagpipe tunes as a way of contributing to the poignant moments. *Marian,* Brooke's second comic opera, which is similar to *Rosina,* was produced at Covent Garden on 22 May 1788. The lovely music, gentle sentimentality, and pastoral scenes and story appealed again to the London audience. Though expectations for it were extremely high, it was something of a disappointment. *Town and Country Magazine* called it "so long wished for, as being the production of Mrs. Brooke," but "very barren of incident" (20 {May 1788}: 235). It had four performances in the 1787-88 season and fourteen in 1788-89.

In the last five years of her life, Brooke was also at work on *The History of Charles Mandeville,* a sequel to *Lady Julia,* which continues the life of Anne Wilmot and narrates the life of Charles, older brother of the dead Harry. Charles has been shipwrecked on a utopian island, Youngland. This novel shows Brooke's continued engagement with English values, ethics, religion, and politics and with theories of government and education. In one episode, she emphasizes that the feather the Younglanders award for a virtuous action is of greater value than the load of jewels they give Charles upon his departure. Although Defoe had Robinson Crusoe reflect similarly upon the relative value of money and wealth when marooned on his island, Brooke is far more emphatic on this point. As in a number of utopias by women writers of Brooke's time, of which the best known is Sarah Scott's *Millenium Hall* (1762), human relationships, status determinants, and local government come in for detailed critique. Hayden White writes in "The Value of Narrativity in the Representation of Reality" that "the social system . . . creates the possibility of conceiving the kinds of tensions, conflicts, struggles, and their various kinds of resolutions that we are accustomed to find in novels and some kinds of histories."[84] These utopian novels by women and indeed all of Brooke's novels hold up the possibility of relationships governed by a sense of community and of values and resolutions outside the social system.

In 1785 Brooke left London for Sleaford, Lincolnshire, within six miles of her son's two livings in Folkingham and Helpringham, where he was respectively rector and vicar. Her husband continued to work in his parish in Colney, Norfolk. He died there 21 January 1789. Brooke survived her husband by only two days, and the two are buried in the parishes in which they died. Their son was Brooke's executor, saw her last novel through the press (published by W. Lane in 1790), and was buried in 1798 next to her in St. Denys Church, Sleaford. Her memorial plaque reads in part, "The union of superior literary talents with goodness of heart, rendered her works serviceable to the cause of those virtues of which her life was shining example" (quoted in McMullen, 212).

Brooke's was a life of adventure, achievement, and, indeed, virtue. Her struggle to remain a part of theatrical London during one of its most competitive times, her trip to Canada, and her varied, often pioneering, literary output offer a fascinating glimpse of an unusual woman's life. Her contribution to the development of the English novel deserves special attention. When she wrote, "formal realism," as Ian Watt called it, was not yet the dominant mode for the novel. Writers, among them a strong corps of women writers, were actively exploring the kinds of "truth" novels could tell, the ways novels could be made relevant and important to the larger culture, the kinds of authority they might have, and the forms and structures they might take. Brooke indicates her share in this endeavor in *The Excursion,* which has several short passages that comment on or ridicule forms of fiction then popular. At the time her novels were published, she was one of the many women who contributed to the new respectability of the form and established the novel as a chief "moral access to the public." By the time of her death, the novel was a major site for the testing and contesting of the great ideas of the era, including those of Rousseau, Paine, Burke, and Adam Smith. Her novels participate in these movements.

NOTES

~

1. Respectively, quoted in Lorraine McMullen, *An Odd Attempt in a Woman: The Literary Life of Frances Brooke* (Vancouver: Univ. of British Columbia Press, 1983), 127; *Monthly Review* 50 (April 1774), 243; Laetitia Barbauld, *British Novelists* (London, 1810), 27:i.

2. McMullen, *An Odd Attempt in a Woman*, 1. Unless otherwise noted, biographical information is from this source, hereafter cited as McMullen.

3. "Memoirs of the Life of Mrs. Brooke," *The Edinburgh Weekly Magazine* (13 November 1783), 193.

4. According to Thomas Moore's will, the daughters received a total of £35 a year for their maintenance and £1000 *to be divided* when they reached their majority. I am grateful to Elizabeth Larsen for this correction of the long-standing opinion that Brooke received £1000.

5. *The Gentleman's Magazine* 59 (September 1789), 176. When she died, the major periodicals of the time gave considerable space to accounts of Brooke's life; the content, even the phraseology, is highly similar. See *The European Magazine and London Review* 15 (February 1789), 99-101; *Town and Country Magazine* 21 (March 1789), 114-15; *The Universal Magazine of Knowledge and Pleasure* 87 (August 1790), 84. See also *The Edinburgh Weekly Magazine* 58 (13 November 1783), 193-95.

6. Wilkinson is quoted in McMullen, 10.

7. See Margaret Ezell, *The Patriarch's Wife* (Chapel Hill: Univ. of North Carolina Press, 1987), 62-100. Many examples survive of manuscripts sent to friends and discussed; the most famous is Samuel Richardson's *Clarissa*. See Tom Keymer, *Richardson's Clarissa and the Eighteenth-Century Reader* (Cambridge: Cambridge Univ. Press, 1992).

8. On Haywood's changing reputation, see Jane Spencer, *The Rise of the Woman Novelist* (New York: Blackwell, 1986), 75-77.

9. These novels, especially Haywood's, show the marked influence of Henry Fielding. Haywood's fiction was consistently popular; her late novels were the subject of discussion for propriety-conscious women's groups. For example, Mary Granville writes that her group's "next important reading will be Betty [sic] Thoughtless" (letter dated 18 January 1752, *The Autobiography and Correspondence of Mary Granville*, ed. Lady Llanover, 3 vols. {London, 1861}). She comments at some length on Jessamy, noting that Jemmy is not worthy of "pretty Jenny, who is really a good girl" with a "pretty" character (3:220, 223).

10. Jane Barker, for example, wrote in 1723 that Aphra Behn should not be named with Katherine Phillips. Because so many of these earlier women wrote ferocious political propaganda and also continued the tradition of short, amorous tales, they were easy targets for the moralists of a generation unfamiliar with either the political wars between 1680 and 1725 or the collections of French, Spanish, and Portuguese novellas that had been written by such still-respected writers as Cervantes.

11. Cowley, "An Address," *A School for Greybeards* in *The Plays of Hannah Cowley*, ed. Frederick M. Link, 2 vols. (1786; New York: Garland, 1979), 2:v-vi. The evidence for this small period of grace around mid-century is abundant; for instance, a column in the *Critical Review* joins many others in praising the English "Sapphos" and their achievements in a variety of genres (1 {1756}: 276). In fiction, the later limitations are well demonstrated by recent critics. See Mary Poovey, *The Proper Lady and the Woman Writer* (Chicago: Univ. of Chicago Press, 1984); Nancy Armstrong, *Desire and Domestic Fiction* (Oxford: Oxford Univ. Press, 1987); and Janet Todd, *The Sign of Angellica* (New York: Columbia Univ. Press, 1989). Todd argues that women gained moral authority and easy access to print by accepting this situation.

12. Walter Jackson Bate, *Samuel Johnson* (New York: Harcourt, Brace, Jovanovich, 1975), 336 and 350.

13. Brooke, Preface to *Virginia* (London, 1756), vii.

14. See Kevin Berland, "Frances Brooke and David Garrick," *Studies in Eighteenth-Century Culture,* ed. Leslie Ellen Brown and Patricia B. Craddock, 20 (1990), 222-23; Berland describes the exchanges between Brooke and Garrick in detail, 217-30. On the discouragements and experiences encountered in the theatre by her contemporary, Elizabeth Griffith, see Betty Rizzo, "'Depressa Resurgam': Elizabeth Griffith's Playwriting Career," in *Curtain Calls: British and American Women and the Theatre, 1660-1820,* ed. Mary Anne Schofield and Cecilia Macheski (Athens: Ohio Univ. Press, 1991), 120-142.

15. The records of the Society are in the British Library (hereafter cited as BL), Add. Ms. 6190; the Mansion House proposal, with the suggestion that Robert Harley's ten thousand books be its foundation, is BL Add. Ms. 4254, fol. 79. Millar paid Henry Fielding the unheard-of prices of £600 for *Tom Jones* and £1000 for *Amelia,* and owned all or part of Tobias Smollett's translation of *Don Quixote* and James Thomson's *The Seasons.*

16. *The Old Maid,* p. 11. I have used the microfilm of the Burney collection copy, BL, which is numbered sequentially.

17. Alvin Kernan, *Printing Technology, Letters and Samuel Johnson* (Princeton, N.J.: Princeton Univ. Press, 1987), 59; Cynthia L. White, *Women's Magazines, 1693-1968* (London: Michael Joseph, 1970), 25; John Feather, *A History of British Printing* (London: Croom Helm, 1988), 93-115.

18. Quoted in Antonia Forster, "'The Self-Impanelled Jury': The Reception of Review Journals, 1749-1760," in *Studies in Newspaper and Periodical History,* ed. Michael Harris (Westport, Conn.: Greenwood, 1993), 29.

19. Manley may have written for the *Female Tatler* and took over the *Examiner* from Jonathan Swift; Haywood wrote the *Female Spectator* and the *Parrot.*

20. Reading this periodical beside the others of the 1750s reveals its old-fashioned nature. It has dialogues very much in the style of those in Defoe's conduct books, such as *The Family Instructor* and *Religious Courtship,* and uses some of their titles ("Conjugal Lewdness" and also the subtitle of Defoe's book, "Matrimonial Whoredom," appear in its second number). "Nestor Druid" is probably a take-off on Steele's "Nestor Ironside," persona of *The Guardian. The Lady's Curiosity* was

being published in 1738, and perhaps earlier, by Rayner; this periodical deserves detailed study, including collation of the 1738 and 1752 runs. Roy Wiles is one of the few students of periodicals to list the 1738 publication. See R.M. Wiles, *Serial Publication in England before 1750* (Cambridge: Cambridge Univ. Press, 1957), 314.

21. I would guess this paper to be written by a man; many of the stories are from a strongly masculine point of view and other items, such as one on how flogging should be done and its "history" (no. 10), reflect distinctly male experiences and interests. This violent voyeurism was not unique; *The Ladies' Magazine,* produced by Jasper Goodwill in 1749, specialized in grisly descriptions of crimes and legal punishments, many allegedly written by eyewitnesses.

22. Lennox published her novel *Sophia* in the paper; see Alison Adburgham, *Women in Print* (London: George Allen and Unwin, 1972), 117-19.

23. *The Old Maid* by Mary Singleton, no. 1 (15 November 1755), 1-2.

24. The Seven Years War had just begun, William Pelham died in 1754, and the stability that the Pelham ministry had given Great Britain would not be re-established until the William Pitt-Duke of Newcastle ministry took control in 1757. W.A. Speck, *Stability and Strife* (Cambridge, Mass.: Harvard Univ. Press, 1977), 258-74.

25. Robert Spector, *English Periodicals and the Climate of Opinion during the Seven Years' War* (The Hague: Mouton, 1966), 178.

26. The essays on *King Lear* have received some recent critical attention. See, for example, Berland, "Frances Brooke and David Garrick," 219-21, and Gwendolyn Needham, "Mrs. Frances Brooke: Dramatic Critic," *Theatre Notebook* 15 (1961, 47-55, who points out that Brooke praises Garrick generously. Needham notes that, among other things, Brooke wishes that foreigners would see Garrick "in Richard, or some equally striking part," for she is sure they would then have a high opinion of English entertainment (50). As these critics note, Garrick's next production of *King Lear* restored many of Shakespeare's lines.

27. See *The Old Maid,* 103-6. Gwendolyn Needham usefully sets her criticism in context in "Mrs. Frances Brooke: Dramatic Critic," 48-49.

28. *Excursion* 2:7:8; quotations are identified throughout by volume, book, and chapter and, unless specifically noted, references are to the first edition.

29. "Imitation" signalled to the eighteenth-century reader a translation that departed freely from the original text to create a new poem in the spirit of the original. Dryden's Preface to the *Sylvae* is the great statement on translation. Battista Guarini, a contemporary of Tasso and Shakespeare, was a sixteenth-century courtier and professor of rhetoric and poetry at the University of Padua. He is best known for his poetry, his tragicomedy, *Il Pastor Fido* [The Faithful Shepherd], and the essays he wrote about dramatic theory. In defending his tragicomedy, he became one of the first writers to challenge the Aristotelian notion of unmixed dramatic forms. Thomas Sheridan translated *Il Pastor Fido* in the 1730s; the exact date is not known, but the editors of Sheridan's translation speculate an early 1730s date, and an anonymous 1735 translation could be Sheridan's. Robert Hogan and Edward A. Nickerson, Introduction to *The Faithful Shepherd: A Translation of Battista Guarini's Il Pastor Fido by Dr. Thomas Sheridan* (Newark: Univ. of Delaware Press, 1989).

30. McMullen, 9.

31. McMullen, 41-45, notes that the manuscript of the pastoral is in the Houghton Library, Harvard University. Among Brooke's Irish connections with interests in the drama was John Boyle, earl of Orrery.

32. Hostilities and rivalries for territory in North America were important causes of the Seven Years War, which quickly became global. England and France fought in North America, Africa, India, Westphalia, and along the French coast. The Peace of Paris was signed in February 1763.

33. *The Old Maid,* see nos. 27, 30, and 34. Robert Spector describes the national mood and periodical response in *English Literary Periodicals,* see especially chapter 2.

34. It is the general opinion that "America was the principal object of the war," and the British were excited about their new territory. Spector, *English Literary Periodicals,* 109; see also 88-110 and 113-14. Linda Colley writes, "The Seven Years War was the most dramatically successful war the British ever fought." *Britons* (New Haven, Conn.: Yale Univ. Press, 1992), 100-3.

35. Brooke, *The History of Lady Julia Mandeville,* ed. E. Phillips Poole (London: Scholartis Press, 1930), 156-57. Subsequent references are to this edition.

36. Joan DeJean, *Tender Geographies* (New York: Columbia Univ. Press, 1991), 124-25. Jean-François de La Harpe included Riccoboni and only three other women writers in his *Lycée ou cours de littérature ancienne et moderne* (1797-1803), according to DeJean, 193-94.

37. Joan Hinde Stewart, *The Novels of Mme. Riccoboni* (Chapel Hill: North Carolina Studies in the Romance Languages and Literatures, 1976), 18-19, and 1 n.1. Information about Riccoboni's life and career comes from this source and Emily A. Crosby, *Une romancière oubliée Madame Riccoboni* (1924; Genéve: Slatkine Reprints, 1970).

38. The histories of the French and English novels are inseparable in the longer eighteenth century. In 1762, Riccoboni published her translation of Henry Fielding's *Amelia,* which appeared in new editions in 1763, 1764, 1772, and 1775.

39. Crosby, 141; here and throughout the translations are mine.

40. Quoted in Joan Hinde Stewart, *The Novels of Mme. Riccoboni,* 16.

41. Alan Kendall, *David Garrick: A Biography* (New York: St. Martin's Press, 1985), 157; David Little and George Kahrl, *Letters of David Garrick* (Cambridge: Harvard Univ. Press, 1963), 1:392 n.5 and 2:886 n.2.

42. *Mme Riccoboni's letters to David Hume, David Garrick and Sir Robert Liston, 1764-1783,* ed. James C. Nicholls, *Studies on Voltaire and the Eighteenth Century* 149 (1976), 45-46, 48. In 1770, Garrick had to reassure Riccoboni that he and Becket would "procure the best translator" for *Lettres d' Elizabeth Sophie de Valliére* after Arthur Murphy declined the job (letter dated 13 June 1765). Little and Kahrl, *The Letters of David Garrick,* 2:461.

43. Quoted in Stewart, *Novels of Mme. Riccoboni,* 16.

44. Lorraine McMullen and others compare the Julia-Harry plot to Shakespeare's Romeo and Juliet. See McMullen, "Frances Brooke's Early Fiction," *Canadian Literature* 86 (1980), 35-36.

45. This type of novel analyzed the beginning, experience, and moods of love and depicted the dynamics of relationships and the private and social implications of them. Some of the best known are Marie-Madeleine de Lafayette's *La Princess de Clèves* and Jean Jacques Rousseau's *Nouvelle Héloïse*. They are sometimes called "novels of analysis" and have a decidedly psychological bent. See Ros Ballaster, *Seductive Forms: Women's Amatory Fiction from 1684 to 1740* (Oxford: Clarendon, 1992), 59-64.

46. Good treatments of major elements in *Emily Montague* are Barbara M. Benedict, "The Margins of Sentiment: Nature, Letter, and Law in Frances Brooke's Epistolary Novels," *Ariel* 23 (1992), 7-25, and Katharine M. Rogers, "Sensibility and Feminism," *Genre* 11 (1978), 161-65.

47. Brooke's husband was described as needing her help; one correspondent wrote, "it is to be lamented, that this Gentleman [Brooke] does not understand French" (quoted in McMullen, 78).

48. *Town and Country Magazine* 2 (1770), 547; *Gentleman's Magazine* 40 (October 1770), 621; *Critical Review* 30 (December 1770), 420, and *Monthly Review* 43 (1770), 365, respectively.

49. William Kenrick was the author of *The Whole Duty of Woman* and translations of Rousseau's *Émile* and *Sophia*.

50. Both the *Monthly Review* and the *Critical Review* doubted her authorship, and, given the small London literary circle in which she and the reviewers moved, I take this as powerful evidence against the attribution. Moreover, Brooke was never shy about publishing or owning her work, even in the face of criticism.

51. Ann Messenger, *His and Hers* (Lexington: Univ. Press of Kentucky, 1986), 169.

52. The term is from Sandra Gilbert and Susan Gubar's *Madwoman in the Attic* (1979; New Haven, Conn.: Yale Univ. Press, 1984); they distinguish the female coming-of-age novel from those that follow the shape of a male hero's life and define it as "a story of enclosure and escape," movement toward "an almost unthinkable goal of mature freedom [through] symptomatic difficulties Everywoman in a patriarchal society must meet and overcome" (339). Gilbert and Gubar identify the female *bildungsroman* with *Jane Eyre*, which I see not as a pattern-setting novel but a brilliant example of a kind of novel already well established. Margaret Doody reminds us that a *bildungsroman* about a woman at this early date is still rare in her *Frances Burney: The Life in the Works* (New Brunswick, N.J.: Rutgers Univ. Press, 1988), 45-46.

53. I would argue that, by using a married woman, Fielding can create a female *bildungsroman* in which the heroine can have experiences not possible for the usual unmarried protagonist of the form.

54. Nancy Armstrong relates the conduct books, the novel, and these social demands well in her *Desire and Domestic Fiction*, see especially chapters 2-4; see also Katherine Hornbeak, *Richardson's Familiar Letters and the Domestic Conduct Books* (Northampton, Mass: Smith College Studies in Modern Languages 19, 1938); Joyce Hemlow, "Fanny Burney and the Courtesy Books," *PMLA* 65 (1950), 732-61; and Sylvia Marks, *Sir Charles Grandison: The Compleat Conduct Book* (Lewisburg, Penn.: Bucknell Univ. Press, 1986), 35-40.

55. Rogers, "Sensibility and Feminism," 167, and see her useful discussion, 165-70.

56. Chris Jones, for instance, writes that the concept of sensibility "poses an intriguing problem for the historian of ideas" ("Radical Sensibility in the 1790s," in *Reflections of Revolution*, ed. Allison Yarrington and Kelvin Everest {London: Routledge, 1993}, 68), and William Empson devotes sixty pages to it in *The Structure of Complex Words* (London: Chatto & Windus, 1951), 250-310. For further discussions of this term see Jones, "Radical Sensibility," 68-82; R.S. Crane, "Suggestions toward a Genealogy of the 'Man of Feeling,'" *ELH* 1 (1934), 205-30; Jean Hagstrum, *Sex and Sensibility* (Chicago: Univ. of Chicago Press, 1980); John Mullan, *Sentiment and Sociability* (Oxford: Clarendon, 1988); and Syndy Conger, ed., *Sensibility in Transformation* (London: Associated Univ. Presses, 1990).

57. It is a common modern misconception that novels such as Frances Burney's were written for women. Men and women alike read romances and courtship novels, discussed them with each other, and did not fall into the kinds of reader categories we have today. On English familiarity with French novels and early English writers, see Ros Ballaster, *Seductive Forms*.

58. Du Plaisir, *Sentiments sur les lettres et sur l'histoire avec des scrupules sur le style* (Paris, 1683), 52.

59. See, for example, *The Autobiography and Correspondence of Mary Granville*, ed. Lady Llanover, 3 vols. (London, 1861) and its three-volume "second series" (London, 1862), for Granville's comments on *Clelia*, which the ladies read aloud "for the amusement of the society at the Bishop of Killala's" (1:363), *Cleopatra* and *Pharamond* (1:472), and *Zaide* (1:356). Granville also read *Lady Julia* (4:23-24) and Brooke's translated *Letters from Lady Catesby* (3:604).

60. Ellen Moers, *Literary Women* (New York: Oxford Univ. Press, 1985), 42. The publication history of this book is interesting; copyrighted in 1963, it was not published until 1976.

61. James Raven, *Judging New Wealth: Popular Publishing and Responses to Commerce in England, 1750-1800* (Oxford: Clarendon, 1992), 51-52; John Feather, *A History of British Publishing*, 93.

62. See Paul Langford, *A Polite and Commercial People* (Oxford: Clarendon, 1989), 565, and 586-87.

63. Newspapers and periodicals also reported alleged debauchery and sexual scandals, purported bigamies, and even a wager over which sex a prominent person really was. See Paul Langford, *A Polite and Commercial People*, 571-72 and 582-87.

64. The phrase is Langford's, 602; see his discussion of the growing anxieties about women's public conduct, 602-6.

65. Among a number of plays that took the fashionable world for their subject, David Garrick's *Bon Ton: or, High Life above Stairs* (1775) was certainly known to Brooke and most of her readers.

66. Locke, *An Essay Concerning Human Understanding*, ed. Peter Nidditch (1975; Oxford: Clarendon, 1987), 2:11:2, p. 156.

67. Brooke describes gamesters as having "no age, no country, no party, no religion," 1:2:5.

68. Women writers, too, had produced these satires. Charlotte Charke's *The Art of Management; or, Tragedy Expell'd* (1735) shows Charles Fleetwood, then manager of Drury Lane, producing a comedy called *The Union of the Bear and Monkey* and offering to pay Merry Andrews £3 per week and the greatest tragic actress of the time 20 shillings a week, in other words one-third of his salary. Over a year, 20 shillings per week would be half a middle-class living wage.

69. Goldsmith, *An Enquiry into the Present State of Polite Learning in Europe* (London, 1759). The second edition of this essay appeared in 1774, and it is not surprising that Brooke read it. *The Works of Oliver Goldsmith,* ed. Peter Cunningham, 10 vols. (New York: Putnam, 1908), 6:88.

70. The authorship of this review is verified by Benjamin C. Naugle, *The Monthly Review* (Oxford: Clarendon, 1934), 16-17, and 67; and by Antonia Forster, correspondence, 6 May 1995.

71. *Monthly Review* 57 (August 1777), 145.

72. Quoted in McMullen, 165. Here and throughout, she transcribes "y" with a superscript "e," the period's abbreviation for "the," as "ye"; I have corrected this error. The entire letter is in Little and Kahrl, *Letters of Garrick,* 3:1163.

73. Little and Kahrl, *Letters of Garrick,* 3:1172, in which he calls Brooke and Yates "wretches" and "Devils." McMullen lists other instances of bad feeling between Garrick and Brooke, 176-77.

74. *The Early Journals and Letters of Fanny Burney,* 3 vols., ed. Lars E. Troide (Montreal and Kingston: McGill-Queen's Univ. Press, 1988), 2:4. Later Burney would express pleasure about her home's proximity to Brooke's (2:94), and in 1783 Brooke would propose that they collaborate on a new periodical. Burney refused, giving as her reason that she was "at present so little disposed for writing." Quoted in Margaret Doody, *Frances Burney: The Life in the Works,* 158-59. Burney may have in mind Sarah Scott's translation of *La Laideur amiable by Pierre-Antoine de La Place* (*Agreeable Ugliness,* 1754).

75. Quoted in McMullen, 197 and 196 respectively.

76. Jane Barker's Galesia novels represent the experiences of women writers and invite comparison. In Barker's time, the character of women writers was undergoing change and reevaluation, and identity as a writer is a more absorbing, difficult issue for her characters. See *Love Intrigues* (1713), *A Patch-work Screen for the Ladies* (1723), and *The Lining of the Patch-work Screen* (1726); these novels are being edited by Carol S. Wilson for Oxford and the Brown Women Writers Project series.

77. Paula McDowell makes a persuasive argument for the empowering effect on women of seeing themselves as part of a "social, collective" "Member of the Body of the Nation," a sense of identity that was both older than and above the conception of the autonomous, unique individual. *The Women of Grub Street: Press, Politics and Gender in the London Literary Marketplace,* forthcoming.

78. I have discussed women, genius, and creativity in my *Spectacular Politics* (Baltimore: Johns Hopkins Univ. Press, 1993), 101-2; women often refer to the urge to write as a "disease" or a "fever."

79. Apparently intended to preface *Charles Grandison* if not an edition of Richardson's collected works, the biography became a piece in the *Universal Maga-*

zine of Knowledge and Pleasure (January 1786), McMullen has speculated (187-89). There is no evidence that such an edition appeared near this time with Brooke's or anyone else's biographical introduction.

80. *Universal Magazine of Knowledge and Pleasure* 68 (February 1781), 63.

81. Whether the accusations against them were factitious or Harris as director or Arthur Murphy, the writer of the epilogue, set up Brooke and Yates cannot be known.

82. McMullen, 202; she also records performances in Jamaica, the United States, and a 1966 recording by the London Symphony Orchestra, 202-3. Among many interesting testimonials to its popularity is the *Overture to Rosina. Adapted as a Lesson for the Harpsichord or Piano Forte* (1805).

83. Alison Adburgham, *Women in Print,* 116; McMullen says that it is "a direct translation" of Favart's second song, 200.

84. Hayden White, *The Content of the Form* (Baltimore: Johns Hopkins Univ. Press, 1987), 14.

CHRONOLOGY OF EVENTS

IN

FRANCES MOORE BROOKE'S LIFE

~

1724, 24 Jan.	Frances Moore, daughter of Thomas and Mary Knowles Moore, is baptized in the parish of Claypole, Lincolnshire.
1725	Her sister, Catherine Moore, is born.
1726	Her father becomes rector of Carlton Scroop, Lincolnshire.
1727	Another sister, Sarah Moore, is born. Thomas Moore dies. Family moves to Peterborough to live with Sarah Knowles, Mary Moore's mother.
1736	Sarah Knowles dies.
1737	Mary Moore dies. Sarah Knowles Steevens, wife of Roger Steevens, rector of Tydd St. Mary, Lincolnshire, takes in the sisters. Catherine Moore dies. Katherine Steevens is born.
1748	Frances is in London. Sarah is living with her mother's brother, Richard Knowles, curate of Thistleton, Lincolnshire.
1755, 15 Nov.	First number of *The Old Maid*, Brooke's weekly periodical, is published, under pseudonym Mary Singleton.
1756	Marries the Rev. John Brooke. *Virginia: A Tragedy with Odes, Pastorals, and Translations* is published.
1757	John Brooke is appointed acting chaplain to British army and spends three months as chaplain on a

1757 *(cont'd)*	hospital ship, then arrives in America, where he serves as deputy chaplain to a regiment of foot soldiers.
10 June	A son, John ("Jack") Moore Brooke, is born.
1758, Aug.	John Brooke is garrison chaplain at Fort Louisbourg on Cape Breton Island, Nova Scotia, Canada.
1760	*Letters from Juliet, Lady Catesby, to her Friend, Lady Henrietta Compley*, a translation of Marie Jeanne Riccoboni's novel, is published (first and second editions).
July	John Brooke arrives in Quebec.
27 Dec.	John Brooke unofficially appointed chaplain to Quebec garrison.
1761, 28 Oct.	John Brooke officially commissioned chaplain to Quebec garrison.
1763	Third edition of *Letters from Juliet, Lady Catesby* appears. Publication of *The History of Lady Julia Mandeville*.
6 July	Brooke leaves for Quebec with her son and her sister, Sarah Moore.
5 Oct.	Brooke arrives in Quebec.
1764, autumn	Brooke visits London and presents a petition to the Reverend Dr. Burton, Secretary of the Society for the Propagation of the Gospel in Foreign Parts from the Protestant residents of Quebec asking that John Brooke be appointed their missionary.
1765, autumn	Frances Brooke returns to Quebec; Sarah Moore returns to England.
1768, Aug.	The Brookes return to London, but John is paid as chaplain of the Quebec garrison until his death.
1769	Publication of *The History of Emily Montague*.
1770	Brooke's translation of Nicolas Framery's *Memoirs of the Marquis de St. Forlaix* appears.
1771	Publishes a translation of Claude Millot's *Elements of the History of England*.
1773, May	Richard and Mary Ann Yates and James Brooke, Frances's brother-in-law, purchase King's theatre.

1773, May (*cont'd*)	Frances becomes co-manager with the actress, Mary Ann Yates. Seeks license from the Lord Chamberlain to introduce plays at King's, but is denied.
29 Nov.	Opening of King's Theatre, commonly called the Opera House.
1776, Mar.	Jack Brooke graduates from St. Paul's School, Westminster.
1777, early summer	Thomas Cadell publishes *The Excursion.*
1778, 24 June	Richard Brinsley Sheridan and Thomas Harris purchase the Opera House.
1779	Brooke works on a life of Samuel Richardson.
1780	Jack Brooke receives his B.A. from Trinity College, Cambridge, and is ordained deacon at Norwich, Lincolnshire.
1781, 4 Jan.	Jack is ordained as priest at Norwich.
31 Jan.	Production of *The Siege of Sinope* at Covent Garden.
8 Feb.	Publication of *The Siege of Sinope* by Cadell.
1782, 31 Dec.	*Rosina* is performed at Covent Garden.
1783	*Rosina* is published by Cadell; Jack receives his M.A. from Trinity College, Cambridge.
1784	Jack becomes Vicar at Helpringham, Lincolnshire.
1785	Second edition of *The Excursion* is published; Brooke moves to Sleaford, Lincolnshire, near her son.
1787	Jack becomes rector of Folkingham-cum-Laughton, Lincolnshire.
1788, 22 May	*Marian* is produced at Covent Garden.
1789, 21 Jan.	John Brooke dies at Colney, Norfolk.
23 Jan.	Frances Brooke dies in Sleaford.
1790	*The History of Charles Mandeville* is published posthumously by Brooke's son, her executor.

NOTE ON THE TEXT

~

The text reprinted here is that of the first edition, published by Thomas Cadell in 1777, along with the preface to the second edition, which was published by Cadell in 1785. The novel was carefully proofread and printed in Brooke's time, and, except for the correction of a single typesetting error ("Vallony" for "Vallouy") and the elimination of quotation marks at the beginning of every line of quoted dialogue (an eighteenth-century convention), the text appears here as it was originally printed.

I have collated the two editions, and the list of textual emendations supplies Brooke's revisions for the second edition. Three substantive reworkings include that of the famous Garrick scene.

THE
EXCURSION

∼

Preface to the Second Edition

"I appeal to the people," was the celebrated form in which a citizen of ancient Rome refused his acquiescence in any sentence of which he felt the injustice.

On giving a new edition of The Excursion to the public, I find myself irresistibly impelled to use the same form of appeal from an illiberal spirit of prejudice, and perhaps of affectation, which has lately endeavoured not only to depreciate works of imagination in general, but to exclude from the road of literary fame, even by the flowery paths of romance, a sex which from quick sensibility, native delicacy of mind, facility of expression, and a style at once animated and natural, is perhaps, when possessed of real genius, most peculiarly qualified to excel in this species of moral painting.

It confers the highest honour on this branch of composition, as well as on this age and kingdom, that some of the brightest ornaments of literature amongst the other sex* have not disdained the meed of inventive fancy; and that the novel, which in other times, and other countries, has been too often made the vehicle of depravity and licentiousness, has here displayed the standard of moral truth, and breathed the spirit of the purest virtue.

In naming Richardson as an illustrious example of my assertion, I silence the voice of prejudice itself. What tasteless critic shall dare to attempt rending the palm from the brow of him, "who" (in the words of a writer whose recent loss a nation joins in regretting) "has enlarged the knowledge of human nature, and taught the passions to move at the command of virtue*?"

"Of him, who in his beautiful histories of the world, and of human nature, those histories in which virtue instructs us by the hand of genius, has communicated at once all that experience can teach? To read his works without a wish to be better, I might add, without the accomplishment of that wish, is impossible*."

---

*Richardson, Johnson, Mackenzie, Goldsmith, &c.[1]
*The Rambler, No. 97.[2]
*Memoirs of the Marquis de Roselle by Mad. Élie de Beaumont, the amiable consort of the generous defender of the family of Calas.[3]

What is here said, with so much justice, by authorities more important than mine, of the moral tendency of Richardson's divine writings, is not less true in general of the more select novels of the present age; the writers of which, like him, have pursued the noble purpose of alluring the heart to virtue, and deterring it from vice, by well-drawn pictures, and striking examples, of both.

In this laudable pursuit, if the female sex have not been undistinguished, if they have unlocked the stores of imagination, and employed the well-wrought fable, to paint moral rectitude in the glowing colours lent by truth; far from acquiescing in the wild and inconsiderate censure of a late critic*, it appears to be a circumstance which places our sex in the fairest point of view, and of which the most timid modesty may be allowed to boast.

To govern kingdoms, to command armies, to negotiate, to fight; to investigate the hidden powers of nature, to traverse the abstruser regions of philosophy and science, to bend the stubborn mind to the yoke of rational obedience, be the province of man. To sway the softer empire of private life, to cultivate the milder powers of the understanding, to impress the gentler, the social, duties, on the hearts of the rising generation, by presenting them to their notice, adorned with their native graces; to watch the opening infant mind, necessarily committed at that early season to our tender cares, to explore the latent spark of generous emulation, to expand (as well by writing as conversation) the bud of reason,

And teach the young idea how to shoot,[5]

Be the task, as it is a pursuit not unworthy the retired dignity, the feminine softness, of woman.

Whilst those are her views, let the female to whom Heaven has lent a ray of the animating fire of genius, content with the pleasing reward of public approbation, with the accompanying tear of sympathy, and the praise of sensible minds, continue to intermix such studies as become her station in the scale of rational beings, with the domestic duties which those studies will diversify, but not interrupt; and, leaving the chilly critic to his uncomfortable remarks, in full confidence of the indulgence which candor never refuses, make her appeal at the unprejudiced bar of the Public.

---

*"There must be a profligacy of manners before women can so utterly forget all sense of decency and propriety as to turn authors." Preface to Select Scotish Ballads.[4]

The Excursion

~

First Edition

~

VOLUME THE FIRST

Book I

~

Chap. I.

On a mild evening in September last, as the two nieces of Col. Dormer, a gentleman of small fortune, in Rutland,[1] were leaning over the terrace wall of their uncle's garden, admiring the radiant lustre of the setting sun, the mixed gold and azure which played on a rustic temple belonging to a neighboring villa, praising the heart-felt pleasures of retirement, and the tranquil joys of a rural life, the lovely Lady H——, whose charms had raised her to the most distinguished rank, happened to pass by, in a superb carriage, with a numerous train of attendants, in her way to the North.

The sisters, for which we shall hereafter account, were differently affected: Louisa beheld this splendid equipage with languid admiration, and returned to contemplate the objects which had before engaged her attention.

The eyes of Maria, on the contrary, followed the coach till it was out of sight: she continued some time after gazing at vacancy: awaking at length from her reverie, she looked at her sister in silence; she sighed; her bosom beat with an emotion unknown before; she forgot "the radiant lustre of the setting sun, the mixed gold and azure which played on the rustic temple, the heart-felt pleasures of retirement, the tranquil joys of a rural life;" and felt, for the first time, the poison of ambition at her heart.

She walked slowly, with her sister, towards the house; she stopped—after a short pause—"Don't you think, Louisa?"—she hesitated—conscious of the idea which filled her whole soul, she fixed her eyes on the ground; the rising blush of modesty expanded on her lovely cheek.

The supper-bell now made them quicken their pace; but, before they obey its summons, let me introduce to the acquaintance of my reader the two heroines of my story, with the respectable man under whose roof they had passed the last ten years of their lives.

Chap. II.

Louisa and Maria Villiers were the twin daughters of a country gentleman; or, to use a phrase more suited to his character, a *squire*,[2] a race happily almost extinct, who was descended from a worthy family in Nottinghamshire.[3] To give his history in few words, before he arrived at the age of thirty-two he had wasted a decent estate in the elegant pleasures of racing, cock-fighting, and drinking, with beings as much below the standard of humanity as himself; and sent out of the world, with a broken heart, an amiable wife after two years marriage.

He died himself, happily for his daughters, whilst they were still of an age to profit by the excellent education given them by their mother's brother, Col. Dormer; who, in every literary pursuit becoming their sex, had been himself their preceptor; and who had gone even beyond the bounds of his little fortune to procure them, as far as his remote situation and retired manner of living made possible, those external accomplishments on which most grave people are apt to set too little value; or, in the words of a late noble writer,[4] to give them "The Graces."[5]

This gentleman, the worthy protector of our heroines, was the younger son of the younger son of a very noble family in a distant part of the kingdom: he had entered early into the army, where he had served with honour; but a weak constitution, some military disappointments, a native love of retirement, a quarrel with the head of his family, and the death of a wife he loved to adoration, had determined him to quit the service at thirty, though he had every thing to hope from continuing in it: he had bought a small house, with an estate of about five hundred pounds a year, at Belfont, a delightful village in Rutland; where, as the human mind must always have a pursuit, he acquired a passion for gardening; a passion which filled up those hours which might have lain heavy on his hands, and chased the monster *Ennui,* to avoid whose chilling embrace, men turn rakes, heroes, gamesters, politicians, and hunt Folly through her ever-varying circles.

But to return: the shattered remains of Mr. Villers's estate, after paying a heavy load of debt, produced about three thousand pounds;[6] which, with good birth, and a more than common share of beauty, composed the whole patrimony of our amiable orphans.

CHAP. III.

I have said, my heroines were handsome: they were much more; they had the soul, as well as the outward form, of beauty: they had countenance,[7] character, expression.

Louisa was fair, her features regular, her hair auburn, her eyes the celestial blue of the poets: she had a look of blended softness, languor,[8] and indolence, which strongly painted the native features of her mind.

Maria—But as she is to stand on the foreground of the picture, she deserves a more particular description.

Chap. IV.

Maria then—

Her face was oval, her complexion brown,[9] her eyes dark and full of fire, her nose Greek, her mouth small, her teeth regular and of the most pearly whiteness, her under lip a little pouting. Her chestnut tresses would have waved (if the despotic tyrant Fashion had allowed them the liberty of waving) in natural ringlets down her bosom. She was tall, and elegantly formed; her every motion exquisitely graceful: but it was a gracefulness I know not how to define; it was what courts may improve, but cannot bestow; it was native, I had almost said *wild;* it was unstudied, spontaneous, and varied, as the lovely play of the leaves when gently agitated by the breath of Zephyr.[10]

Natural in all, she had, when conversing with those she loved, a smile of bewitching sweetness; but, when injured, a look of ineffable disdain; a look which however became her, because it evidently arose from the occasion.

Warm, sincere, simple, unaffected, undisguised, every turn of temper and of sentiment was painted instantaneously on her countenance.

She had one charm, which is of infinitely more importance than is generally supposed; I mean, that luxurious melody of voice in speaking, which passes irresistibly to the heart.

Though beauty was the portion of each, yet nothing could have less resemblance than the persons of these sisters; though virtue formed the basis of each character, yet nothing could differ more than the features of their minds. Louisa was mild, inactive, tender, romantic; Maria quick, impatient, sprightly, playful: nor were their views and wishes less opposite; Louisa fancied Happiness reposed on roses in the shade, Maria sighed to pursue the fugitive goddess through the brilliant mazes of the world. Each had the bloom of health; but it glowed more vivid on the cheek of Maria.

Col. Dormer, their uncle and guardian, though he had passed his youth in the mixed society of mankind, still retained that beautiful simplicity of character which is generally the companion of very exalted understanding: he was well-bred, as much from his early intercourse with the great world (an intercourse which had been long almost entirely suspended), as from the feelings of a heart naturally desirous to please; but that good-breeding never passed the bounds of the most exact and undeviating sincerity. Generous to the extent of his income, frank, hospitable, chearful, his table was the seat of decent plenty and convivial delight.

An enthusiastic admirer of truth, nature, and genuine beauty; his house, his gardens, his fields, every thing around him, reflected his own mind.

Simplicity, neatness, elegance, were the characteristics of his little domain: delicate in his choice, attentive in his culture, his flowers bloomed more fair, his fruit had a more delicious flavour, than those of his more opulent neighbours.

Indeed his most striking failing was that of valuing himself rather too much on this subordinate merit: he would, I am afraid, have been better pleased with the reputation of being the most skillful gardener, than the best officer, or even the worthiest man, in the kingdom.

He was tall, had fine eyes, a dark and rather pale complexion; with the air and deportment of a man who had seen that world from which he had long withdrawn.

Chap. V.

Mr. Dormer this evening perceived a thoughtfulness and constraint in Maria's behaviour, which, being unusual, exceedingly alarmed him: he told her so; she pleaded, what she really felt, the headach, and retired early to her apartment.

She passed the night without rest; the ideas of coaches, coronets, titles, filled her mind, and effectually murdered sleep. She rose, determined to pass the winter in London, the only place where, according to her new-born idea, beauty and merit were allowed their sterling value; but greatly perplexed in what manner to propose to her uncle a design which she was absolutely certain he would disapprove.

Col. Dormer, though he knew the human heart, had yet never thought of taking his nieces into more active scenes of life: he had fallen into the common mistake of people past the meridian of their days, who, feeling tranquillity their greatest good, do not sufficiently reflect that it is insipid at that season when expectation and the wish for novelty are the springs which actuate the mind; when all opens fair on the dawning imagination, and a thousand ideal pleasures play in the chearful rays of hope.

Youth is of itself gay and vivacious; Maria possessed in a superior degree every charm of that enchanting age; her conversation exceedingly amused him, and it never occurred to him that his might not equally amuse her, or that she could have a wish beyond the little paradise of Belfont.

CHAP. VI.

M aria wished to methodize her plan, a plan she was however resolved at all events to pursue, before she proposed the journey to her uncle. After waiting two months, a conjuncture presented itself, which seemed favourable to her wishes: by the will of a relation she was, though not of age, to receive immediately a legacy of two hundred pounds, which she was to employ in whatever manner she thought proper, without accounting to her guardian.

A favourite servant of her late mother, a woman of worthy character, had just before taken a house in Berners-street,[11] and had written to entreat her recommendation of some single lady to hire her best apartments, which she assured her were fitted up with the utmost elegance.

And, what made this house particularly agreeable to her, it was in the next street to a lady with whom she had made an acquaintance the preceding summer; a lady whom she extremely loved, and under whose protection she hoped to be introduced, with every advantage, into the brilliant circle for which her heart now so ardently panted.

This lady, Mrs. Herbert, was a young widow of fashion and unblemished character; rich, good-humoured, lively, dissipated, and a little capricious; she had spent the summer with a family in Col. Dormer's neighbourhood, and, finding no being half so pleasing in the little *coterie* with whom she lived when in the country, had distinguished Maria by a very flattering preference; a preference which her young heart, then unemployed, ever on the *qui vive*,[12] and not absolutely satisfied with the calm though steady affection of her sister, returned by the most animated friendship.

Nor was Mrs. Herbert insensible to Maria's regard; on the contrary, she had her perpetually with her, and found a thousand charms in her conversation: she had indeed taken such an amazing fancy to her, that nothing but this amiable girl's being fifty times handsomer than herself, could have prevented her giving her an invitation to her house in town.

Mrs. Herbert really loved Maria, as much as she could love any thing except admiration; but that was her primary object, and she well knew, the science of light and shade was as necessary a study to a beauty as to a painter.

She therefore chose for her constant companion, particularly in public, a long, lean, brown, young lady, of good family, and not ungenteel, but with a face about three scruples handsomer than that of Medusa;[13] doated on the Opera[14] and Ranelagh[15] because there were no two places where people looked so well; and abjured the Pantheon,[16] not because it was *triste,*[17] but because it was unbecoming.

To this friend Maria would at first have communicated her design, had she not pleased herself with the idea of surprizing her by an unexpected visit.

She was a little tempted to ask Louisa to accompany her; but when she reflected, that by so doing she should leave her uncle in absolute solitude, she waved[18] the idea, and determined to undertake the journey alone.

Had she asked her concurrence, she had however probably been refused. Louisa's blue eyes had not been turned on the rustic temple merely to admire the radiant lustre of the setting sun, but to contemplate *the human face divine,* in the person of a very handsome youth, the only son of the squire of the parish, but who, happily, had not an atom of squire-ism in his composition.

In short, Louisa loved; Maria's hour was not yet come; a distinction which will sufficiently account for the different manner in which they had been affected by the brilliant object which had banished peace from the bosom of the latter.

After settling the plan with herself, Maria determined to pursue it the moment she could assume sufficient courage to disclose to Col. Dormer her wish to pass a few months in London.

She knew he would remonstrate, but she had previously resolved it should be in vain: she was clear his disapprobation would be only temporary; and painted to herself in glowing colours his rapture and surprize, when he should see her return to Belfont, after an absence of two or three months, with a ducal coronet[19] on her coach; an event of which she had not the remotest doubt.

Chap. VII.

To recount all Maria's timid efforts to unveil her purpose to her uncle, and to observe how often her heart failed her, would be exceedingly uninteresting to the reader. Suffice it then to say, that, after several weeks of irresolution, during which the agitation of her mind exceedingly affected her temper, and in some degree her health, Maria proposed the journey with hesitation, and her uncle resisted with firmness; till, at last, wearied out, not convinced, and at once distressed and softened by seeing the gloom continue, which he hoped would have passed over like a light cloud before the summer breeze, he, after a thousand cautions against the arts of a world to which she was a perfect stranger, reluctantly gave his consent.

He cautioned her, not against the giants of modern novel, who carry off young ladies by force in post-chaises and six[20] with the blinds up,[21] and confine free-born English women in their country houses, under the guardianship of monsters in the shape of fat housekeepers, from which durance they are happily released by the compassion of Robert the butler;[22] but against worthless acquaintance, unmerited calumny, and ruinous expence.

The first dangers he knew were generally imaginary, the latter, alas! too real.

After many long conversations, in which this amiable old man drew a faithful picture of the various evils to which she was going unnecessarily to expose herself; and which she heard with the attention generally given by presumptuous, believing, unsuspecting youth to the prudent lessons of wary experience; her journey was fixed for Tuesday the 10th of January; and an old grey-headed footman, who had lived twenty years with Mr. Dormer, was ordered to prepare to go with her, and attend on her whilst in town.

Chap. VIII.

Behold her at length in possession of her uncle's consent, though obtained in a manner which did not quite satisfy her feelings.

His arguments appeared to have some weight, though she was predetermined not to be convinced by them. She saw something like just drawing in the dark shades of his pencil, though the lines seemed a good deal exaggerated: she reflected, she doubted; but, after settling a balance in her mind, she found her own scale preponderate; and easily obviated all the dangers he had so elaborately displayed, by determining to make no new acquaintance to whom she should not be introduced by her friend, Mrs. Herbert; and to return, if unsuccessful, to the tranquil shades of Belfont, as soon as the legacy, which she had appropriated to the execution of her plan, should be expended.

As to calumny, such was her knowledge of the world, that she thought herself secure from its attacks, only by resolving not to merit them.

Chap. IX.

O n Tuesday then, the 10th of January, about ten o'clock, Col. Dormer's post-chaise (for he would not trust her to any other conveyance) drove up to the door.

The tears of her sister, the benevolent concern on the countenance of her uncle, with her own involuntary horror at leaving what was almost her paternal roof, and parting with friends so tenderly attached to her, a little shook her resolution: but her desire of pursuing this ardent impulse of her soul, was a resistless torrent, which her own good sense, and her respect for the opinion of the man on earth whom she believed the wisest and best, in vain opposed.

Louisa prest her to her bosom; neither of them were able to speak. Mr. Dormer led her to the chaise; he kissed her cheek, "My dear child," said he, "as I cannot prevent your embarking on the tempestuous ocean of the world, I have only this to add; when beat by the storm, remember you have a safe port always within your reach."

The chaise, attended by John on horseback, had proceeded through half the village, when, on turning the corner of a street, the terrace of her uncle's garden struck Maria's sight: the tears gushed from her eyes, her heart reproached her with ingratitude, she felt her uncle's excess of goodness, she felt the happiness she was going to quit, and was on the point of ordering the servants to return: she had even let down the fore-glass of the chaise for that purpose, when the fond deceiver, Hope, painted to her lively imagination the gaudy scene which had originally misled her. Her sister's attention, her uncle's accumulated kindness, the silent language of her own heart, every whisper of discretion and of sentiment, the pictures drawn by Truth and Nature, faded away before the dazzling blaze of a coronet.

She drew up the glass, and proceeded on her journey, her bosom beating with mingled regret and expectation. We will leave her on the road, and return for a moment to Belfont.

Chap. X.

M r. Dormer and Louisa stood some time at the window without speaking: at length the latter put an end to the silence, by venturing to ask her uncle a question, which probably the reader may have been inclined to ask already; "Why, if he foresaw such dangers in her sister's being in London unprotected, he had not himself accompanied her?"

He was struck by the question, as it had more than once obtruded itself on his own mind: he answered her as he had before answered himself: he pleaded his decline of life, his indolence of temper,[23] his delicate health, his disgust of the world, his love of tranquillity and retirement.

He did not perhaps himself really perceive the governing spring of his reluctance to quit Belfont.

At another season he would not have hesitated a moment; but to leave his garden during the three most important months of the year—his early flowers, his hyacinths then ready to blow, his tulips, his anemonies, his auriculas; his lovely new polyanthus, the invaluable present of a curious friend at the Hague—all the blooming hope of the genial spring, the floral pride of the rising year—all, all, would too probably perish, if he left the tender nurselings, or (to speak in technical terms) the *babes,* at this critical juncture.

Gentle Critic, if thou art not a Florist, reflect one moment, that the ruling passion is, in its effects, the same, has the same art of throwing a veil over our reason, whatever happens to be its object.

Man of the World, consider, that the pursuit of the Florist is, at least, innoxious: no ruined virgin, no agonizing parent, weep his blameless pleasures: he pursues beauty without the wish to destroy it: tender of his lovely charge, he resembles the vernal breeze, thou the chilling blight which marks its progress by destruction.

But to resume our story. Louisa was unwilling to carry the subject too far; she trembled lest her uncle should return her question by another—it was so natural *she* should have desired to accompany her sister—so natural Col. Dormer should be surprized she never made the offer.—She therefore changed her style, spoke of Mrs. Herbert's attachment to Maria, of the immense advantage of having such a friend to consult on every occasion, a friend in possession of general esteem, and able to introduce her with *eclat*[24] into the best company; of the great faithfulness of John, and the good woman in whose house Maria was to reside; and concluded by observing, that her sister's excursion would amuse and perhaps improve her; and could have no further ill consequence than dissipating a part (or what if all) of the legacy which seemed to have been left her for that very purpose.

They passed into the garden, and from the terrace cast a tender look at the great road, where they endeavoured to trace the wheels of Maria's carriage.

Mr. Dormer was absorbed in thought; Louisa perhaps stole, unobserved, a look at the rustic temple.

CHAP. XI.

Maria's chaise flew along with a velocity almost equal to her impatience, till it stopped at the Bell at Stilton;[25] where, reflecting on the inconvenience her uncle, must suffer by being without a carriage, she, though contrary to his express injunction, sent it back, and took a post-chaise the rest of the way.

In compassion to old John, who found some difficulty in keeping up with her, she slept that night at Biggleswade,[26] and got into London about five the next afternoon, without meeting with any adventure worthy the dignity of history to recount.

Mrs. Merrick, with whom she was to lodge, a little, fair, fat, honest, loquacious, good-humoured, good sort of personage, of about forty-six, met her at the door with a thousand curtesies, a thousand smiles of undissembled affection, and conducted her to her apartment, where she had scarce entered, when she dispatched a card to inform Mrs. Herbert of her arrival, and to beg to see her immediately.

Her heart danced with hope, she counted the moments with impatience: John returned; she met him on the stairs; when he informed her, the lady was at Paris, and the time of her being in England uncertain.

It is not necessary to paint her disappointment; she was however constrained to submit; she drank her tea, she supped, she retired to rest; she passed the next day, and the next, in solitude; it was the first time in her life she had been alone; she sat down pensive to her silent meal; the shades of evening came, but came unattended by the chearful voice of domestic pleasure; the enlivening smile of friendship, the social, the convivial hour was far away.

She listened, in expectation of she knew not what; she heard a thousand coaches, but they passed her door; she saw crowds, but to these crowds she was unknown: she seemed a solitary being, cut off from the society of human kind; she sighed for the shades of Belfont; the promised scene of happiness she found a dreary void.

CHAP. XII.

A thousand moralists and philosophers have declaimed on the joys of solitude, on the advantages of silent contemplation. May I be allowed to suspect them of affectation, if not of falsehood? For my own part, I had rather be a beggar happy in the converse of my fellow beggars, than a princess condemned to solitary greatness.

My heroine, for which I love her, thought, or rather felt, in the same manner: unable to bear any longer that divine state of heavenly solitude and contemplation so praised by the wise men of whom I have been speaking, she on the fourth evening invited Mrs. Merrick, the good woman of the house, to sup with her; she thought any company better than none, and she thought justly; if it was only for the pleasure of hearing the sound of one's own voice—if only—In short, a human being who can live without conversation must be little better than a beast, and ought to be driven out to eat grass with Nebuchadnezzar.[27]

CHAP. XIII.

In the course of the evening's conversation, Mrs. Merrick had hinted her surprize at Maria's coming to town to live by herself; and, on being acquainted with her disappointment in respect to Mrs. Herbert, had begged leave to introduce her to a mighty agreeable widow lady, to whom this good woman had formerly been housekeeper, and who lived in the same street. This lady was, to use Mrs. Merrick's own phraseology, one of *the quality,* and kept the very best *of* company.

Maria's heart bounded with joy at the proposal; she had no time to lose; her money might be all spent before Mrs. Herbert returned; the resource of which I shall speak presently might fail; and though there were several ladies then in town who visited at Col. Dormer's, yet she was not sufficiently intimate with any one of them to expect the kind of protection she wanted.

Mrs. Merrick waited on the lady in the morning; who, after a very minute enquiry into Maria's situation, family, character, and connexions, and on hearing she was a particular friend of Mrs. Herbert's, whom she happened to visit, readily undertook the office of her *chaperon,* and invited her to a rout[28] at her house in the following week; first passing through the necessary introductory form of rapping very hard at her door, and leaving a card,[29]

Lady Hardy at home Jan. 19th.

CHAP. XIV.

Behold her now happy, on the eve of being introduced into the world, that world for which her little heart panted: the radiant picture drawn by Hope again started into ideal existence, and resumed its pristine glow.

As she wished to proportion the means to the end, she went to her bureau, and counted her wealth: she found it amounted to an hundred and ninety-four pounds thirteen shillings and six-pence, a sum which she supposed would last her a good part of the winter.

But, should it be expended sooner, she had another resource: a mine unopened; and to all but herself, undiscovered; a mine she thought inexhaustible.

To be explicit, she had *genius,* that emanation of the Divinity, that fatal gift of heaven, pleasing to others, ruinous to its possessor.

From almost infancy she had

"Lisp'd in numbers, for the numbers came."[30]

but had never found sufficient courage to own this circumstance, even to her sister, to whom she had no other secret.

Her portmanteau[31] was her only *confidante;* and it now contained a novel, an epic poem, and a tragedy.

Though she had expectations from the two first, yet it was on the last she placed her dependence.

Diffident as she was by nature, that enthusiasm inseparable from true genius, broke through the veil which modesty would have thrown over the merit of this piece; she felt she had succeeded beyond her warmest hopes: the fable was interesting and pathetic, the characters strongly marked, and the language at once mellifluous and sublime.

Certain of her tragedy being received with rapture by the managers, if her affairs should oblige her to offer it, she had no difficulty, but in determining to which house to give the preference.

The shining talents of Mr. Garrick,[32] of which she had heard and read so much, would have left no room for doubt, had she not been accidentally informed this great actor had left off playing himself[33] in new pieces; a circumstance extremely mortifying to her self-love, as she had drawn the hero of her piece with a view to his performing the character.[34]

At length she determined to take every possible opportunity of seeing tragedies at both theatres,[35] and to regulate her conduct by the different degrees of merit in the performers.[36]

As she had however no present intention of entering the lists of fame,[37] she descended from the heights of Parnassus[38] to consult Mrs. Merrick (with whom we will leave her for the present) on the œconomy[39] of her dress for Lady Hardy's rout, the expected era of a new life of happiness.

Book II

~

Chap. I.

I know not which, of two very common errors, most merits reprehension, the thoughtless passion of young ladies in the country to see London, or the short-sighted wisdom of their papas and mammas, such I mean whose situations give them the power to comply, in neglecting to indulge this very pardonable inclination; an inclination founded on the restless curiosity of the human mind, and never dangerous but when controlled.

Let your children, ye careful parents, see this world of which they entertain such fallacious ideas. Let their own experience, for they will never grow wise from yours, break the gay bubble which fond imagination had formed; let them run the giddy round of fashionable amusement unrestrained, and satiety will soon be the certain effect of your complaisance.

Let them see this boasted world, but be yourselves their guides through the whirling maze; be constant sharers in all their pleasurable pursuits; and, whilst you lead them through the flowery road of dissipation, shew them the rocks and precipices by which it is surrounded.

Inspire them with a disgust of bad company, by introducing them into good; and prevent their mixing in diversions dangerous to morals, by suffering them to enjoy freely such as have a contrary tendency; such as, whilst they improve and inform the mind, contribute to elevate, to enlarge, to refine the heart.

In order to secure this important point, you need in general only leave them to themselves; they will almost always chuse better than you; their taste is natural, yours too often acquired. *they will make their own decision.*

They will never voluntarily offer incense at the shrine of *Pam;*[1] they will be cold to that destructive passion, Play;[2] that passion which levels youth and age, wisdom and folly, dignity and meanness, vice and virtue; which quenches every spark of the divine fire within us; blunts the edge of wit, renders knowledge useless, undermines the empire of beauty, and tears the palm from the brow of honour; that passion which contracts the understanding, hardens the heart, annihilates all the finer feelings of the soul, and renders human society a state of selfish uncomfortable warfare.[3]

restless curiosity is okay, so don't try + get rid of that in children because it will only make it more tempting forbidden.

when they encounter something new, talk w/ them about it.

You have your wisdom which can sort of mess you up. Enlightened belief in naturalness.

But they will run with avidity to the theatres of every kind: with the noble enthusiasm of uncorrupted taste, they will worship the sister Muses, the lovely Powers of Poesy and of Song.

Hurried away by the charms of declamation and of harmony, their bosoms will beat responsive to the magic sounds; sounds rendered more interesting by all the graces of action.

Their souls will be harrowed up by Lear and by Medea,[4] nor will they refuse a tear to the expiring Montezuma.[5]

They will weep with Romeo; and from your relation of the past, regret that Juliet's grave is not ideal.

They will not be equally delighted with the Comic Muse. Youth are better judges of the Passions than the Manners.

But a truce with reflection. We left Maria, with the officious Mrs. Merrick, assorting ornaments for Lady Hardy's rout.

We should premise that she had, as in politeness bound, paid her ladyship a morning visit, had found her at home, and had been most graciously received.

Chap. II.

The 19th of January at length arrived. Maria, to her native charms, had added all the adventitious advantages of dress in her power: she had exhausted a third part of her little treasury in preparing for this important moment.

John being dispatched to call a chair, we will dedicate the interval, till his return, to Lady Hardy.

This worthy dowager, under whose happy auspices our heroine was to be introduced into the *beau monde*,[6] was the relict[7] of an ancient baronet, of one of the best families in the kingdom, who, observing her a handsome healthy country girl, whilst dairy-maid at his seat in ——shire, took a fancy to her, and kept her several years.

As she was at once artful and imperious, she gained such an ascendant over her antiquated lover, that at the end of fifteen years, during which he had turned her out of the house, and taken her in again, at least fifteen times, he, in the first kind moments of reconciliation, after a quarrel which had lasted longer than usual, very generously made her an honest woman, and about a year from the date of this honourable alliance was kind enough to make his exit, leaving her in possession of two thousand pounds a year, half of which was in her own disposal.

As the people of distinction in the neighbourhood shewed no very striking propensity to cultivate her Ladyship's acquaintance, she very sensibly determined to transplant herself to London, that seat of true hospitality and universal benevolence; where any lady, who has a large house, an elegant carriage, well drest footmen, will play gold loo,[8] and now and then give a supper,[9] may with very little difficulty, and without producing a certificate of her virtuous life and conversation (unless her deviations from the rule of right have been very public indeed), make her way into *company*, often into *good company*, and sometimes, but this is rather uncommon, into *the best*.

But, that we may not rate her ladyship's sagacity too high, it is proper to observe, that this plan was not originally her own, but was first suggested to her by a gentleman, with whom, whilst he was on a visit to the late Sir John, she had contracted a friendship of the most interesting kind.

This gentleman, who, from having been a lieutenant in the East-India Company's[10] service, had assumed the title of Captain, was so admirable an œconomist, that he maintained a carriage and two footmen, drest well, and kept *pretty good company*, on an annuity of sixty pounds a year.

We will suppose her Ladyship fixed in town, aspiring to *bon ton;*[11] her house, her equipage, her dress, her parties, her suppers, arranged in due form by her friend Captain Wilson.

We will suppose, that, by the assistance of this worthy gentleman, who had represented her to his female card acquaintance as a woman of good family and connexions, the widow of a baronet, with a great estate and a large sum of ready money in her own disposal, fine diamonds, an elegant equipage, and a perfect ignorance of the mysteries of the card-table (a circumstance which greatly facilitated her admission), she had been received into, and was become one of the principal ornaments of, a society, which merits, and therefore shall have, a chapter devoted to its service.

Chap. III.

Those of our readers who know the world, or, to speak with more propriety, the town, and especially those who play much at loo, that sovereign leveller of all distinctions, need not be told, that, besides the various circles and semicircles into which people of fashion are necessarily divided and subdivided, in a capital so immense, so opulent, so full of *noblesse,*[12] as London, there is a *coterie* which may, not improperly, be considered as the intermediate state between good and bad company, as it touches the two extremities, and partakes something of the nature of both; and, whilst it is frequented by some persons of rank, fashion, and character, admits without scruple well-drest men of whom nobody ever heard, ladies of equivocal fame, and gamblers of almost every denomination.

This heterogenous mass of unknown gentlemen, self-made captains, demireps,[13] neglected coquets, antiquated virgins, and dowagers *sur le retour;*[14] in which however the women are both in rank and reputation greatly superior to the men; is by their enemies (and who have not enemies?) distinguished by the appellation of *a certain set.*

If fortune, if dress, if diamonds, if equipage, if even title alone, abstracted from all regard to character, or to the qualities of the head and heart, could constitute good company, *a certain set* would undoubtedly merit that name: but if its ever-open gate stands ready to admit all who, from whatever cause, are either utterly rejected, or coldly received, in more estimable society, we may, without hesitation, venture to refuse it, collectively, that honourable appellation.

Nobody will be offended at this refusal, for nobody will allow themselves to be of *a certain set.*

Chap. IV.

Our digression being ended, we beg leave to resume Lady Hardy.

This amiable protectress of the blooming Maria was, at the time when our history commences, about the age of forty-three, from which she had the modesty to subtract only eleven years.

She was, as to her person, what in the country is called a hearty, hale, comely, portly, woman; tall, large made, plump; with coarse features, a ruddy complexion, and an air and manner not very expressive of feminine softness.

Her tone of voice was strong and masculine; her address forward and self-sufficient; she had an easy confidence, which nothing could disconcert, a good natural understanding, with that instinctive cunning which in the common concerns of life is of more importance than all the understanding in the world.

She was vain, ignorant, insolent, assuming, vociferous, and satirical; which last quality she found of infinite service in intimidating all who were once unfortunately enrolled on her visiting list, from daring to drop her acquaintance.

She was gallant, but without much delicacy of choice; her first favourite, from a similarity of sentiment, was Captain Wilson; but though he was her *home,* yet her heart sometimes deviated into a temporary *visit,* when she met with a handsome ensign whose time hung heavy on his hands.

She was however so disinterested a lover of virtue, that though she has now and then, as we have already said, ventured to disobey its dictates herself, she would not allow any of her acquaintance to transgress its smallest law with impunity; nor was she ever known to give quarter to the minutest degree of female indiscretion in another.

Chap. V.

John and the chair arrived; Maria set out; Lady Hardy received her at the top of the stairs, praised her beauty, criticized her dress, laughed at her *mauvaise honte*[15] (for she blushed, trembled, and stammered like an idiot), and led her into the assembly.

Maria entered the rooms, equally agitated by pleasure and apprehension: on advancing, a cold tremor seized her, she turned pale, she stopped; she felt, and felt painfully, the disadvantage of not having been earlier introduced into the world; she wanted that happy self-confidence which is the indulgent companion of unblushing folly, but which those of strong sense and quick feelings can only acquire by being, almost from infancy, in a crowd.

She looked round her with a timidity which for a time suspended all her powers: the lights, the numerous company, the glare of dress, the impertinently enquiring eyes of the women, who had been apprized they were to see a new beauty; the more complacent, but not less curious, regards of a few of the men (the greater part being too much engrossed by their cards to have afforded a glance even to Venus herself, if she had descended *in propria persona*)[16] disconcerted, and almost turned her to a statue.

She was awed, she was intimidated by a set of beings in the aggregate, whom considered individually she would probably have despised; at least if she had known their true characters.

A confused murmur of admiration, as Lady Hardy led her through the apartments, added at once to her embarrassment and her charms.

As beauty was a flower not very common in this autumunal *parterre,*[17] the lovely Maria excited astonishment; she would have excited more animated sensations had any men but gamesters been present: but I need not inform my Reader that a true gamester is not a *sensitive,* but a *frost* plant.[18]

He is of no *sex;* as he is of no *age,* no *country,* no *party,* no *religion;* he is, literally speaking, an *individual.*

Chap. VI.

A quarter of an hour had elapsed, our heroine had recovered her presence of mind; her apprehensions had given place to unmixed pleasure; her ideas were still in some degree tumultuous, but it was the tumult of delight: when Lady Hardy offered her a card for one of the gold quadrille[19] tables; she was too happy not to be inclined to comply with any thing: but had not this been the case, though she hated play, yet she wanted resolution to refuse.

She sat down without having dared to enquire into the stake, and was surprized at being asked for twenty guineas to put into the pool.

As she carried her little exchequer in her pocket, she was however amply prepared, and had the good fortune to rise from the table thirty guineas richer than she sat down: a circumstance which, it may be supposed, did not diminish her happiness.

She had just cut out, and was passing from one room to another, Lady Hardy leaning with an air of intimacy on her arm, when a servant announced Lord Melvile.

She turned hastily at the sound of a title; a sound for which she had listened impatiently the whole evening in vain.

This young nobleman, the only son of the Earl of Claremont, whose rank and character intitled him to shine in more distinguished circles, happening to dine in the neighbourhood, had accidentally, in his way to Arthur's[20] rambled into Lady Hardy's, whose parties he generally honoured with his presence about once a year.

The first object that struck his sight was Maria, her countenance drest in smiles of undissembled pleasure, talking earnestly to Lady Hardy.

So much beauty, under such protection, must necessarily attract the notice of every man who was at all its votary.

Lord Melvile's eyes met those of Maria; she blushed; he regarded her with an attention the most flattering possible to her charms; but in which, if she had known the world, she would probably have observed a mixture of something like hope, not quite so flattering to her virtue.

If the well-known character of her *chaperon,* "whom (to borrow the admirable definition of Fielding) every body knew to be what nobody chose to call her,"[21] might naturally encourage ideas unfavourable to Maria's honour, her own present appearance was not very well adapted to destroy them.

The transport of seeing herself in the chearful haunts of men after a week of uncomfortable solitude, the admiration she had excited, perhaps her success at play which pointed out a new source of *ways and means,*[22] with the revival of that brilliant imagination which had a first seduced her from Belfont, and the sight of a man she thought formed to realize her fairy dreams of greatness; all conspired to give a glow to her complexion, a fire to her eyes, a gaiety, I had almost said a *levity,* to her air, which it was not difficult to misinterpret.

Fresh and blooming as Hebe,[23] playful as the Mother of the Loves,[24] her form, her manner, invited the spoiler, whom the purity of her heart would, if known, have repelled.

If she appeared charming to Lord Melvile, he did not seem less so to her.

Amongst such men as composed Lady Hardy's assembly, he seemed, what indeed he was, a being of a superior order.

To a countenance full of expression, eyes that anticipated all he meant to say, and a form more perfect than that of the Belvedere Apollo,[25] Lord Melvile added that air of distinction, that easy dignity, compared to which, beauty alone is a meer dead letter.

His address was polite, spirited, insinuating;[26] his conversation that happy mixture of good sense and frivolousness which makes the most pleasing of all compounds, and is so particularly agreeable to women.

He had read, he had traveled; he knew books and mankind; but the latter had unfortunately been shewn to him through the wrong end of the perspective.

His father, Lord Claremont, besides being naturally of a gloomy and suspicious turn of mind, had seen the world in the way most likely to give him unfavourable impressions of it; he had stood high in administration; and, on a change of men, had figured not less conspicuously on the side of opposition:[27] the school of modern politicks not being the purest school of rectitude, he had found a great part of those with whom he co-operated knaves, and therefore naturally enough, though very falsely, concluded knavery to be the characteristic of mankind.

For such a world he had endeavoured to form his son, and had, in this view, spared no expence or trouble to improve and adorn his person, polish his behaviour, cultivate his understanding, and corrupt his heart; in all which points his labours had been crowned with tolerable success.

He found it however impossible to eradicate, and very difficult even to suspend, a warm susceptibility of soul, and an extreme good-nature, both which strongly opposed those cold, uncomfortable, selfish maxims, on which he endeavoured to form Lord Melvile's character.

He read him unceasing lectures on the universal depravity of mankind, the supposed total selfishness of the human heart; and, to confirm his precepts by the more forcible language of example, he introduced him early into the intimate society of a set of men, whose general principles were as profligate as their outward conduct was regular and decent; and of women who practised every vice with impunity, under the mask of hypocrisy, and the sanction of *bon ton.*

To pursue my favourite allusion: in the variegated garden of human life and manners, he industriously pointed out the weeds to his son's observation, and concealed from him with not less sedulous anxiety the flowers with which it at least equally abounds.

Though he had instilled these destructive principles into the young bosom of Lord Melvile, principles calculated not only to loosen the bonds that hold society together, but to rob it of all its sweets, he had instructed him to conceal them with the utmost care.

He had taught him to "smile without being pleased, to caress without affection;" to profess friendship for the man he regarded with aversion, and respect and esteem for the woman he beheld with contempt: to dress vice in the graceful garb of virtue, and conceal a heart filled with the deepest design, under the beauteous veil of honest unsuspecting integrity.

He had succeeded in making him one of the most pleasing men in the world; he had not absolutely failed in making him one of the most artful. But, though his system of conduct was formed on his father's plan, his heart frequently revolted against it: his principles were narrow and selfish, his feelings generous and humane.

In short, he had learned to *smile and smile,* but he had not yet learned to *be a villain.*[28]

CHAP. VII.

Such was the man who now addressed Maria, with that insinuating respect, that graceful ease, that gentleness of manner, that softened tone of voice, that mixture of every thing seducing, which good sense and good breeding equally dictate to the man who wishes to gain the heart of woman, and which was so peculiarly adapted to ensnare that of our heroine.

Lady Hardy pressed him to play: he pleaded an engagement, which obliged him, however unwilling, to go in a quarter of an hour.

She again offered a card to Maria—the timid Maria now found courage to refuse: Lady Hardy smiled maliciously; her young friend blushed, and sat down.

Lord Melvile took the chair next her, he talked, she found a thousand charms in all he said; the subjects of his conversation were trifles, but those trifles from him were so interesting!—

"Then he would talk—good gods, how he would talk!"[29]

Her heart felt sensations to which she had till this instant been a stranger—she did not doubt he was actuated by the same emotions—he had asked, with an air of the utmost anxiety, where so much beauty had been till then concealed—that countenance could not deceive—he certainly loved—all she had heard, all she had read, of sympathy,[30] was realized—she anticipated the joy her uncle and her dear Louisa would feel on receiving her next letter—she blessed the happy impulse that had brought her to town.—These were the first moments in which she could be said to live—they danced away on downy pinions.[31]

We will suppose Lord Melvile's quarter of an hour, which he had however more than doubled, was expired, we will suppose he had left the assembly; we will imagine Maria, after having followed him to the door with her eyes, sitting pensively gazing on her fan, insensible to all around her, when she was suddenly awakened from her *reverie* by Lady Hardy's presenting her to some of her female friends, who were dispersing their cards of invitation with a liberal hand. She exchanged a profusion of civilities, and found herself invited to sixteen card parties in the course of the coming eight days.

My Reader will perhaps be surprised at the facility with which she had made all this acquaintance, as she was an utter stranger to all the company: it may be therefore necessary to observe, that, besides her being represented as much richer than she really was by Mrs. Merrick, who did not know the extent of her old master's extravagance, and her playing ill enough, though she had won to-night, to promise their avarice a harvest; *a certain set* pique themselves more on the quantity than the specific quality of their visitants, and therefore pay a constant attention to the great object of encreasing the number of their tables.

The difficulty in respect to many *coteries* is how to *get in;* may we be permitted to say, the only difficulty in respect to this truly hospitable one is how to *get out?*

Miss Villiers's chair came, and was in due course announced: as the party was beginning to break up, and she felt herself untuned, as to play, for the evening, she gladly embraced the opportunity this event presented of making her escape, as we shall do of concluding the chapter.

Chap. VIII.

Maria returned from her visit, full of a thousand pleasing ideas. She sat down, and wrote a short letter to Louisa.

"She had passed a delightful evening in the best company, at the house of a very respectable lady, the widow of a baronet; had been invited by half a dozen ladies of the most estimable character, to parties where she should see only persons of the first fashion; had attracted the notice of the most amiable young nobleman in town, the heir of an immense fortune.—But his rank and fortune were the least considerations—she had found the man she should have chosen had she seen him in a cottage—the man on earth formed to make her happy—had found him in the most distinguished rank—had found him possest of that bewitching delicacy of sentiment—that dear sensibility[32]— that perfect honour—that noble simplicity of character—that dignity of manner—his looks exprest such benevolence of heart—such candour was painted on his countenance—it was Virtue adorned by the Graces—his eyes spoke the language of truth and tenderness—their souls were formed for each other—it was his least merit to be the most lovely of mankind."

She would have filled a folio sheet in this Pindaric style,[33] the style of a girl bred in shades, who loves for the first time, if the bellman[34] had not reminded her to seal and send away her letter.

She retired to bed, but joy kept her waking: the idea of Lord Melvile pursued her; she endeavoured to recollect every syllable he had said; his disinterested sentiments, so resembling her own; his tone of voice; those expressive changes of countenance—the eyes were the index of the mind—his had said—Good heavens! what had they not said?

she is expecting that all consuming love that wollstonecraft is worried about.

Lady Hardy had told her in a whisper at parting, that Lord Melvile wore her chains: she wished it too ardently not to have believed it on much slighter evidence.

She was now clearly convinced of what she had always believed, that there is between certain souls a secret sympathy, which it is almost impossible to resist.

CHAP. IX.

We should be happy if that scrupulous regard to truth, which is the first duty of an historian,[35] and from which it is our firm resolution never to deviate, would permit us to say, this wonderful sympathy was as strong on the side of Lord Melvile: but the plain fact is, he went from Lady Hardy's to Arthur's, played deep, won a very considerable sum, retired home at two, in all the pride of triumphant success, to Mademoiselle Dorignon, and forgot, before he reached Grosvenor-street,[36] that there existed such a being as Miss Villiers.

CHAP. X.

How then account for his Lordship's temporary attention to the latter, or for his having lengthened his quarter of an hour at Lady Hardy's?

Nothing is more easy. Whilst he continued to see Maria, and for some hours after, he thought her charming; but he was too much inured to beauty, to receive from it very forcible or very lasting impressions, though it never failed to excite his admiration for the moment.

His attention to her was natural: she was the only very handsome woman in the room; she was young; she was new; she had, though educated in the country, an air of fashion, an elegance of manner as well as of person, which the rest of this respectable company in some degree wanted; she had fine sense, and sprightliness, mixed with a very interesting style of sentiment; she had with him, that lively desire to please which seldom fails of attaining its end; and what was of still more importance, she had distinguished him, the moment she saw him, in the manner most flattering to his self-love.

His coquetry had therefore given the additional quarter of an hour; he had observed her refusal to engage at quadrille; and, on the information of her blush, and Lady Hardy's very intelligible smile, had justly placed it to his

he's just not that into you.

own account; he thought this complaisance[37] demanded some little sacrifice on his part, and what less could he make than an idle quarter of an hour?

In short, he wished to secure, though his present engagements left him without the least intention to pursue, his conquest.

He even quitted her with a kind of half reluctance, and went so far as to enquire her name.

As his chair past along the streets, he recollected her with pleasure; it was indeed that tranquil, languid, unimpassioned style of pleasure with which he had formerly comtemplated the statue of the Medicean Venus;[38] but still it was pleasure.

He thought of her, it is true, without emotion, but he *thought of her;* her image, in all its native loveliness,

"Played round his head,—"

though it

"Came not to his heart."—[39]

It accompanied him to St. James's-Street, mounted the stairs, seated itself by him at the table, nor absolutely retired till the last decisive throw, by making him master of unexpected thousands, banished every idea but that of his good fortune.

Chap. XI.

Lord Melvile hastened home, as we have said, with his prize, to Mademoiselle Dorignon; a female more distinguished by her spirit than her charms; but possest of that happy *je ne sçai quoi*[40] which so effectually answers the end of beauty: a female who, to use the emphatical words of the sweet swan of Twickenham;[41]

Was just not ugly, and was just not mad:
Yet ne'er so sure our passion to create,
As when she touch'd the bounds of all we hate.[42]

His Lordship, having found this *jewel of a woman* a noxious weed in the capital of a neighbouring kingdom, had kindly condescended, such is the empire of caprice, to transplant her into *his own fair garden.*

She presided at his table, and did the honours of his house; a situation, however, for which neither her birth or education had very distinguishingly fitted her.

This amiable object of his Lordship's present inclination was the daughter of an artizan at Paris, had fallen early into the hands of an officer in the Swiss guards,[43] had completed her studies in the Rue St. Honoré,[44] where, after a variety of adventures, she had attracted the notice of an old French nobleman, who, after entering into a convention with her as his declared mistress, being disgusted with a few little vivacities to which the warmth of her temper made her sometimes unhappily subject, obligingly contrived to transfer her to *mi Lor Anglois*,[45] as the easiest way of getting rid of her, without altercation, trouble, or expence: a circumstance which we beg leave to submit to the consideration of every English gentleman when he sets out on his travels.

Lord Melvile found an elegant supper, ready to be served, *et des convives*,[46] the younger sister of Dorignon, just arrived, and a little Marquis, who, on pretence of joining his regiment, then in garrison in the Provinces, had left Paris, with all the money he could procure, and eloped to London with *la petite Janeton*.[47]

The countenance of Dorignon was drest in smiles, which, being unusual, had the greater power of attraction.

Lord Melvile, who, as he had made supper wait an hour, expected a storm, was enchanted with his reception. He entered with ardour into the interests of *la petite Janeton,* and prest her earnestly to fix her residence in his house; an invitation she had too much *politesse*[48] to refuse.

Dorignon was this evening uncommonly brilliant: she had carried her point in respect to her sister, without even having had the trouble to signify her commands.[49]

She was in some pain about Mons. le Marquis, who might be an impediment to her sister's advancement, and who could be of no further service, as the voyage was made, and his *louis'*[50] reduced almost to the singular number: she however considered she was in a country of liberty, where nothing in nature was more easy, if he should grow troublesome, than to give him his audience of dismission.

She might even, by a little *tour d'addresse*,[51] make a merit of delivering him up to his father.

Full of these agreeable ideas, and a thousand more which presented themselves to her fertile imagination, she put in practice all her convivial powers of pleasing, the fruits of her extensive knowledge of the heart of man, and the various roads by which it is accessible.

The divine creature! What engaging vivacity! What fire! What *piquantes caprices!*[52] What were a thousand Villiers's to the enchanting Dorignon!—Not handsome, it must be confessed, nor very young; *mais, si enjouée! si amusante! si eveillée!*[53]

Her sallies indeed were sometimes a little eccentric; but did not those very sallies stamp a greater value on her paroxysms of good humour? Could any thing be so insipid as meer youth and beauty? *so ennuieuse*[54] as eternal complaisance?

She was ruining him, it is true; *mais n'importe;*[55] was he the first man of fashion she had ruined? To say nothing of her French conquests, had not Sir George—— and Lord Y—— worn her chains?

And was it not the *ton* to be a little *derangé?*[56] Would not a wife, at any time, retrieve his affairs?

Such a proof too she had given of her disinterested attachment! had she not for him (for so he had been taught to believe) abandoned Mons. le Duc—— in the very first month of their arrangement? Mons. le Duc, it must be owned, was old and poor; but still it was a sacrifice, and he ought to be grateful.

To be grateful? We know not what idea this phrase may present to our reader; but to us it seems to want no comment.

His Lordship was not however sensible his passion for the fair stranger was on the decline: perhaps he did not chuse to perceive it, as he felt he had not sufficient resolution to give her her *congé,*[57] though he knew his submission to her impertinent tyranny had extremely lowered his character.

A little inclination, and more caprice, had at first forged those chains which habit and indolence had now riveted too strongly for common efforts to break: his good-nature too contributed to render it difficult for him to make those efforts.

And wherefore should he undertake so painful a task? If she had, in some little degree, ceased to interest, yet she still continued to amuse, him; and to be amused was of infinitely more consequence than people in general imagined.

Besides, his bondage could not be of long continuance: his father, who wanted money to pay off a mortgage, would necessarily marry him, and then the affair would die a natural death, without any unpleasing exertion on his side, or any pretence for altercation or reproaches on hers.

She could not expect him to disobey his *cher pere;*[58] and if she did, he should yield to his *cher pere* the task of bringing her to reason.

Chap. XII.

We will leave Miss Villiers to enlarge the circle of her very estimable friends, to become in due form one of *a certain set,* to make her fortune at gold quadrille, to draw designs for her future coronet, and to dream of the all-accomplished Lord Melvile.

We will leave the all-accomplished Lord Melvile to amuse himself with the *enjouement, les piquantes caprices, et les petites vivacitez,*[59] of the enchanting Dorignon; to endeavour at twining festive wreaths round the galling fetters he finds himself unable to break, whilst we make a short visit to our deserted friends at Belfont.

But let us first do justice to our heroine's skill in physiognomy, by observing, that as Lord Melvile was by nature all she had represented him in her letter to her sister, she could not fairly be accused of having painted him ill.

His virtues, though in a great degree expunged from his mind, by the very worst of all possible educations, had left their amiable traces still visible on his countenance; a countenance which might have imposed on a person of much greater sagacity and keener observation than the innocent and inexperienced Maria.

BOOK III.

~

CHAP. I.

It was one of those clear frosty mornings in January*, which make us often forget the season, the blue serene almost rivaling the brightest tints of a summer sky, when Col. Dormer and Louisa, impatient to hear from their dear wanderer, drove, as soon as they had breakfasted, to meet their letters at Stamford.

Col. Dormer was surprized at receiving no answer from Mrs. Herbert; to whom he had written the day after Maria left Belfont, to recommend her in the strongest terms to that friendship she had so warmly professed for this amiable girl, which he began to fear absence had totally destroyed.

He was not less surprized that Maria had not mentioned this friend of her heart in either of the two letters which he had already received from her.

He considered the scene of dissipation in which Mrs. Herbert was immersed, and therefore excused that silence for which he was prepared; but could not account for so blamable an inattention in Maria: he had, this very day, written to chide her gently for so unpardonable a neglect, and to ask a thousand questions respecting her fair friend.

As Maria abhorred every approach to deceit, she had herself reflected on this omission, and thought herself obliged in honour to communicate to her uncle a circumstance, of which, for his own tranquillity, she could have wished him to remain ignorant: she had done this in the letter that now waited him at Stamford; she however softened the information by saying what was true, that Mrs. Herbert was every day expected in England; and that, in the mean time, she was under the protection of a lady who was so happy as to be of her acquaintance.

This letter, having been written the day of her visit to Lady Hardy, and sent away before she left her own house, arrived at the same time with that to Louisa, giving an account of the delightful evening she had past in *the best company,* and of her new-born passion for Lord Melvile.

---

*The 21st of January, 1775.

Louisa, who, though romantic, was less subject to receive sudden impressions, and a thousand times more discreet than Maria, saw a great deal to disapprove in her sister's letter; she therefore made use of that liberty to which every human being, of every age and sex, has an unquestioned right, and in which her uncle had always indulged them, even when children, of never communicating their letters, except from choice: she read it attentively, folded it up, and, saying her sister was well, put it with great seeming composure in her pocket.

CHAP. II.

Louisa was, however, alarmed. She knew the purity of Maria's heart, the dignity of her sentiments; but she also knew her indiscretion: she knew she was much less beloved in the little circle of their acquaintance than herself, and that any imprudence of hers would therefore be infinitely more fatal.

There was a regularity in the mind of Louisa, which set her amiable qualities in the clearest and most favourable light: the virtues of Maria, on the contrary, though perhaps stronger, were wild and Pindaric, and therefore too often mistaken or overlooked.

Louisa's attention was always at home; she was polite to every creature with whom she conversed, and polite almost equally to all: Maria's soul was on wing to oblige the few she loved; but she was subject to little absences in the common intercourse of life; absences which wore the appearance of a pride to which her heart was a stranger, and which very naturally made her a thousand enemies whom she had never thought of offending.

From a similar inattention, Maria was indiscreet: she overlooked, perhaps she despised, those trifling forms, which mask vice, and protect virtue.

Conscious of her own integrity, and true even to excess, she disdained every species of disguise.

Had she faults? they appeared in their native colours to every eye.

Had she virtues? she left them to shine by their own unborrowed lustre.

Her mind, not less pure and unsullied, was obvious and transparent as the clear rivulet in the sequestered vale.

Maria should have avoided with care that world in which she was so fond of mixing: of the whole human race she was least formed to be safe and happy in the undistinguished general mass of society. Sincere, rash, credulous as an infant, she invited deceit, and stood a ready prey to the arts of the selfish and designing.

CHAP. III.

These were Louisa's reflections (nor were her uncle's very dissimilar) during the remainder of their morning's airing; reflections, only interrupted by two or three very uninteresting visits to as many very uninteresting gentlemen and ladies (uninteresting we mean to our Readers, who are strangers to the chit-chat and politicks of the little, though lovely, county of Rutland), whose houses they must necessarily pass in their way home.

The more Louisa considered her sister's situation and turn of mind, the more she found herself alarmed for her.

She trembled at dangers of which she could however form only a very indistinct and inadequate idea; and, as she had a high opinion of her own *comparative* discretion, was almost resolved to propose to her uncle passing a month with Maria in town, and endeavouring to bring her back to Belfont as soon as that month should be at an end.

Nothing could be better concerted, or more kind, than this determination, which continued firm to the very entrance of their own village.

She hesitated a little as she passed the manor-house, and saw the sunbeams glitter on the dear rustic temple, which was constantly honoured with her passing glance.

She began, as the chaise turned the corner of her uncle's garden wall, to think her design a little absurd; and condemned it as absolutely wild and extravagant, on seeing Mr. Montague, who was to spend only a month longer at his father's, ring the bell at the court-gate, in order to pay his customary morning visit, a visit he seldom omitted.

He was to go back to College in a month: that month—that little month—He was not to return to Belfont till June—there would be time enough to go to her sister after.

CHAP. IV.

Mr. Montague was the gentleman of whom we made a slight mention *en passant* in the beginning of this our history, as the magnet which drew Louisa's eyes to the rustic temple, and the latent cause of her attachment to the shades of Belfont.

He was the only son of the lord of the manor,[1] to whom the whole village, except Col. Dormer's estate, belonged.

He had been educated at Eton[2] till seventeen; and at the time when we have chosen to begin our narrative, being exactly one-and-twenty, was a fellow-commoner of Trinity College, Cambridge,[3] where he had the reputation of being a young man of uncommon genius, and an excellent classical scholar.

His father, a man of strong sense, a kind of rural philosopher, who held the present *macaroni* race[4] in the utmost horror, had taken infinite pains to accomplish him in all those manly exercises, of which force, agility, and health, are generally both the consequence and the reward.

He was of opinion, in which we entirely agree with him, though against great authorities, that strength of body had a natural tendency to produce strength of mind.

Active and light as air, Mr. Montague danced, fenced, walked, rode, played cricket, and shot flying,[5] better than any man, of whatever rank, in the next seven counties: nor was he quite untaught in the less gentleman-like exercises of quarter-staff,[6] boxing, and wrestling; exercises which the good old man insisted, by multiplying the means of defence, were calculated to increase courage, a consideration of no little importance.

As his father had the best pack of hounds in the neighbourhood, and was himself a keen sportsman, he had early inspired him with the ambition of being *in at the death:* and though hunting was not his favourite amusement, yet in these degenerate days, when the robust race of hardy Nimrods[7] are dwindled to

"Puny insects shivering at a breeze—"[8]

he might very well pass for an excellent fox-hunter.

By the way, it might not be amiss at present, to encourage the race of *squires,* in order to keep up that of *men.*

But to Mr. Montague; his accomplishments were not all of the corporeal kind; he was passionately attached to the enchanting sisters, Poetry and Music; had written odes and sonnets which Horace[9] and Petrarch[10] need not have blushed at owning; and was no mean proficient on that graceful and elegant instrument the *viol de gamba.*[11]

He was generous, humane, open, brave; disdaining disguise, as below the dignity of man, yet detesting that affected blunt impertinence which is generally the mask of a villain.

He was easy, courteous, attentive, well-bred; but without the high Parisian varnish.

➤ Though he set little value himself on this species of merit, yet he might, without being accused of presumption, have enrolled himself on the list of handsome men.

Nothing could be more interesting than his countenance; a countenance on which candour, benevolence, and truth, were pictured in the strongest colours.

His eyes were dark, and expressive of the utmost sensibility of heart; his complexion brown, his hair the most beautiful chestnut; his smile insinuating almost beyond description.

Tall, genteel, and finely proportioned; he had the easy mien and unconstrained deportment of a gentleman, though he had never breathed any air but that of his native country.

His father, a determined enemy to the modern system of education, was of opinion *the Graces,* if they must be sought abroad, might be purchased infinitely too dear.

He dared to assert, they might be acquired without leaving England; and that a man naturally formed to become their disciple, might find them in the lore of ancient days, or sporting on the banks of Cam[12] or of Isis.[13] "Where," he observed, "should we seek the Graces, but in the seats of their allies, the Muses?"

He thought Horace, not to mention Pope, a better teacher of urbanity than the best dancing-master Paris, or even Versailles,[14] could produce; and that more politeness might be learned from the conversation of a well-educated English woman, of fashion and of honour, than by the strictest attendance at the *ruelle*[15] of *Madame la Presidente,*[16] the highest distinction at which a travelling Englishman, unless of the first rank, almost ever arrives.

He observed, and his observation was not the less true for having been made before, that our *boy* travellers generally culled the follies and vices of every clime, and with the most happy dexterity contrived to leave the national virtues of every country behind.

"I had rather," said he, "my son should come ungracefully into a room, than that he should violate all the ties that hold society together, and wound the bosom of domestic happiness.

"But I see no occasion for either: I think a man may be exceedingly well-bred, without endeavouring to seduce the wife of his friend, or even of the man by whom he has been hospitably entertained.

"I think love the most likely means to refine the heart, and soften the manners; but I think, the more estimable the object, the more forcibly the means will operate on the mind.

"Of this at least I am certain, that the worst-bred men that have fallen within the circle of my acquaintance, have been in general the most profligate and unprincipled."

CHAP. V.

The amiable young man we have been describing, had from almost childhood regarded Louisa with a partiality which had insensibly grown up into the most ardent and tender affection, though from being habitual he had never suspected it to be love.

When a boy, he never returned from school without bringing his dear Louisa a present to the utmost extent of his little finances.

The first partridges he ever shot were carried to his Louisa; his air of triumph was a little checked by the fear of her thinking him cruel.

As he grew towards man, Louisa was the subject of his sonnets, his constant partner in the dance.

In short, from twelve years old to the present moment, he had persisted in shewing her those thousand almost unnoticed attentions which steal so imperceptibly on the soul.

Louisa was much better acquainted with the state of her own heart.

More retired, less amused, less distracted by variety of objects and of pursuits, she had leisure for reflection, and was not to learn that she loved; but, as the dear object of her affection had never declared any attachment to her beyond the bounds of friendship, she had with the utmost care concealed her sentiments even from her sister, though she could not from herself.

Mr. Montague saw her with a delight of which he had never asked himself the source; but which he found so pleasing, he was willing to indulge it at all events.

He would perhaps have been long before he discovered the nature of his affection, had not a man of such fortune, as it was scarce to be imagined Col. Dormer would refuse for his niece, seen her at a ball, and declared his intention of addressing her.

From this moment jealousy opened his eyes to the passion which had lain almost unperceived in his heart; and he determined on endeavouring immediately to explore that of Louisa.

Having taken this resolution, he hastened to Col. Dormer's, and met them at the door, as we have already said, returning from their airing.

We will leave him there, and make the best of our way to Berner's-street.

CHAP. VI.

Joy, we have already observed, had, after her evening's adventure at Lady Hardy's, banished sleep from the bright eyes of Maria.

We would not however wish to be literally understood; she slept, but her slumbers were short and interrupted.

Those broken intervals of rest had charms which she had never found in the calmest moments of perfect repose.

Tranquillity had bid adieu to her agitated bosom; but a more interesting, a more pleasing, guest had taken possession of the vacant place.

Lord Melvile, respectful, insinuating, tender, attentive; Lord Melvile, triumphant in all the pride of youth and manly beauty; Lord Melvile, crowned with wreaths of myrtle by the Graces, presented himself incessantly to her creative imagination.

She awaked, she regretted the fleeting phantom; she again resigned herself to sleep, the enchanting vision returned more lovely than ever.

How delightful must these enthusiastic slumbers have appeared to a heart like hers! a heart formed with the quickest sensibility; a sensibility which had never yet found its object! a heart which recoiled at the state of apathy and inaction in which it had hitherto vegetated!

She arose at nine, and prepared to arrange the business of the day.

The first two hours were devoted to her *friseur*[17]: she had a morning visit to pay afterwards to Lady Hardy; and was to be introduced in the evening by this indulgent friend to a brilliant card party, for which she had received an invitation at her house the preceding night.

The lady by whom she was invited had been particularly distinguished by Lord Melvile; she had asked him to be of this party, and he had made a bow of acknowledgement and assent.

She meditated during breakfast on the events of her little life of *bon ton;* she counted her winnings at play; she read over again all her cards of invitation; she recollected every particular of her conversation with the *most lovely of mankind;* and regretted the time she had so unfortunately lost in the country.

She made her morning visit to Lady Hardy: she returned; Mons. De——— arrived; she was *frisée comme une ange.*[18]

She sat down to her toilet: she studied her dress with the minutest attention; an attention she had never before given to this very important business of female life.

She was too much in earnest not to succeed. Lady Hardy called at seven; our fair heroine accompanied her, more radiant than the star of morning.

She entered the rooms; she mixed in the circle who were not at play; she found almost the same faces as the night before; she did not however find the same admiration; as she was no longer new, she attracted very little notice.

She looked round with a glance of enquiry; that glance of enquiry was vain; alas! the *most charming of mankind* was far away. Her cheek glowed with a blush of wounded sensibility and disappointment.

She sat down to quadrille; she knew not a card she played: her eyes were continually turned towards the door; her heart fluttered at the sound of every carriage which stopped.

The second pool ended, she was pressed to play on; she played, not from inclination, but that childish, that timid flexibility, which is the source, not only of half the follies, but of more than half the vices, of mankind.

She lost considerably: but her loss was not the subject nearest her heart.

The hours past on; she grew impatient; she looked every moment at her watch: ten o'clock came; no Lord Melvile appeared.

She found the women displeasing, the men detestable; she was out of humour; she had the head-ach, she had the spleen.[19]

The lady of the house saw her uneasiness, and relieved her; she arose from the table, made an apology to Lady Hardy, and retired.

Politeness would perhaps have advised her waiting for her friend; but a stronger principle of action than politeness impelled her to quit the assembly.

She hurried home; she asked with eagerness if any person had called; if any message—not a human being had been there.

It was strange—she had overheard him ask her name and address: he knew she was to be that evening at Mrs. M——'s; he had been asked; he had appeared to accept the invitation.

He might at least have sent to enquire after her health.

Could he love her, and not endeavour to see her? She had not had a doubt of meeting him at Mrs. M——'s.

She sat down to supper; her chicken was ill drest, it was not eatable—she could not conceive how Mrs. Merrick could be so mistaken. She could not taste it; she ordered John to take away: she shed tears of regret and vexation.

CHAP. VII.

We should little amuse the Reader in going through the uninteresting detail of half a dozen more such parties; where the blooming Maria suffered the martyrdom of mixing with people, for whose society (if society is a name to be given to this species of intercourse) she had not the smallest taste; and of passing her whole time at the card table, though play was the thing on earth she most detested.

She suffered this too without any event to enliven and vary the scene; without any change of situation, except a very sensible and alarming diminution of her finances; and without so much as hearing the name of the man, in the dear hope of seeing whom she had made these engagements.

After about a fortnight spent in this amiable, this very interesting style of life; a style of life so congenial to the feelings of her soul; so admirably adapted to youth, beauty, and sensibility; she was proceeding to determine, in a fit of disgust, to leave London immediately, and return to the bosom of domestic happiness, when Lady Hardy came in, and, observing her chagrin, asked her to go with her that evening to the opera.

"There, my dear," said she, "you will hear Rauzzini[20] in a new opera of Sacchini;[21] there you will see the brilliant Baccelli.[22] It is, I am told, a divine opera; it is the second night; it is Saturday; *all the world will be there.*"

"And there, my dear," added she with a significant glance, "you will be certain of seeing Lord Melvile, who is languishing for an opportunity of telling you to what a degree you have charmed him."

A stroke of electricity could not have had a more instantaneous effect than this last sentence.

Maria's gloom was dissipated; her eyes re-assumed their fire, and London all its powers of pleasing.

"But I thought, my dear Madam, your ladyship had been engaged this evening on a charitable party, to play loo with a sick friend."

"Yes, child, but the party is broke; my sick friend, who was turned of fourscore, has done the most impertinent impolite thing in the world, she chose to die last night, sitting up in her bed, in a fit of coughing, with a flush of trumps in her hand.

"They say, but I don't believe a syllable of the story, that there were three Pams found, after her death, under her pillow."

Maria looked astonished; and Lady Hardy proceeded.

"She has used that young Ensign extremely ill: she promised, in my hearing, to provide liberally for him in her will; and I find she has not left him a shilling.

"I hear she has settled annuities on all her dogs except Julio (who had disobliged her by taking notice of a little citizen's wife in the park), and that she has left her chambermaid executrix.

"There is no accounting for the caprices of old women: for my part, I think Julio, except the Ensign, the only supportable being in her house.

"The dear little creature! a true Bolognese![23] such eyes! and so much the air of a dog of quality!

"I will allow that a citizen's wife is not a proper acquaintance for the dog, and the favourite dog too, of a woman of fashion; but his motive was pardonable, for this citizen's wife had been his first protectress, and had brought him to England.

"But I must leave you, my dear Miss Villiers: I have only just time to dress and dine. Remember to put on all your charms."

Maria had not perfectly understood that part of the conversation which related to Mrs. T——.

She saw no great harm in her being innocently amused at fourscore; on the contrary, she thought fourscore the age at which amusement was particularly necessary; and what amusement more innocent than cards with a few chosen friends?

What surprised her most was Lady Hardy's contemptuous manner of speaking to-day, of that very friend for whom she had heard her express the warmest affection last night.

That friend too just expired; a circumstance which should rather have silenced the voice of disapprobation.

She disbelieved the anecdote of the three Pams; admired (though she was sorry for little Julio) Mrs. T——'s diffusive humanity, which extended even to her canine dependants; but execrated her unjust severity to her grandson, for such she very naturally concluded the neglected Ensign to be.

CHAP. VIII.

It may appear extraordinary, that Maria had been a month in town without having been once at the Opera.

It was much more so, considering one part of her plan, that she had never been at the other theatres; but she was entirely under the guidance of Lady Hardy; and the ladies of *a certain set* look on going to public places as so much time lost from the important business of the card-table.

Nor was it now Montezuma, though *all the world was to be there,* which drew this accomplished dowager to the Opera.

The little accident of her dear friend's decease had broke the loo party, when it was unfortunately too late to make another; and the approaching evening was a burden she knew no other way to get rid of.

She might indeed have gone to the Play; but—good heavens! the Play on an Opera night—not a creature there whose name one has even heard—she had besides not the least interest with Johnson.[24]

The Opera was therefore her *pis aller.*[25]

CHAP. IX.

They went early, and seated themselves between the two centre pillars in the pit.

Lady Hardy amused her young friend till the Opera began, with telling her the names of all the company as they came in.

The overture was played, and the curtain drew up; the opera advanced; Rauzzini appeared; he sung an air; our heroine was enchanted.

Maria adored music; the first passion of her heart was the theatre: she had never heard Italian music but at her own harpsichord;[26] she had never seen any theatrical representation but in a country town.

My reader will therefore imagine her transport: she gave attention still as night to the whole.

The music (worthy of Sacchini); the voice, the taste, the blooming youth, the animated action, of Rauzzini; the beauty of the theatre; the splendor of the decorations; the force, the execution, of the brilliant Baccelli; the grace of Vallouy;[27] and let me add, what is not the least ornament of an opera, the striking *coup d'œil*[28] of the assembled audience; an audience which the world cannot parallel, composed of all that is great and lovely in the kingdom; struck her young mind with an extasy almost too great for words.

Absorbed in pleasure, she did all but *forget* Lord Melvile.

Just at the moment when Rauzzini, expiring in Montezuma, shews himself not less an actor than he is an accomplished singer; at the moment when her whole soul was employed in admiration; the god of her idolatry appeared in Fop's alley,[29] leaning carelessly, with an air of the most philo-sophic indifference, but in an attitude of infinite grace, against the corner box, with his friend, Sir Charles Watson, on his left hand.

He was to-night drest with the most critical elegance: his cloaths were from France, and in the *buon gusto*[30] of Versailles; his *cheveux flottant*[31] rivaled in studied negligence the waving tresses of Fierville, or of Vestris himself.[32]

osho ✳ Lady Hardy interrupted our heroine's attention to the hero of the drama, by whispering softly in her ear the still more interesting name of Lord Melvile.

She turned her head quick, she saw him, she blushed, her foolish heart fluttered; the opera was in its turn forgotten; his eyes met hers, he observed her confusion, he enjoyed his triumph; inspired by coquetry, not less the weakness of one sex than of the other, he came forward into the pit; after some efforts, he reached the seat on which she sat; he addressed her with the most submissive, the most persuasive, air; his eyes assumed that insinu-ating, that deceitful softness, which had already misled her inexperienced heart.

He said then thousand flattering things, which she too easily believed; he begged permission to visit her, which she had not resolution to refuse; he engaged himself to meet her the next night at Lady Hardy's.

He returned to his friend: they retired together to the coffee-room, where the following conversation took place.

"*A propos,* Melvile, who is that immense fine girl to whom you was talking just now in the pit?"

"The very woman, Charles, of whom I was speaking to you last night. Don't you think her lovely?"

"Lovely? She is enchanting—will you introduce me?"

"With pleasure! I love to communicate happiness."

"But when?—how!—to-night—now—this very instant—as they go out."

"A little patience, my good friend; tomorrow night you shall see her at Hardy's. This good lady keeps Sunday; and your acquaintance, as you are the *ton,* will be an acquisition of which she will be proud, and for which I shall receive her thanks."

"I may depend on you?"

"Do you doubt my honour? She may be worth *your* attention, as you are at present unemployed."

"But pray? I want the *carte du pais.*[33] This divine girl? is she kind?"

"I should think not: though her manner is a little equivocal. She is at least, you see, *en bon train.*" [34]

"She is in good hands certainly. But to be plain; you have no designs there yourself? for I would by no means interfere."

"None, upon my word; though I think her angelic, and her behaviour to me has not been discouraging: but I have too much on my hands already."

"Who, and what, is she? I never saw her before. Is she of fashion? she has that air."

"All I know of her, I learnt from Hardy's *maitre d'hotel,*[35] of whom I enquired. She is just come from the country, is alone in a lodging, and her name is Villiers. This is all the fellow himself ever heard about her. You know Hardy is not very scrupulous in her acquaintance, nor indeed has she a right to be so."

"Alone in lodgings? That circumstance is promising: she is certainly nobody: therefore one may hazard breaking through forms."

"O fear nothing, Charles: the conquest will not be difficult."

"You know I am naturally timid with women."

"Your timidity here would be absurd. She seems to me a little adventurer, who is looking out for men of a certain rank: I know not with what design, nor is it material. You will best learn her views from herself: perhaps they may differ from yours, but you will probably bring her to reason."

In these terms of respect, esteem, and tender veneration, did *the most amiable of mankind* speak of a woman, who thought *him* all but a divinity, and who amused herself with the idea of their hearts having been formed for each other.

Yet let us be candid: Lord Melvile might in some degree stand excused.

The impropriety of her unprotected situation, and her apparent intimacy with a woman of Lady Hardy's very equivocal character, were sufficient pleas to justify suspicion.

Had he only silently doubted her conduct, we would have forgiven him; but the very unfeeling manner in which he endeavoured to awaken those doubts in the mind of another, was equally mean, unjust, and unmanly.

Nor was he less culpable in attempting to ensnare her into an inclination which promised to make her unhappy, and which could afford no advantage to himself, situated as he was, but the gratification of a contemptible selfish vanity, the lowest of all human passions.

After encountering some little difficulties in getting to their coach, the ladies drove to Miss Villiers's lodgings, where they supped together.

A new world had opened on the mind of Maria. How different was this evening from those spent at cards, with the society in which she had lived the last fortnight!

She was enchanted with the entertainment, and not less with the audience.

With all her partiality for Lord Melvile, she could not avoid observing, that though he really looked much handsomer this evening than when she had first seen him, yet that the striking air of easy dignity, which had so particularly charmed her, was not, as at Lady Hardy's, solely appropriated to his Lordship.

He had there appeared a being of a superior order; he was here only an elegant man of fashion amongst his equals.

He retained the same air of distinction, the same graces of deportment; but he shared these advantages with a thousand others; whereas at Lady Hardy's they were peculiar to himself.

She felt also, but she felt it without envy, of which not an atom entered into her composition, that she was not the only handsome woman in London.

Lady Hardy to-night, by the whole tenor of her conversation, endeavoured to fan into a flame that spark of inclination which Maria, who was sincerity itself, had confessed for Lord Melvile: an attempt in which she succeeded but too well.

She did this with no more important view than that of bringing a man of his rank oftener to her house; as she was a little ashamed, and not without reason, of the general style of her male visitants.

As to the cruelty of sacrificing the peace, and perhaps the honour, of a young, innocent, unsuspecting woman, who regarded her as her guide and protectress, to so very trifling an interest of her own, it weighed little with her: she was a woman of the world, and consequently above the weakness of feeling for any thing but herself.

Had she been questioned on this point, she would have said coolly, "'Tis her affair!"

Chap. X.

On Lord Melvile's return from the opera, he found a message inviting him to breakfast with his father the next morning.

He went at ten; and found his Lordship, in an elegant *dishabille*,[36] reclining on a sopha, reading a political pamphlet, with a dish of chocolate[37] in his hand.

"Good morrow, Melvile: you looked like an Adonis[38] last night at the opera: I never saw you so well drest."

"Your Lordship is partial—I really thought I looked ill."

"You are mistaken. There was in your whole air and manner a well-fancied *nonchalance,* which could not fail of its effect. "Your second attitude[39] in Fop's alley was enchanting."

"O, my Lord, you flatter."

"No, indeed—the women were all of my opinion.

"But to business.—I believe, Melvile, I shall marry you in about six weeks."

"As you please, my Lord; you know I never interfere in family affairs."

"And in those of the heart, you will do me the justice to own, I never take upon me to dictate.

"But to our marriage.—The lady I think of is the only daughter of a Nabob,[40] who is just returned from making the tour of Europe with his family.

"The fellow, to be sure, is a scoundrel; but no matter. He has offered us eighty thousand pounds down; a handsome sum, for which we have great present occasion.

"You know the mortgage is large; I want to build a house in Mansfield-street:[41] and you, I fancy, can dispense with a little ready money."

"Why, certainly, my Lord—at my time of life, you know—"

"I understand you; and will comply with every thing reasonable.

"But pray, Melvile, what do you intend to do with Dorignon? She must positively abdicate."

"I should be glad to make some provision for her, and to get rid of her without noise: but I intend to leave that to your Lordship's management."

"You will do well. I have a West Indian[42] in my eye for her, who is worth her attention; and have planned an excursion of ten days to my house in Yorkshire, where I hope to settle the arrangement.

"I would have you go with us, stay one day; contrive to quarrel with her, which is not difficult; pique her vanity, which will naturally put her on coquetting with our West Indian; pretend business, come to town, leave them both behind, and the rest will follow of course."

Some company arriving, put an end to the visit.

Lord Melvile returned home, to think of his marriage, settle the sum necessary to pay his debts, dine with Dorignon, and prepare to introduce his friend, Sir Charles Watson, at Lady Hardy's assembly in the evening.

CHAP. XI.

The unbounded complaisance of that inconsistent monarch Charles the Second[43] to the prejudices of his good friends the Dissenters[44] (prejudices which were however the constant objects of his ridicule), having shut the door on all rational and innocent amusements on a day evidently intended by the beneficent Lord of all, not only as a day of public worship, but of relaxation from care and labour; a London Sunday is generally passed by people of fashion at cards—by the better sort of mercantile inhabitants in parties out of town—and by the lower class, consisting principally of mechanics and young apprentices, either in absolute sotting at clubs of choice spirits, or in cultivating an acquaintance with ladies *of the town,* and gentlemen *of the road,* at those seminaries of virtue the various tea-drinking places of entertainment in the *environs* of this metropolis; to the unspeakable improvement of religion and morals, and the great emolument of a certain very respectable personage.[45]

But to wave a subject which calls for other animadversion, and on which no person of humanity can reflect without a sigh; let us return to our heroine, and to the *conversazione* [46] at the house of her friend, who, from a caprice for which we cannot account, never suffered play on a Sunday, though her company in general had not an idea which did not originate from the card-table.

CHAP. XII.

A *conversazione* without cards, being in England, and perhaps every where else, if the company is numerous, the dullest of all possible things, and the least productive of conversation; it is usual for those ladies who do not play on Sundays, to run incessantly from one house to another; by which means they are themselves at least amused with the sight of different faces; and the rooms through which they pass in perpetual review, by presenting a constantly moving picture, are rendered less melancholy than they would appear if composed of the same unvarying circle of half-animated, and almost vegetative, beings.

About nine o'clock, the tide of company at Lady Hardy's being at the highest, Lord Melvile, and his friend Sir Charles Watson, entered the rooms.

After introducing his friend to the lady of the house, Lord Melvile advanced alone to the place where Maria, whose cheek was suffused with the blush of pleasure at his sight, sat impatiently expecting his arrival.

He approached her with the most respectful air, assumed a look of the most insinuating tenderness; said little, but with that irresolute tone of voice, that seeming timidity, so exactly resembling love, and so dangerous to women who do not know the world.

His coquetry redoubled at Sir Charles's approach; he even thought her more lovely on seeing her so much the admiration of another.

He entreated permission to visit her, which he obtained; he asked the same permission for his friend, which she declined granting, meerly for the pleasure of marking more strongly the preference she gave him to all the rest of his sex.

His eyes sparkled with the joy of conquest, and of triumph over Sir Charles; which was not unobserved by the latter, who redoubled his assiduity, but without the least effect; and at length, piqued at his ill success, left the field in possession of his rival.

Inebriated with gratified vanity, Lord Melvile staid very late, and left Maria fully convinced of the reality of her conquest.

She returned home, in the greatest harmony of temper imaginable; she asked Mrs. Merrick a thousand questions about her family and affairs; promised her *her* protection, with the most condescending goodness; destined her eldest son, then at Paris, for my Lord's valet de chambre; thought of her daughter for her own woman; and, in short, considered every light in which Lady Melvile could be useful to this worthy creature; and anticipated, with delight, her future power of exercising the native beneficence of her heart.

Chap. XIII.

Lord Melvile, who felt himself uneasy and constrained in the presence of Dorignon, from the consciousness of his intention to part with her, and of the plan laid to make her engage in another connexion, and whose vanity was agreeably flattered by the artless attention, and very obvious partiality, of the young, the lovely, the unaffected, the innocent, Maria, paid a visit to the latter on Monday, in his way to Cavendish-square, where he was to dine with Lord Claremont, and settle the preparations for their journey into Yorkshire, which was to take place the next morning.

He found her alone, he made a long visit, he led her to talk more, and on a greater variety of subjects, than she had had an opportunity of doing at Lady Hardy's.

The pleasure of seeing him, and the lively desire of fixing a heart on the possession of which she felt her own happiness depended, called forth all her native vivacity, and gave new graces to an understanding naturally strong, and improved and polished by the cares of her excellent uncle Col. Dormer.

He found the charms of her mind not less attractive than those of her form; and, if he had possessed a heart, it would have been undoubtedly in the greatest possible danger.

He was however safe: the dissipated life to which he had been long accustomed, the false principles he had imbibed in the course of a very ill-directed education, and his early connexions with the most abandoned of the other sex, which naturally gave him unfavourable ideas of the best, had destroyed all the finer feelings of his soul, and rendered him almost a Stoic to every species of beauty.

Charming as Maria was, and pleasing as he found her conversation, she amused and flattered, without interesting, him.

He felt infinitely more pleasure in the idea of triumphing over his friend Sir Charles, than in that of being beloved by a woman whom he thought of all women most lovely.

Dead to the genuine transports of love and delicate friendship, incapable of the tender ties of affection, of those endearing relations which strew the thorny paths of life with unfading roses, vanity was the only sentiment of which he really felt the empire; and Dorignon herself had only held him by that imperious caprice, those well-dissembled variations of temper and of character, of which women of her wretched profession know the effect, and which, by keeping the mind in continual agitation, the passions in perpetual play, prevent their subsiding into that torpid calm which is the mortal, the incurable, disease of inclination.

He left the unexperienced Maria fully persuaded of his tenderness: he had looked passionately, talked incoherently, and during the whole visit had addressed her in that equivocal style which self-love, especially when attended by ignorance of the world, never fails to interpret to its own advantage.

He had vowed there was enchantment in her form, in her conversation, in her smile, which it was not in man to resist; had left the room three times with well-dissembled reluctance, and had returned as often to bid her *once more* adieu.

She had not the remotest doubt of his intention to marry her: a mind like his must be incapable of any views, but such as were dictated by the most perfect honour.

She fondly imagined the journey he was going to take with his father had been concerted by himself, in order to secure a favourable opportunity of confessing a passion which her birth and connexions (we mean her *family* connexions) gave Lord Claremont no pretence to disapprove.

She therefore depended on his Lordship's acquiescence; for as to fortune, she thought that a consideration infinitely below the attention of a man of his elevated rank.

Hope and joy at present filled all her soul; her heart, devoted to Lord Melvile, supposed Lord Melvile existed only for her.

Alas! how fatally was she deceived! Her beauty had indeed made some impression on his senses; but it was an impression as light, and as easily effaced, as the flying footstep on the falling snow.

CHAP. XIV.

On Tuesday morning the fourteenth of February, Lord Claremont and Lord Melvile in one chaise, the West Indian and Mademoiselle Dorignon in another, set out, *with a grand retinue,* for the seat of the former in Yorkshire.

Their journey was attended with no remarkable circumstance, except a kind of half revival of Lord Melvile's passion for Dorignon.

As this foreign fair had two points in view, one of which it was absolutely necessary she should carry, to revive the expiring fires of an old lover, and fan the just beginning flame in the heart of a new one, she played off the whole artillery of her charms on the road: she was more sprightly, more *eveillé,*[47] more enchantingly capricious, than ever; and, far from being in danger of failing in her two grand designs, seemed almost certain of succeeding in both.

She was, it must be confessed, uncommonly amusing: but this was not all: such is the folly of the human heart, that we are apt to value whatever we seem in danger of losing; and Lord Melvile was unable to bear the idea of another's possessing the affection of the woman whom he himself had the day before been so eagerly anxious to get rid of.

Her being in the chaise with the West Indian gave him a thousand pangs, and it was with difficulty he restrained himself from desiring an exchange, a proposition which he knew his father, who had a great deal to say to him, would not easily have forgiven.

We will leave our travellers to pursue their journey, to be met some miles from the village by the tenants, to be conducted by these faithful vassals to the mansion-house of this once adored family; to that mansion heretofore the seat of elegant hospitality and convivial pleasure; that mansion to which in better days Lady Claremont, the lovely, the amiable mother of Lord Melvile, had led the Virtues, the Muses, and the Graces.

BOOK IV.

~

CHAP. I.

Poor Maria! This journey was a stroke she did not expect. How give wings to the lazy-footed time? How pass the tedious hours of Lord Melvile's absence from London?

Lady Hardy came in, laughed at her gravity, and, though with great difficulty, seduced her to a card party: she lost fifty guineas[1] at loo, found the company detestable, and came home determined to play no more; her little exchequer was wasting away, and she was in danger of being distrest before her great plan was accomplished; a plan in which her heart was now interested, though vanity had been its primeval source.

She could indeed have applied to the managers of one of the theatres, in respect to the tragedy she had brought with her to town; but rather wished, unless her affairs should oblige her to precipitate her measures, to wait till she was Lady Melvile before she allowed it to be represented; as the performance of a woman of quality would naturally attract general attention, and appear with double eclat.

If this event, of which she had little doubt, should take place, it was her determination to give the profits of her play to a public charity; a circumstance which would alone, she was convinced, secure its reception; especially with the acting manager[2] of Drury-Lane, of whose extensive benevolence, and disinterested protection of the drooping Muses, she had read, with tears of undissembled pleasure, a very warm and elaborate encomium in that impartial vehicle of truth and candour, the Morning-Post.[3]

All concern for her loss at cards being absorbed in these agreeable reflections, she took out a pencil, and drew a sketch of a dress for the heroine of her play.

This important affair finished, she resigned herself to the God of slumbers, who, to sooth her soul to peace, twined myrtle and laurel with his poppies:[4] in other words, she dreamed of Lord Melvile, and her tragedy.

CHAP. II.

Maria's latent passion for the theatre being, by this train of thinking, awakened, she determined on going to see the new tragedy of Braganza,[5] which was announced for the following day; and to which, as it was the *ton,* Lady Hardy had promised to accompany her.

Whilst she was at breakfast therefore she sent John to Drury-Lane to take a box; or, if that could not be had, places, for the new tragedy.

John returned, with this answer, that every part of the house was taken, and not a single place to be had for Braganza till the thirtieth night.

Great as her disappointment was, she could not help feeling infinite pleasure at such a proof of the taste of the present age for dramatic entertainments of superior merit.

She anticipated her own success in that of this estimable author; and congratulated herself on the happiness of having written for the theatre at a time when it was so evidently the interest of the managers to take new pieces,[6] since this tragedy had already ensured them thirty full houses.

CHAP. III.

Just at the moment of John's return, Lady Hardy entered the room; she heard his message, and Maria's reflection, with a smile.

"My dear," said she, "you know nothing of these affairs; the house being engaged for thirty nights is a jest, as there are not so many nights during the season on which it is possible this tragedy can be played; but there are a set of people, favourites of the housekeeper,[7] many of them people whom nobody knows, who are to be served first; and till they have determined on what nights to go, no other person can be admitted: you will perhaps imagine this preference is given to rank and consequence; not at all: I have known a countess refused a box, which has been given to the wife of her linendraper.

"You look incredulous, my dear: I will convince and oblige you at the same time: I have a friend who is on the favourite list, she shall send for a box for to-morrow night, and we will be of her party: give me pen, ink, and paper, this moment.

"La Rose, step to Mrs. H———, and bring an answer to this note."

La Rose returned with Mrs. H——'s compliments, that her ladyship might depend on a box for Braganza the next night, or any other she chose.

"You must know, my dear," pursued Lady Hardy, "that this incomprehensible conduct of the managers is one reason why people of fashion have, in some degree, deserted the playhouses, and devoted so many of their evenings to cards: my good friend Pam has infinite obligations to the politicks of Drury-Lane.

"But, my dear Miss Villiers, I have something much more important to say to you: you are young and inexperienced, and want the advice of a sincere friend like me: you are playing a losing game, with every winning card in your hand.

"You expect to fix Lord Melvile (for I am no stranger to your most secret views) by waiting at home in solitude for his visits. Nothing can be so absurd, believe me, as this conduct: if you wish to attract the attention of a man of fashion, it must be by becoming a fashionable woman.

"You are in a road where you promise to go far, if you do not unfortunately mistake your way.

"You have youth, beauty, politeness, understanding; and, wherever you acquired it, an air of the world: you have every personal requisite to make an *éclat,* but you want that exterior splendor which alone can set your perfections in full day.

"If you wish to carry your point, you must have a house, servants, carriage, and a thousand other necessary *et ceteras,* without which you will ever be regarded as one whom nobody knows, and be admitted into good company by a kind of courtesy which is exceedingly humiliating.

"Your poor old John, with his lank grey locks, and antique civility, trotting before a hackney chair, is a sight more ridiculous than you, who know little of this town, can imagine.

"Let me send you my coach-maker to-morrow; I will find you a ready-furnished house, and a footman with the true insolence of a domestick of condition. Pursue this plan, give cards and suppers; be at every fashionable place of amusement, drest with the most studied elegance, draw a crowd of men about you, be talked of all over the town as a new beauty, and in less than six weeks I shall see Lady Melvile's carriage at my door."

Ideas so consonant to Maria's wishes, could not fail of being attended to with delight: she forgot the state of her almost exhausted finances, and consented to all Lady Hardy proposed: after a moment's reflection, she objected to taking a house, as she was determined on no account to leave Mrs. Merrick;

she agreed, without hesitation, to take a more fashionable footman, but without parting from her faithful John, and to hire a chariot by the month.

She was particularly anxious to make this new arrangement before Lord Melvile returned from the country: Lady Hardy undertook the whole; and it was agreed between them, that her carriage and new footman should attend her the Saturday morning following.

Behold her then on the eve of appearing, besides an apartment at three guineas a week, with a carriage and two footmen, on an income of less than an hundred pounds a year.

Perfect madness!—I readily grant it, and it would be happy for society, if this madness was confined to the young, the inexperienced, the sanguine, bosom of our heroine; whose reliance, however ill founded, on Lord Melvile's honourable passion was such, that she thought a month the longest time this imprudent expence could continue; nay, she determined it should be the longest, and resolved absolutely to leave London the latter end of March, if she was not before that time Lady Melvile.

She also considered that, if necessary, she had a considerable sum in bank in her portmanteau: she estimated her epic poem at 100*l.*, her novel at 200*l.,* and her play, including the copy, at 500*l.*; on the whole 800*l.*; a sum, in the aggregate, to which the little additional expences she was going to incur bore no manner of proportion.

She had some little debts to milliners, hairdressers, &c. but they were trifles; she had money remaining in her bureau; into the precise sum she had not had the courage to scrutinize.

CHAP. IV.

She rose next morning to prepare for Braganza: she was to be in a stage-box, and therefore her friend had advised her to give great attention to her dress.

It was of importance that she should strike; she had been only seen at a few card parties, where beauty is of all qualities the most useless, and the least regarded.

This exhibition of her figure might, with great propriety, be called *her second appearance in public:* she had been once at the opera, but she had been at no other place of amusement.

She was impatient for six o'clock; six o'clock came; Lady Hardy called for her; they joined their party in the stage-box of Drury-Lane.

Maria was absorbed in expectation; she forgot herself; she thought of nothing but the entertainment she was going to receive.

She had heard much of the tragedy which was to be performed; she had heard still more of the admirable actress[8] who was to play the principal character.

Whilst the other ladies of the party were laughing, talking, whispering, and looking round with their glasses to reconnoitre their acquaintance in the boxes, Maria was eagerly listening to the play.[9]

The first act passed, the second began: the hero and heroine of the piece had not yet appeared; Maria expected them with the warmest impatience.

The beautiful description of the triumphant entry of the royal pair, a description adorned with all the flowery charms of diction, raised her ideas of the bright Louisa very high; nor were those ideas in the least degree disappointed: she found descriptive colouring, in this instance, rivaled by truth.

The bright Louisa[10] of the theatre appeared; she came forward.

The beauty of her form, the easy majesty of her deportment, secured Maria's partiality before she spoke;

"Grace was in all her steps, heaven in her eye;
In every gesture dignity and love."[11]

The play proceeded, the heroic dutchess of Braganza strove to awaken the latent flame of public virtue in the bosom of her Juan.

Maria was collected, she was silent, she sat with attention still as night.

She found her judgement satisfied, but her heart was still unmoved: the author's thoughts were bold, sublime, and sometimes uncommon: his style was manly,[12] nervous,[13] poetic; but the whole was hitherto unimpassioned.

She felt the strongest degree of approbation, but she felt no more; she was pleased, but not enraptured.

The part of Louisa was fine writing, delivered indeed with all the graces of which meer poetry is susceptible; but it was still only fine writing: the tragedy and the actress excited her admiration; but even the highest degree of admiration alone is a sentiment too cold to fill a mind awakened and ardent like that of Maria.

The last scene arrived; the distress rose; the great actress, whom Maria had so eagerly expected, pierced the veil which the languid power of declamation had thrown round her; she burst forth in a blaze which aroused every dormant spark of sensibility, even in the most inattentive of her auditors.

Filled with the noblest enthusiasm, the divine fire of genius, she appeared almost more than mortal.

It was Louisa herself, the indignant queen, the tender wife, the steady heroine, the generous victim to the happiness of her people.

Her voice, her look, her attitude—the whole *tableau* was striking beyond description.

But you must have heard her, grasping the tyrant's arm, pronounce,

"Feel! do I shrink, or tremble?"

to form any adequate idea of the excellence of her performance.

Every heart was chilled with terror, respiration was suspended through the whole house; the dagger seemed pointed at each particular bosom, and the shout of exultation on her breaking from the traitor (whose part was admirably sustained)[14] almost spoke the danger real.

The beautiful, the expressive, the picturesque, change of her countenance, on finding herself in safety with her Juan, calls for the vivid pencil of Raphael[15] himself.

Maria was satisfied; her warmest ideas of theatrical perfection were realized; she was on fire to give her tragedy to the public; she forgot her design of waiting till she was Lady Melvile; and resolved to send to the Manager the next morning.

CHAP. V.

Miss Villiers returned from the theatre happy in having found an actress capable of filling the character of her poetic heroine.

Determined not to lose a moment in her application, she sketched half a dozen letters to the Manager; none of which pleased her, though they would perhaps have satisfied the most critical judges.

On reflection she thought a personal application would be best, and therefore threw her letters into the fire.

One only difficulty remained, that of finding some respectable man of learning; for a man of learning she determined it should be, who could with propriety introduce her to the acting manager.

As she was now absolutely resolved to have her tragedy performed immediately, she was under no concern about her finances.

She looked on her expected third-nights as a bank already established, on which she might almost venture to draw at sight.

Perfectly easy therefore on this very important point, she took courage to count the remains of her exchequer, which to her astonishment amounted to no more than twenty-nine pounds eleven shillings.

Her heart recoiled, even through all her gay dreams of future prosperity; she was agitated, she was alarmed at her situation: she had her frizeur, her milliner, her mantua-maker, and her lodgings, to pay.

She was on the point of plunging into an immoderate encrease of expence, without any adequate income to support it.

Too proud to submit to being in debt, she ordered John to call in all her bills the next morning.

She sat down to supper; she rose without tasting it; she felt terrors she had never before experienced.

She went to her bureau; she took out her play, she read it once more; all her sanguine hopes returned; she retired to bed in a more tranquil state of mind than could have been expected from the view of her treasury.

CHAP. VI.

As Miss Villiers was drinking her second dish of tea in the morning, she recollected the story of Moliere's Old Woman.[16]

It occurred to her that she might be mistaken as to the merits of her piece; her own judgement was least of all others to be depended on.

She rang her bell, she desired Mrs. Merrick to walk up stairs.

After some little hesitation, she assumed sufficient courage to trust this worthy woman with a secret, to her of the utmost importance; and on her earnest request to read her tragedy.

She began several times, was intimidated, and laid down the manuscript; her courage however came by degrees, and the play received infinite advantage from the fine tones of one of the most mellifluous voices in the world.

Mrs. Merrick's tears, the genuine tribute of unfeigned and native sensibility to real genius, gave Maria the purest, the most exquisite delight.

She communicated to her the extreme embarrassment she was under in respect to the manager, which she was, unexpectedly, so fortunate as to remove.

One of the sublimest poets, and most judicious critics, this enlightened age has produced, had, it seems, lived a year in her house before she came to Berner's-street.

The candor and beneficence of his mind, his advanced time of life, his birth (for he was of a noble family), and the extreme respectability of his character, to which Maria was no stranger, rendered him the properest person on earth to consult.

He was the more so, as he had himself declined writing for the theatre, and had consequently no interest to warp his judgement.

It was therefore settled that Mrs. Merrick should that day wait on Mr. Hammond, the name of this amiable man; should give him the tragedy to read, and invite him to dine the next day with Miss Villiers.

Chap. VII.

The next day came; Mr. Hammond was announced.

He entered the room: Miss Villiers saw a little man, about sixty, plainly drest, but with a neatness which, if neatness could be *outré*,[17] would have been so. His eyes were quick and penetrating, his countenance expressive, and his air that of a gentleman, and a man of the world.

Maria's cheeks were suffused with crimson at his approach; she trembled; her voice faltered; and she felt all the disadvantage of strong sensibility and modesty united: guilt itself could scarce have affected her more painfully than consciousness of Mr. Hammond's having seen her tragedy.

Timid, bashful, fearful of having committed an absurdity, she was afraid to meet his eyes.

She might have judged too favourably of her own production; she might be mistaken, so might Mrs. Merrick. A thousand terrors crowded on her imagination; she would have given the world to have recovered her play unread.

A criminal before his judge never felt more than the blushing Maria before the gentle, the indulgent critic, who entered the room, impressed with the most lively sentiments of admiration for her genius; and who, struck with her beauty, would have forgiven her an offence of a much deeper dye than that of possessing talents on which she would have had a right to pride herself, if pride was a passion becoming the state of humanity.

He observed her confusion, and endeavoured to dissipate it by the most polite attention, and by turning the conversation, after thanking her for the pleasure she had given him, to other subjects; till dinner relieved her from the very irksome constraint under which she suffered.

It has been said, the most unpleasant instant of our lives is the quarter of an hour before dinner is served: no person perhaps ever experienced this more strongly than Miss Villiers.

Dinner was at length served, and was removed: the coffee was on the table, where constraint had given place to mutual confidence.

After Mr. Hammond had, by imperceptible degrees, led Maria into the subject on which his visit was founded, he addressed her in the following terms:

"I have read your tragedy, young lady, with astonishment; the fable is interesting, the conduct such as the severest judgement must approve; the manners painted in the most glowing colours, and the style even luxuriantly poetical; but what I most admire are those little strokes of tenderness and passion which seize so instantaneously on the heart.

"You have literally a *Muse of fire* [18]; and had you lived in those happy days when the dramatic Muse, like her enchanting sisters, trod the flowery paths of Parnassus unfettered, you promise fair to have rivaled even the great Poet of Nature."

Miss Villiers blushed, her eyes sparkled with pleasure; Mr. Hammond proceeded:

"But, alas! you have many difficulties to surmount, of which you have not at present the remotest idea: you will perhaps be astonished when I tell you, it requires no small degree of interest even to get your play read. Just this degree of interest I believe I possess; and you may command my utmost services."

"You will then, Sir, be so obliging to accompany me"—

"No, my dear madam, I will take upon myself the disagreeable task of seeing the manager: the delicacy of your sex and character make it highly improper you should wait, which might probably be the case, amongst the unhappy train whom dire necessity oblige to submit to humiliations, from which the free spirit of genius flies with horror.

"I am obliged, though with reluctance, to leave you: in a week I will wait on you with your tragedy, and shall be happy if I bring you the answer you wish.

"Do not, however, be too sanguine in your expectations; if I am not mis-informed, it is only by servilities, of which I already pronounce you incapable, or by the weight of great connexions, that access can be had to the theatres."

Maria was delighted with the first part of this speech; the latter she looked on as the peevishness of age, and perhaps of disappointment.

Mr. Hammond retired; Miss Villiers communicated her supposed success, a success she now thought inevitable, to Mrs. Merrick; who was as much convinced as herself, that it was impossible the manager could refuse a tragedy of such merit, and recommended to him by one of the greatest geniuses of the age.

The character of the heroine too was so calculated to shew all the powers of Mrs. Yates to advantage—this alone, Maria was clear, would ensure its reception.

Whatever knowledge Miss Villiers wanted, she certainly was an adept in that of the world, and especially the little world of the theatre.

Chap. VIII.

On the third day from his leaving London, Lord Claremont, with his son, and his very respectable friends, reached the seat of his glorious ancestors, a line of heroes dear to their country, about ten minutes before dinner was served.

We should have premised that *la petite Janneton,* having business of her own to transact, staid in town, and made no part of this illustrious band.

The noble master of this superb mansion led Dorignon through a suite of magnificent apartments, once honoured by other guests, and, entering the dining-room, placed her at the head of his table, of which he desired her to do the honours.

Lord Melvile blushed, a spark of virtue still remained unextinguished in his bosom; his degenerate passions had not entirely conquered the faithful monitor within; his heart revolted to see this wretched woman occupy the seat once filled by his noble, his amiable, mother.

He ate little, he was gloomy, he was silent; the sprightly sallies of Dorignon missed of their usual effect.

He looked up, the picture of Lady Claremont met his eyes; the blood rushed to his heart, a tear of remorse started; he fancied he saw the picture glow with indignation; he rose from table, pretended illness, and retired.

Neither Dorignon, nor Lord Claremont, had the least idea of the cause of Lord Melvile's emotion, though it was too obvious to escape the eyes of either: both were surprized at his retiring; but, as Lord Claremont took no notice of his absence, Dorignon thought it prudent to observe the same conduct.

No other visible cause appearing, the convivial trio imagined his lordship's precipitate retreat arose from his jealousy of the West Indian, who, full of the same idea, enjoyed his supposed triumph over a rival in every respect so much his superior.

The dinner, the wines, were exquisite; the glass went round; Dorignon, convinced she had riveted Lord Melvile's chains more firmly than ever, displayed all the charms of her *sçavoir vivre;*[19] she was singing a *chanson à boire*[20] when a servant informed the company that Lord Melvile had set out for London in ten minutes after he left the room.

Dorignon did not expect this stroke; it disconcerted all her measures; she hesitated what step to take, turned alternately red and pale, and was on the point of proposing to follow him, when Lord Claremont, who chose to dissemble his surprize, told her his son was gone to town by his order, on some unforeseen business of great importance to himself; but that he and Mr. Martin, the name of her new lover, would do all in their power to amuse her till Lord Melvile's return, which he supposed would be in about a week.

How this week was passed in Yorkshire will hereafter appear. Let us at present attend Lord Melvile to town.

Chap. IX.

Lord Melvile, on leaving the dining-room, retired to his own apartment, his heart torn by contending passions, which banished peace from his agitated bosom; he despised himself for his attachment to so unworthy an object as Dorignon, yet felt not the less strongly the ascendant she had gained over his heart.

He saw no alternative between submitting to resume his inglorious chains, and setting out that moment for London: his inclination pointed out the first; but shame, remorse, his respect for the memory of his noble mother, and perhaps a mixture of jealousy and despight, carried it for the latter.

He found some difficulty in taking this laudable resolution, and, conscious of his own weakness, determined on setting out without seeing Dorignon, and without giving his indignation time to cool.

He threw himself into the chaise, and drove from the door; he looked back, happily for him, his Circé[21] was not in sight.

The chaise drove on; Lord Melvile had courage to persevere in advancing, though Dorignon's idea perpetually obtruded itself on his imagination;

the charms of her form indeed were not such as justified his infatuation; she was, in respect to personal attractions, much below mediocrity; but her sprightly sallies, her *sçavoir vivre,* her *piquantes caprices;* her unbounded, her libertine vivacity, unfettered by the chains of either politeness, decency, or good-nature; her dexterity in varying the scene from storm to sunshine, from rage to softness; in short, those wretched artifices to which beauty need not, and probity will not, descend, held him in a state of willing slavery, from which he scarce had firmness of mind enough to attempt getting released.

CHAP. X.

Lord Melvile reached Grantham[22] that night, though very late; he sat down and wrote to Dorignon; he upbraided, he soothed, he upbraided again; he tore the letter; he determined to break his chains.

He reflected on his life of gallantry; he was dissatisfied; he blushed for the indelicacy of his past attachments; he determined to renounce the pursuit of venal beauty.

He wished to be beloved, to seek an affair of the heart; he did well; refinement in vice is one step, and no inconsiderable one, towards virtue.

This train of thinking naturally led him to remember the blooming, the amiable, the lovely, the innocent Maria, who, with every charm of youth and beauty which the abandoned Dorignon wanted, had the recommendation of having distinguished him from all his sex; she had convinced him of her unaffected tenderness by endeavouring to conceal it, and by a thousand little circumstances, which, though sufficiently perceptible, are difficult to describe.

He therefore determined on pursuing his conquest, and destined Miss Villiers to the honour of being his favourite sultana,[23] as soon as decency, after his marriage, would allow him to make an arrangement.

His heart, for a moment, revolted at the idea of seduction; but he soon silenced the unwelcome monitor.

He was born with better feelings; he was naturally humane, tender, compassionate; but he had, unfortunately for himself, been educated by a father, who, as we have already observed, had taken the most unwearied pains to eradicate from his expanding mind those social affections which the Deity has planted in our bosoms for the wisest purposes.

By the repeated instructions of this father, whom he both loved and revered, he had reasoned himself into the persuasion, that there exists no real principle of action but what is merely selfish; and that the first, indeed the only, duty of every being, is to pursue its own particular gratification.

In respect to the other sex, his reverend Mentor[24] had assured him, that woman is as much destined, by the Creator, the prey of man, as the lamb of the wolf; and that compunction was as little required, and would be as contrary to the rule of right, and the established order of nature, in the one pursuit as in the other.

Allow me to observe, that immorality in the extreme, that abandoned state of mind, in the composition of which hardness of heart makes a necessary ingredient, is seldom attained by the young. Pure, unmixed, unfeeling depravity is the glorious privilege of age.

Lord Melvile's heart, that faithful adviser when we obey its cooler dictates, told him these principles were erroneous; but he had been directed to study morals, as a science, in the admirable writings of the new French philosophers;[25] a race, who, dissatisfied with the beauteous workmanship of heaven, have endeavoured, to the utmost extent of their limited abilities, to mould human nature into a form as distorted, and as different from that which the great Creator gave it, as the head of a North American savage, or the foot of a Chinese woman of quality.[26]

Illustrious ******* ! Scientific ***** ! Bright luminaries of France! who have taken such meritorious pains to convince mankind they are on a level with the beasts that perish! How much are human life and manners indebted to your beneficent labours!

Let it however lower the swelling topsails of your *amour propre,*[27] to be informed, that you are, in this instance, following, and at a great distance, one of the cast[28] modes of England, *les esprits forts*[29] of this kingdom, being at present only to be found amongst the *canaille.*[30]

Free-thinking,[31] to take this respectable word in its perverted modern sense, is, with us, a fashion *passé,* which we have left to the common people, and our domestics.

A few young men, indeed, like Lord Melvile, catch it on the rebound at Paris, whither it has traveled with our one-horse chaises; and a few old ones, like his noble father, retain it because it was the *ton* when they were boys; but it is by no means the fashionable creed of modern English good company.

But to return to Lord Melvile.

Behold him philosophically determined, on principles which appeared to him at once rational, and becoming a man of honour, to break with Dorignon, marry the nabob's daughter, and take Miss Villiers into keeping.

If a sigh of regret escaped him, it was not for the innocent object of his vicious pursuit; it was not for his intended bride, who might for aught he knew, as he had never seen her, be the most amiable of women; it was only excited by the idea of parting with the enchanting Dorignon—

L'amabile donzella! Ah! che farò?[32]
"Che farò senza Euridice?"[33]

Chap XI.

The bright Maria, whose views were diametrically opposite to those of her noble lover, rose early on Monday morning, all-unknowing of the honour intended her, to take a review of the debts she had contracted, and compare them, not with her exchequer, *that* was in a melancholy state of decline, but with the ideal profits of her literary performances.

John, being called upon, produced her bills; which, including mercer, milliner, mantua-maker, hair-dresser, lodgings, and twenty little et ceteras, amounted exactly to one hundred and twenty-eight pounds more than she was at present mistress of.

But what of that? Her first night at Drury-Lane would more than pay it.

At the moment when she was settling (on paper) so discouraging a balance, a balance so extremely in her own disfavour, her new footman, hired by her obliging friend, Lady Hardy, presented himself to her notice; and her new chariot drove up to the door.

Reflection, that sober matron, that unwelcome guest to the young, the gay, the giddy, the enthusiastically sanguine, would fain have obtruded herself at this instant, but was refused; she paid Maria a momentary visit, but no more.

How was it possible to attend to her rigid dictates? The chariot was so elegantly designed, so highly varnished—the colour of the lining so admirably adapted to her complexion—the new footman so well drest, so well powdered, so *degagée*,[34] so very different from poor old John—Lady Hardy had so clearly demonstrated, that it was impossible to exist in London without a carriage—

A little additional expence for only a month was, at all events, so trifling, so uninteresting an object—she had such a variety of resources, and all so certain—

Should even all her hopes of literary success vanish, which was to the last degree improbable, these little demands could be of no consequence, her present prospects considered.

Lord Melvile would, undoubtedly, on their approaching union, make a present of her fortune to her sister,[35] Louisa, who would of course be happy to free her from this temporary embarrassment.

She threw aside the bills, stepped into the chariot, her new footman, with John, behind: drove to Lady Hardy's, who, after saying a thousand agreeable things to her on her new arrangement, accompanied her to Hyde Park;[36] where, after congratulating her on the very proper step she had taken, and assuring her of her eternal and inviolable friendship, she engaged her, by a promise of not asking her to play, to be of a party at her house in the evening.

CHAP. XII.

Maria's chariot glittered, not unobserved, amongst the brilliant carriages at Lady Hardy's door this evening: her two domestics in new liveries, with white wax flambeaux, and her whole exterior regulated by the exactest laws of *bon ton*.

She descended, her little heart fluttering with pleasure, at appearing in a style so becoming the future Lady Melvile.

She had always been accustomed to the convenience of a carriage, but never before to the splendor of one.

Her father's old family landau, and her uncle's plain travelling postchaise, were very different from the brilliant varnish, the superb gilding, the enchanting *tout ensemble*[37] of this resplendent vehicle, which Lady Hardy had ordered in the first taste, meerly because she expected it to be seen often at her own door.

We have said, Miss Villiers had determined not to play; she kept, though with some difficulty, this very laudable resolution.

As it was the first time she ever refused, this circumstance was matter of animadversion amongst the benevolent circle of female gamesters who composed this illustrious assembly.

Her chariot, and new footman, did not less excite the curiosity of the gentle dowagers, who with no friendly eye beheld youth and beauty like hers.

She was sitting, absorbed in contemplation; meditating perhaps on the choice of a subject for her next tragedy, and unconscious she was the subject of attention, when the door opened, and she saw enter the room—no other than the god of her idolatry, the all-accomplished Lord Melvile, whom she imagined far distant, at his father's seat in Yorkshire.

Surprize and joy threw her off her guard: by an involuntary, and to herself almost unperceived, impulse, she started from her seat, and met him in the middle of the room.

His triumphant smile of gratified vanity brought her back, for a moment, to common sense; she recollected she was violating the rules of decorum, and retired, blushing, to her chair.

Lord Melvile seated himself by her, without seeming to know there was any other person in the room.

His softened tone of voice, the pleasure visible in his eyes, Miss Villiers's apparent confusion, the glance of tenderness she could not conceal, all tended to confirm ideas unfavourable to the honour of our heroine; and might indeed have justified them in minds much more inclined to candor than any present.

The point was now decided; nothing could be more clear; she had refused to play in expectation of her lover—the chariot too—the whole mystery was now fully unveiled.

Swift as the electrical fire, the malignant whisper ran from table to table.

Detraction, however, had not yet ventured to speak her own genuine language; she had employed only the small still voice of timid suspicion.

She had just appeared, glided lightly round the rooms, and retired.

CHAP. XIII.

Lord Melvile had arrived in Grosvenor-street at one; had dressed, and dined at home alone.

He found his house a desert without the enlivening caprices of Dorignon.

He traversed the apartments, where solitude and silence reigned.

The festive board, the lively repartee, the song, the dance, were no more.

He felt an involuntary sadness, which he determined to remove by dissipation.

He ordered his chair, called at the Pantheon, spoke to some of his friends, engaged himself to sup with Lady B., heard half a song, and found his melancholy increase.

His bosom still felt a frightful void; the image of Dorignon still haunted him; she still occupied a heart accustomed to her chains; Miss Villiers alone could dispossess her.

To Miss Villiers's lodgings, therefore, he directed his chairmen; where being informed she was at Lady Hardy's assembly, he resolved on honouring this amiable relict with a visit.

Thus much by way of parenthesis, and we proceed.

Chap. XIV.

Lady Hardy, who had overheard some good-natured conjectures in respect to her young friend, was exceedingly alarmed; not for her young friend, but for herself; for her own honour, and the immaculate reputation of her assemblies.

To the fame, as well as to the happiness, of Miss Villiers, considered abstractedly as Miss Villiers, she was most stoically indifferent; but to what might be said to her disadvantage as the acquaintance of Lady Hardy, and by Lady Hardy introduced into the fashionable world, she was even tremblingly alive.

She had found her one *whom nobody knew,* and had produced her as a woman of character and fashion to this respectable set, to whom she was therefore responsible for all which might happen.

She was sensible her own situation in the ever-varying region of *bon ton* was a fabrick raised on a very sandy foundation; and that, if the least atom should give way, the whole superstructure would probably fall to the ground.

She had no other choice remaining than either to support Miss Villiers as a person of family and character, for whose conduct she dare be answerable; or to give her up as a little adventurer, who had deceived her, and was unworthy her future protection.

Had she been able to develop Lord Melvile's real intentions in respect to this lovely girl, she would have found no difficulty in taking her measures: but his behaviour was to the last degree equivocal; he seemed to like her, he shewed her the most pointed, the most respectful attention; and the account Mrs. Merrick had given of Miss Villiers's birth and connexions, seemed to set her above any address inconsistent with honour.

The good lady was, it must be observed, a stranger to his lordship's treaty with the nabob's daughter, which the trump of Fame had not yet announced to the world.

This important secret, had she known it, would have determined her conduct in a moment; but she could not give up the flattering idea of seeing her house graced with the presence of Lady Melvile, who with such personal attractions, if this very probable event should take place, must infallibly be soon at the head of the fashionable world.

In this perplexing uncertainty, as her oracle, Captain Wilson, happened not to be present to give her his opinion, she thought it most prudent to endeavour at silencing the rising murmur of slander, by drawing Lord Melvile's attention from Maria, and engaging him in conversation herself.

"Did your lordship look in at the Pantheon?"

"I did, madam, and staid about five minutes."

"Was there much company, my lord?"

"A great number of people, madam, and some that one knew. Lady B—— was there, and looked like a divinity."

(Here Miss Villiers changed colour, and his lordship proceeded.)

"One goes every where sometimes, but I detest the Pantheon; 'tis the temple of *ennui*—'tis a church over a charnel-house."

Here Lady Hardy being called away, to settle a dispute about a renounce at a whist-table[38] in another room, Lord Melvile, after talking about five minutes in a half-whisper to our heroine, rose rather abruptly, and desired his chair to be called.

Our heroine (truth obliges us to confess her inconceivable indiscretion) rose at the same instant; and the hall re-echoed with "Miss Villiers's carriage and servants!"

A thousand enquiring glances followed them (for they went together) through the *suite* of apartments; a thousand mouths, eager to speak, opened at once; a thousand faded countenances bloomed anew with a momentary glow of malevolent delight.

The potent goddess of detraction now returned triumphant to the charge, expanded her dusky pinions unappalled, and shed her venom on each antiquated bosom.

Three hoary Sibyls[39] formed a private conclave, in a corner of the saloon.

"'Tis too plain, madam; I suspected something when I saw the chariot."

"Who could have believed it?—Such a look of innocence—well—I shall never depend on faces again."

"Is it possible your ladyship should be a stranger to this affair?—the whole town have known it above a month.

"He has dismissed the Frenchwoman he brought with him from Paris; a young person of family* whom he inhumanly seduced, and has taken this creature to supply her place."

"Pray, madam, who is this paragon of Lady Hardy's? I have never been able to discover her origin."

"Nor anybody else, I believe, madam. For my part, I am astonished Lady Hardy *lets such people in.*"

But this indulgent trio were not the only persons whose attention were fixed on Miss Villiers.

Curiosity had her hundred eyes awake.

Half the company at the card-tables wished their respective parties at an end, that they might be at liberty to investigate this weighty affair.

Lady Blast left her pool,[40] unfinished, to the care of a friend, on purpose to have the satisfaction of seeing where Lord Melvile stopped.

She had the transcendent happiness, as her coach crossed the street, to see his lordship's chair and servants at Miss Villiers's door.

Had she waited three minutes longer, she would have seen him go away, as he was engaged to sup with the beautiful Lady B——; but that was not the point at which she aimed.

She hurried home, and dispatched cards to a dozen of her female friends (a venerable band, who had figured forty years before as her sister demi-reps), to drink chocolate with her at twelve the next morning.

She assembled the dread divan,[41] in order to pass sentence of banishment from good company on Miss Villiers.

We will leave this respectable *court of claims,*[42] to examine the charge now preparing by Lady Blast against Miss Villiers, to settle our heroine's pretensions to continue one of the *beau monde,* and to issue their imperial mandate in consequence of their sage determination, whatever that may be;

---

*Lest our readers should be surprized at this account of Dorignon, let it be remembered, she was *dismissed;* and, as these good ladies supposed, on purpose to make room for Miss Villiers.

whilst the lovely victim of their assiduous malevolence, unconscious of the storm impending over her head, soars aloft on the lucid wings of hope; and, far from imagining herself on the point of being degraded from her present moderate rank in life, enjoys by anticipation the charms of a station infinitely more elevated.

 END OF THE FIRST VOLUME.

The
Excursion

~

VOLUME THE SECOND

Book V.

~

Chap. I.

If Miss Villiers was elated with the sudden return of her noble lover, a return which she, with great appearance of probability, attributed to the excess of his affection, and his inability to live longer absent from her; she was still more so on receiving from him the next morning a letter, in which, after some general professions of the most ardent passion, he intreated permission to attend her in Berner's-street any evening she would appoint, when he could have the pleasure of entertaining her, without witnesses, on a subject of the utmost consequence to the future happiness of *his* life, and, he flattered himself, of *hers.*

She read the letter a thousand times; she kissed the beloved name by which it was subscribed: her heart beat with emotions equally new and delightful.

She had *hoped,* but till this charming moment she could not with any propriety be said to have *believed,* the reality of that happiness which now appeared to await her.

She sat down to write; it was the first letter in which she had ever entered into so interesting a subject: Lord Melvile was the first man she had ever suffered to speak to her of love, the first man she had ever regarded even with approbation.

She was embarrassed; she took up the pen; she proceeded; she found the letter too tender; her delicacy was alarmed; she wrote another, she found it too cold.

Dissatisfied with every sentiment which occurred, she determined on sending only a card, to fix an evening when she might have the pleasure of seeing him.

But, what evening? was the question; and a question not easily answered.

Though she would have wished a conversation on which so much depended, in respect to her future days, to have taken place immediately, yet modesty (for she was superior to art), and that bashful timidity inseparable from youth and sensibility like hers, influenced her to postpone Lord Melvile's proposed visit till Thursday.

She therefore wrote him, not an answer to his letter, but a short card, inviting him to tea, and, if he had no other engagement, to supper, on Thursday evening.

Chap. II.

The most perfect ignorance of the world, and the most unsuspecting temper existing, will, in candid minds, but in no other, apologize for Miss Villiers's extreme imprudence in inviting Lord Melvile to a *tete-a-tete* supper; and that, in consequence of a declaration which was far from being explicit as to its tendency.

The exuberance of her joy had once more hurried her beyond the bounds of that indispensable, that cardinal virtue, Discretion; a virtue without which all others lose their exterior lustre, and which is the only adequate guardian of female honour.

The world will judge, and it has a right to judge, by probable appearances; and though innocence may escape the snare it has laid for itself in forming an indiscreet appointment, yet reputation will be the inevitable sacrifice.

The dignity and purity of Maria's mind left her without an idea of danger from such an interview; and even, if a doubt had arisen, her unbounded esteem for, and confidence in, the object of her affection, would have silenced it.

Convinced of the rectitude of Lord Melvile's intentions, the least shadow of suspicion would, in her own opinion, have rendered her unworthy his generous, his disinterested tenderness.

Her imagination represented to her in the liveliest colours his transport at placing the woman he loved in a situation so worthy of her.

She would have almost envied such excess of felicity to any being but Lord Melvile.

Chap. III.

His lordship saw the whole affair through a medium extremely different. Maria's invitation left him not a doubt of success in his design; a design he had been forming with great coolness and deliberation ever since he left his father's seat in Yorkshire.

He therefore sat down, to consider how he should regulate the future household, and state the necessary expences, of our heroine, whom from this moment he regarded as a part of his equipage.[1]

His marriage, the preliminaries of which were settled, though he had not yet seen his intended bride, and which was to be concluded soon after his father's return to town, made it impossible for him to think of taking her to Grosvenor-street.

It was therefore necessary she should have a house, and an establishment of her own.

Naturally liberal in every part of his expence, he was profuse, and with a strong mixture of ostentation, in his pleasures.

As no man of the world marries with any view but that of paying off the old debts of his paternal estate, in order to be able to contract new ones in his turn, a mistress is an almost indispensable part of a matrimonial arrangement in high life; unless, which is a plan attended with some hazard, affairs of gallantry with women in high life should be preferred.

The declared mistress of a man of his rank ought to appear with eclat.

The *declared* mistress it was determined she should be.

As vanity was the predominant passion of his soul, he could not resist the triumph his imagination promised him, in producing (as soon as decency after his marriage would permit) so much beauty, as his property, to the world.

Indeed, this was his most powerful motive for making choice of our heroine, his inclination being much stronger for Dorignon; but Dorignon was not handsome enough to do honour to his choice.

He had however another reason for the preference he gave to Miss Villiers.

The vivacity of Dorignon's temper rendered her the most improper mistress breathing for a man who intended to marry.

There would have been no answering for the manner in which she might have expressed her irascible feelings, if she had met her honourable rival in public.

Mais, a nos moutons.[2]

The fortune of the destined Lady Melvile, and the consequent settlements to be made by his father on himself, would render his situation affluent, and justify a little extraordinary expence in so important an article as a mistress.

Miss Villiers's person, her air, her conversation, her deportment, her *tout ensemble,* conveyed so strikingly the idea of a woman of condition; she was so formed to become an elegant style of life; her present appearance (if we set aside her being in a lodging) was so correspondent to that idea, that he could not think of offering her common terms.

Convinced, as he was determined to be, that she was an adventurer; and that her views corresponded with his own; yet he felt a kind of respect, when with her, for which he could not account.

It was not sufficient to make him desist from his pursuit, but it determined him to make such an ample provision for her as should demonstrate to the world the generosity of his disposition, and, at the same time, give the ostensible goddess of his idolatry that exterior splendor which aims at confounding ranks and characters, and putting humble virtue out of countenance.

A dramatic writer, whose name I forget, says, "Virtuous women walk on foot:"[3] which must not be understood to insinuate, that only vicious women go in carriages; and can certainly mean no more than this, that, if a woman is not born to a coach, she will never acquire one by her virtue.

From which premises we draw a conclusion; a conclusion which may not perhaps be universally subscribed to, that a coach is not, as some people suppose, a necessary concomitant of human happiness; since heaven could never intend its creatures should be less happy in proportion as they deserved to be more so.

In other words, heaven could never ordain, that poverty should be necessarily the companion of virtue;[4] or, that "Virtuous women should walk on foot."

A propos, I have often wondered at the various ideas annexed to this respectable word, virtue; a word which in ancient Rome meant public spirit; in modern Rome means a taste in the fine arts; in England, at least in the female vocabulary, means chastity; and in France has little or no meaning at all.

CHAP. IV.

There are lovers who would have thought it a tedious interval between the present hour and Thursday evening.

Not so Lord Melvile: the opera to-night, and Bach's concert[5] to-morrow—he did not well know how to spare Thursday—if she had luckily fixed on Friday, he had no engagement.

Some true-born Englishman, some genuine son of nature, who has not softened his manners, and hardened his heart, by a French education, may perhaps wonder at the *sang froid,*[6] and stoical deliberation, with which Lord Melvile pursued a mistress, whom he notwithstanding intended to support at an extravagant expence.

He will be surprized that he should coolly sit down and calculate this expence with the precision of a clerk in a merchant's counting-house; and be so methodically discreet in an affair which seems founded in indiscretion.

He will set no bounds to his astonishment when he is told, that this young man, who is not deficient either in understanding or good-nature, chuses to incur the guilt of seduction without even the excuse of passion to alleviate his crime.

But a man of *bon ton* is a man of reason, not of passion; he is invulnerable to the shafts of beauty; and is vicious from principle, not inclination.

It is to the shrine of Vanity, not to that of Love, his adoration is directed.

Not meerly a man of reason, he is a man of snow: or, to express it better in the beautiful lines of one of my fair countrywomen:

> "Cold as the snows of Rhodope descend,
> And with the chilling waves of Hebrus blend;
> So cold the heart where vanity presides,
> And mean self-love the bosom-feelings guides*."

CHAP. V.

A moment, gentle reader, let us step to Lady Blast's. Ten dowagers obeyed her summons; the merits of the cause were fully stated; and after debates which might have done honour to the senatorial abilities of A—— and B—— themselves; debates whence ministers and patriots might equally have culled the fairest flowers of elocution; Miss Villiers was found guilty of having, by her indiscretion, forfeited her title to be one of *the world,* and was, in consequence, adjudged to be degraded from the place she at present occupied in the immaculate coterie into which Lady Hardy had so kindly introduced her.

The dreadful sentence of banishment from what these venerable matrons styled *good company,* was denounced in form by Lady Blast; who, after signifying the decree in writing to Miss Villiers's protectress, Lady Hardy, proceeded to dissolve the assembly.

---

*The Bleeding Rock, a Legendary Tale; written in the true spirit of poetry, by Miss Hannah More.[7]

The benevolent sisterhood, having hurried down their chocolate, dispersed different ways to publish the award of the court, and, to do their *possible*, that from this instant, *nobody should let Miss Villiers in.*

Chap. VI.

Absorbed in her fairy dream, and insensible to every object but Lord Melvile, and her coronet, Maria walked in air.

The crisis so ardently wished was at hand; she was arrived at the smiling summit of hope.

A thousand gay fantoms of happiness, the delusive offspring of credulity and expectation, chaced each other, in her imagination, like the ever-varying tints of the dawn.

The door opened: she started from her reverie, on John's announcing Mr. Hammond.

The amiable old man advanced; a new source of pleasure opened on her mind; he could only come to bring her an answer in respect to her tragedy.

Certain of success in this interesting point, she did not observe the traces of disappointment on his countenance.

But his narrative, which we recommend to the perusal of all young votaries of the Dramatic Muse, will appear to most advantage in a separate Chapter.

Chap. VII.

"In obedience to your commands, madam, I sent your tragedy to the acting manager the very day I had the honour of attending you before.

"I accompanied the packet with a letter, requesting him to read the play, which was written by a friend for whose success I was as anxious as I should be for my own, with attention; and to give me his decisive answer this morning; when I intended to have the pleasure of calling on him to receive it.

"I went accordingly at eleven, the hour which I supposed would be most convenient to him.

"As he loves to keep on good terms with all authors of reputation who have the complaisance not to write for the theatre, as he has measures to keep with me on account of some of my connexions, and as he knows enough of my temper to be assured it is not calculated for attendance, I was admitted the moment I sent up my name.

"I found him surrounded by a train of anxious expectants, for some of whom I felt the strongest compassion.

"Amongst the rest I saw—but I forbear his respectable name: an involuntary sigh escaped me; I could scarce avoid exclaiming aloud, Alas! to what is genius reduced!

"The train which composed this great man's levee[8] all retired on my entrance, when the following conversation took place; a conversation which will convince you I over-rated my little interest, in supposing I could secure your tragedy a candid reading."

"My good sir, I am happy any thing procures me the pleasure of seeing you—I was talking of you only last week"—

"I am much obliged to you, sir, but the business on which I attend you"—

"Why—a—um—true—this play of your friend's—You look amazingly well, my dear sir—In short—this play—I should be charmed to oblige you—but we are so terribly overstocked"—

"I am not to learn that you have many applications, and therefore determined to wait on you in time—You have read the play, I take for granted"—

"Why—a—um—no—not absolutely read it—Such a multiplicity of affairs—Just skimmed the surface—I—a—Will you take any chocolate, my dear friend?"

"I have only this moment breakfasted, sir—But to our play."

"True—this play—the writing seems not bad—something tender—something like sentiment—but not an atom of the *vis comica*."[9]

"In a tragedy, my good sir?"

"I beg pardon: I protest I had forgot—I was thinking of Mr. What-d'ye-call-um's comedy, which he left with me last Tuesday.

"But why tragedy? why not write comedy? There are real sorrows enough in life without going to seek them at the theatre—Tragedy does not please as it used to do, I assure you, sir.

"You see I scarce ever play tragedy now? The public taste is quite changed within these three or four years?"

"Yet Braganza—"

"A lucky hit, I confess—something well in the last scene[10]—But as I was saying, sir—your friend's play—there are good lines—But—the fable—the manners—the conduct—people imagine—if authors would be directed—but they are an incorrigible race—

"Ah! Mr. Hammond! we have no writers now—there was a time—your Shakespeares and old Bens—If your friend would call on me, I could propose a piece for him to *alter*,[11] which perhaps"—

"My commission, sir, does not extend beyond the tragedy in question; therefore we will, if you please, return to that."

"Be so good, my dear sir, as to reach me the gentleman's play: it lies under the right-hand pillow of the sopha."

"He took the play, which was still in the cover in which I had sent it, and it was easy to see had never been opened.

"He turned over the leaves with an air of the most stoical inattention, and proceeded:

"There is a kind of a—sort of a—smattering of genius in this production, which convinces me the writer, with proper advice, might come to something in time.

"But these authors—and after all, what do they do? They bring the meat indeed, but who instructs them how to cook it? Who points out the proper seasoning for the dramatic ragoût? Who furnishes the savoury ingredients to make the dish palatable? Who brings the Attic salt?[12]—the Cayenne pepper?—the—the—a—'Tis amazing the pains I am forced to take with these people, in order to give relish to their insipid productions"—

"I have no doubt of all this, sir; but the morning is wearing away.

"You have many avocations, and I would not take up your time; I have only one word to add to what I have said: I know we are too late for the present season; but you will oblige me infinitely if you will make room for this piece in the course of the next."

"The next season, my dear sir!—why—a—it is absolutely impossible— I have now six-and-twenty new tragedies on my promise-list—besides, I have not read it?—That is—if—if—a—your friend will send it me in July—if I approve it in July, I will endeavour—let me see—what year is this?—O, I remember—'tis seventy-five—Yes—if I think it will do, I will endeavour to bring it out in the winter of—the winter of—eighty-two.

"That is, if my partner—if Mr.———should have made no engagement, unknown to me, for that year, which may put it out of my power."[13]

"I wished him a good morning, madam; and have brought back your tragedy.

"I have related the conversation literally, on which you are to make your own reflections: whatever may be your future determination, you will find me always ready to execute your commands."

CHAP. VIII.

The lively red in the cheek of Maria went and returned a thousand times in the course of this narration; her heart beat thick with contrary passions; fear, a faint ray of hope, uncertainty, disappointment, indignation, took their turns; the latter at length prevailed, and enabled her to bear this unexpected stroke with becoming spirit.

She repressed the tear which was ready to start, the tear of blended resentment and distress.

She determined to make no further application to the theatres till she should glitter in the gay circle as Lady Melvile; and the moment that event, which could not be far distant, should take place, to make a present of her piece to the other house;[14] letting the manager who had treated her so contemptuously know, *whose* play it was he had not condescended to read.

Elated with this idea, she thanked Mr. Hammond for the unpleasing step he had taken in the hope of serving her; and replaced the unfortunate tragedy in her bureau, with an air of tranquillity which effectually deceived him.

He was now convinced of what he had before, from her apparent anxiety, a little doubted, that fame was the only object she had in view, and that no inconvenience would arise from her waiting a more favourable moment.

Perfectly at ease in this point, he proceeded to give her his opinion on the general subject of writing for the theatre; a pursuit in which her sex, her delicacy of mind, her rectitude of heart, her honest pride, and perhaps her genius, were all strongly against her success.

He advised her to keep her piece—not nine years,[15] but till more liberal maxims of government should take place in the important empire of the theatre; an empire on the faithful administration of which depended, not only national taste, but in a great degree national virtue.

"The incoherent jumble of words without ideas, which I have been repeating to you, madam," pursued he, "is, I am told, the general answer to dramatic writers, who are intended to be disgusted by this unworthy treatment, which the managers honour with the name of policy, from thinking of any future applications.

"That vulgar, unenlightened, minds should act with this wretched imitation of craft (for even craft is here too respectable an appellation), I should naturally expect; but that a man of excellent understanding, of the most distinguished talents, the idol of the public; with as much fame as his most ardent wishes can aspire to, and more riches than he knows how to enjoy; should descend to such contemptible arts, with no nobler a view than that of robbing the Dramatic Muse, to whom he owes that fame and those riches, of her little share of the reward, is a truth almost too improbable to be believed.

"Would it not have been wiser, as well as more manly, to have said, in the clearest and most unambiguous terms,"

"Sir, we have no occasion for new pieces while there are only two English theatres in a city so extensive and opulent as London; a city which, in the time of Elizabeth, when the frequenters of the theatre were not a tenth part of the present, supported seventeen.[16]

"We will therefore never receive any new production but when we are compelled to it by recommendations which we dare not refuse: nor will I read the tragedy you bring, lest its merit should make me ashamed to reject it."

"This would have been indeed the language of a thankless son of the drama; the language of a man having no object in view but his own emolument, and wanting gratitude to that publick, and to that beautiful art, to which he was so much indebted; but it would have been the language of a man, and a man possessed of sufficient courage to avow his principle of action.

"Indulge me a moment longer. The person, of whom I have been speaking, deserves, in his profession, all the praise we can bestow: he has thrown new lights on the science of action,[17] and has, perhaps, reached the summit of theatrical perfection.

"I say *perhaps,* because there is no limiting the powers of the human mind, or saying where it will stop.

"It is possible he may be excelled, though that he may be equalled is rather to be wished than expected, whenever (if that time ever comes) his retiring shall leave the field open to that emulation which both his merit and his management have contributed to extinguish.

"I repeat, that, as an actor, the publick have scarce more to wish than to see him equaled; as an author, he is not devoid of merit; as a manager, he has, I am afraid, ever seen the dawn of excellence, both in those who aspired to write for, or to tread, the theatre, with a reluctant eye; and has made it too much his object, if common sense, aided by impartial observation, is not deceived, 'To blast each rising literary blossom, and plant thorns round the pillow of genius'*."

On a favourite theme the garrulous old man would have expatiated much longer, had he not observed an air of impatience in Miss Villiers, who was not inclined to attend to reasoning, on a subject where both her passions and her interest were so much concerned. He therefore took leave, and promised to call on her again in a day or two.

CHAP. IX.

Grateful as Miss Villiers really was for Mr. Hammond's very friendly interposition in favour of her tragedy, she was not perfectly satisfied with his mode of application.

He had depended too much on himself, and on his supposed interest with the acting manager.

He had, besides, even from his own account, conversed with this gentleman in a style far removed from the persuasive, and not a little tending towards the dictatorial.

After all, the manager might not be so much to blame.

Mr. Hammond had neglected adverting to two circumstances, which appeared to her of infinitely more importance to her success than the protection of fifty peevish old fellows like himself.

The circumstances he had thus injudiciously omitted to mention, would naturally have had great weight with a man of genius, who as such

---

*Long after the above Chapter was written, but before it was committed to the press, this great theatrical luminary disappeared from his orbit. As the writer honours his talents, though she disapproves his illiberal maxims of government, she has unaffected pleasure in predicting, that the various excellencies of his performance will be remembered with delight, when the errors of his management, though fatal to literature, shall be consigned to oblivion.

She wishes him a calm and honourable retreat under the shade of his own laurels: laurels which Candour will exult in twining round his brow, and proclaim to have been fairly won.

May she be here indulged in a wish, which she almost ventures to call a prediction, that the dramatic Muse may again raise her head; and new Shakespeares, new Sophocleses, new Garricks, arise, under the auspices of a manager who has sufficient genius to be above envy, and sufficient liberality of mind to be incapable of avarice?

could not fail of being a man of delicate and refined gallantry, and a zealous partizan of female excellence.

He should have urged, that the piece in question was the production of a woman [he might, without the imputation of flattery, have added, of a young and amiable woman, of family and unblemished character], and that the part of the heroine was exquisitely adapted to display in full light the brilliant powers of the actress who filled the first characters at his theatre.[18]

She had hinted both these particulars to Mr. Hammond the first time he had attended her on this business; but a sarcastical smile of disapprobation had prevented her entering further into the subject.

The truth is, he declined using those arguments, because he thought them both extremely unfavourable to the cause.

She was not quite clear she had acted wisely in consulting *this* Mr. Hammond; he might be a very good kind of man, but apparently ignorant of the world; nor did she find that he was a man *anybody knew.*

He was splenetic, fretful; and she could not help believing, from the severe style in which he spoke of theatrical direction in general, that he had, in the early part of his life, been a candidate, and an unsuccessful one, for the dramatic laurel.

In this, however, she was mistaken; as she was in imagining she knew the world better than a man who had passed all his life, and that life not a short one, in the first company of which it is composed.

He had not indeed the honour of being of a *certain set;* but there were coteries rather more estimable, where his merit received the most flattering distinctions.

But to return to Miss Villiers.

She now wished ardently she had pursued her first plan, of writing to, or seeing, the manager herself; she was certain she should have succeeded better; nor should she, in that case, have been without hopes of prevailing on this great actor to perform the character in her piece which she had written on purpose for him.

It was however too late to take this step, and therefore regret was folly.

She had judged ill in trusting this important affair to a stranger, but no matter—Lady Melvile's play would undoubtedly be *received,* though Miss Villiers's had not even been *read.*

She could not recollect this last humiliating circumstance without feeling her resentment against the manager revive.

The blush of anger had not left her cheek, when Lord Melvile, unexpectedly, entered the room.

His Lordship, who had been riding in Hyde Park, had there met the lovely Lady B——, who had insisted so earnestly, before twenty of the most fashionable people in town, on his meeting her at Almack's[19] on Thursday evening, that he must have lost all reputation as a gallant man had he refused.

Not that he had the least inclination for Lady B——, or she for him: on the contrary, she was strongly suspected of giving the preference to her Lord; but she was amazingly *the ton,* and therefore to be distinguished by her was of the utmost consequence.

What was to be done in this perplexing situation? To have postponed an assignation, would have been as great a solecism in gallantry as to have refused Lady B——'s challenge: to anticipate it, would have a much better air.

He settled it with himself, to call on Miss Villiers before he went home; to dissemble a little impatience, and to prevail on her, if possible, to change the time she had fixed for their *tete-à-tete,* and permit him to sup with her the approaching evening, after the opera.

He addressed her with that persuasive easy grace so natural to him on all occasions, and so extremely useful on most, and found very little difficulty in carrying his point.

Her present situation, setting her love aside, made procrastination extremely inconvenient to her: she had failed in one of her great pursuits; it was therefore indispensably requisite she should be clearly informed what she had to expect as to the other; and an eclaircissement, though her modesty would have deferred it, could not arrive too soon.

Lord Melvile returned home to dress; and Maria sent for Mrs. Merrick up stairs, to order her supper.

She explained herself no farther than by saying, she should have a friend to sup with her, and desiring to have the table set out with elegance.

Mrs. Merrick supposed the expected guest to be Lady Hardy, who had more than once supped with our heroine before; but had too much respect for her young lady (so she always called Miss Villiers) to ask the question.

She withdrew, to make the necessary arrangements for the evening; and Miss Villiers retired to her dressing-room, to prepare for the most important hour of her life; an hour, on the events of which depended the good or ill of her whole future days; an hour, which was to decide whether she was destined to be the most wretched, or the most happy, of womankind.

Sanguine as she naturally was, the disappointment of the morning had a little abated her presumption.

She had been, in idea, quite as certain of success in the one point as in the other; and yet she had failed.

But then—there was a very essential difference—She was a stranger to the manager, and it was therefore easy to mistake his character and turn of thinking.

She had supposed (and she might perhaps, if any manager had elevation of mind sufficient to try the experiment, be justified in this seemingly Utopian idea), that the director of a theatre must at the same time taste the most refined pleasure, and reap the most permanent advantage, in encouraging genius and gratifying the publick, by giving pieces of superior excellence, without regard to any consideration but that excellence itself.

On this supposition, after Mr. Hammond's very favourable judgement of her tragedy, she had looked on it as certain it would be received.

She had therefore only formed illusive expectations by the commonest error in the world; that of reasoning right on principles which, unhappily, were wrong.

In respect to Lord Melvile the case was very different; she was almost as well acquainted with his heart as with her own.

Could that countenance deceive—But away with suspicion—Lord Melvile's mind was as faultless as his form.

His soul was an emanation of the divinity: a lively image of the *first good, first perfect,* and *first fair.*

Besides, on this interesting occasion, her own opinion, or rather her own heart, was to direct her conduct.

Mr. Hammond, with his chilling, suspicious, superannuated policy, had, thank heaven! nothing to do in this affair.

Her hair-dresser interrupted this train of reflections: he was desired to exert his utmost skill; he obeyed, but she was far from being satisfied: he had never dressed her so well, yet never found it so impossible to please.

His work finished, he observed, with a very respectful bow, that her ladyship had had the goodness to order her bill; he should not have taken the liberty to remind her of this, had he not been in great distress to make up a payment the next morning.

Both her own temper, and the education given her by Col. Dormer, had inspired her with the laudable pride of disdaining to be in debt.

She therefore paid him, however inconvenient, and found she had only twenty pounds remaining.

She had still an hundred and twenty to pay, the greater part of which she every moment expected to be asked for.

She repented having been so precipitate in calling in her bills.

Yet it was necessary to form some judgement of her situation in respect to money; and who could have supposed her tragedy would not have been received?

Alas! the ideal source of wealth, on which she had so fondly relied, was no more!

She did not dare to think—should Lord Melvile deceive her—But it was a degree of sacrilege even to suppose it possible—

At all events she determined on a truce with care for the approaching evening.

So disinterested[20] a lover deserved that she should meet him drest in smiles.

The day past on; my reader will judge of her anxiety.

She dined; that is, she sat down to table—she drank tea—the hours past heavily along.

She traversed her apartment, she changed her seat a thousand times; she attempted to read—the book might have been Greek—

Ten o'clock came; he had promised not to stay the whole opera—the watchman went the half hour—she had never known half an hour so long— eleven—she looked peevishly at her watch—at a quarter past eleven, Lord Melvile made his appearance—

A thousand apologies—the croud—his carriage could not get up—he had met with ladies in distress in the passage, and could not refuse his assistance—Nothing was ever so unlucky—She might judge what must have been his impatience—

He presented her with a *bouquet* of roses from his father's villa in Kent,[21] praised her dress, and told her all the little anecdotes of the opera.

She talked too, as soon as that mixture of anxiety and diffidence, which had taken possession of her on Lord Melvile's entrance, would give her leave.

She talked—good gods! how she talked! Could he be otherwise than charmed!—she talked of him.

She praised his dress; every thing he wore was so exquisitely fancied.

He was in all so superior to other men!

She flattered, without herself perceiving it, his taste, his understanding, his politeness, his knowledge of the world, his refined connoisseurship in the elegant arts.

He was enchanted—with the subject at least.

He listened to her with the most gentle complacency, found she had infinite wit, though she had not yet said one word which merited such an appellation; and applauded himself for having once made a choice for which he should not have occasion to blush.

He repaid her in kind the incense she so liberally bestowed; the conversation was consequently pretty dull, and, as it could entertain only themselves, may be omitted without any loss to the reader.

This mild, inoffensive chit-chat filled up the interval, a very short one, between his lordship's arrival, and the appearance of supper.

They sat down; Lord Melvile ate amazingly, found every thing excellent, asked if her cook was French, and was with difficulty convinced of the contrary.

Mrs. Merrick had really this evening surpassed herself; and she was by no means unlettered in the fashionable science of good eating.

Miss Villiers, inebriated with the pleasing hope of finding Lord Melvile the man of honour she had always believed him, and happy at seeing him appear pleased with her entertainment, forgot the important crisis of her fate was arrived.

She forgot that her future life must probably take its colour from the hour that was on the wing; and found her anxiety, before the supper was ended, give way to modest confidence and convivial delight.

She recovered that chearful ease, that something above serenity, which is so absolutely necessary to render our social moments pleasing; and gave way, by degrees, to all the natural vivacity of her temper.

The bewitching melody of her voice; the softness of her manner; that lovely femininity so conspicuously wanting in his Dorignon; her sprightly sallies, chastised by delicacy and good-breeding; commanded Lord Melvile's admiration through all his *sang froid,* and threw a new lustre round the attractive graces of her person.

Poisoned as his taste unhappily was by the boundless licence of vicious conversation, he yet found a thousand unexpected charms in that of our heroine.

here is another time when Brooke is trying to sudar us in.

He even found her amusing, of which till this moment he had not conceived the remotest idea.

As his self-love was gratified to its utmost extent by her very assiduous attention to please, by her smiles of undissembled affection (for she really loved him), it found its account almost as much in her perfections as in his own; and he therefore contemplated them with almost equal satisfaction.

He had, he was convinced, nothing to fear from avowing his design, therefore why not avow it? He even fancied she expected a proposal of the kind which he intended making.

Her tenderness for him was too evident to be mistaken.

Yet, strange as it may seem to some of our readers, that very tenderness, which merited the utmost delicacy on his part; her unaffected modesty; the elegance of her manners; her apparent innocence (whether real or assumed he was not at present able to determine); all together awed him into a temporary silence on the subject which had occasioned his visit.

He talked of love, it is true; but it was in such general terms as could not have alarmed the most scrupulous, the most apprehensive virtue; in such terms as confirmed Maria in the unhappy delusion which had betrayed her into the imprudent part she was unfortunately acting.

CHAP. X.

They had supped, the conversation was beginning to grow interesting. Lord Melvile, after a thousand protestations of the most sincere attachment, had gone so far as to declare that the happiness of his future life depended entirely on passing it with her.

He had proceeded, in expressions which were rather equivocal, to offer her *carte blanche* [22] in respect to settlements. [23]

As her idea of the word settlement differed very essentially from his lordship's, she looked on their marriage as concluded, [24] and could with difficulty restrain the transports of her heart.

She blushed, looked abashed, dropped a tear of mixed tenderness and gratitude, and was for some time unable to speak.

She at last assumed sufficient courage to tell him, though with hesitation, that she had the most lively sense of his lordship's generosity and nobleness of sentiment; but that she loved him for himself alone, and was indifferent to every other consideration.

As he looked on these as words of course, which meant nothing, he pressed her to be more explicit.

She was going to refer him to Col. Dormer for an answer, when the door opened, and a very genteel man, about twenty-five, in regimentals, entered the room, with an air of the most perfect ease and unconcern, humming a part of one of the favourite songs in Montezuma.

He stopped short, appeared confused, looked round with astonishment, and, addressing Maria with the most respectful air, attempted to apologize for an intrusion which he had not intended.

"Can you forgive me, madam? I found the street-door open, and mistook it for my own apartment, which is in the next house.

"I am ashamed of my indiscretion, but you have nothing to fear from it."

He hurried down, after he had said this, without waiting for an answer.

Neither Miss Villiers nor Lord Melvile could speak; they were both petrified with surprize.

His lordship's was, however, a surprize mixed with uncertainty and chagrin.

He knew not how to give credit to the stranger's story of mistaking the house; it was very improbable, to say no more.

He might be a lover, and a favoured one; or, at least, one who had been favoured, and was still in the list of her friends.

His familiar manner of entering the room, his unembarrassed address to Maria, his retiring without waiting an answer, gave Lord Melvile, who had been taught to think ill of the human heart, suspicions still more injurious to both.

He even fancied, and how creative is fancy! that he had seen mutual glances of intelligence.

He thought it more than possible he was in danger of becoming a dupe to the most infamous artifice; and that Maria, in her seeming attachment to him, had been only acting an assumed character, in order to deceive.

His vanity combated, but could not conquer, this very mortifying idea.

Unable to recover his good-humour, or to resolve in what manner to take this extraordinary adventure, he found it impossible, and indeed he thought it impolitic, to resume the conversation.

Miss Villiers, who was still more disconcerted, without having merited to be at all so, had an air of perplexity and self-condemnation, which added strength to Lord Melvile's suspicions.

She was much more at a loss than his lordship, how to behave in so uncommon a conjuncture.

The confusion she felt on the stranger's entering the room, gave her the first idea of her own imprudence in allowing Lord Melvile's midnight visit.

The stranger's apology for his intrusion, though apparently respectful, shewed too plainly the light in which he regarded the party.

She was alarmed, she was determined to be more guarded for the future; she entreated Lord Melvile to retire.

She was not without apprehension as to the continuance of his esteem.

She dreaded losing his good opinion by that very indiscretion of which her too great anxiety to oblige him had been the sole cause.

The delicacy inseparable from real affection taught her to be the more careful of her own honour because it was soon to be his.

In short, without knowing well how to develop her ideas, she found them crowd upon her too fast for expression; nor indeed were they such as she would have chosen indiscriminately to communicate.

The continuity of the scene being broken by this unexpected event, and both feeling an embarrassment which made it very difficult to recover the thread of their discourse; each found a thousand plausible reasons for separating, and deferring the subject, on which they were just entering, to another opportunity.

His lordship's politeness, however, and that art which he had taken so much pains to acquire, got so entirely the better of his displeasure, that he left her without her entertaining the slightest suspicion that he attributed to her any share in this mysterious adventure.

He was really extremely at a loss, as well how to determine on this important point, as how to form a just idea of her general character.

He hesitated whether to pronounce her the most artless, or the most designing, of her sex.

As he very naturally, in which we wish he had more imitators, looked on his father as his firmest friend, and the person most interested in his happiness, he with great prudence resolved to suspend the present negotiation till Lord Claremont's return to town; to give his lordship, without disguise or palliation, a circumstantial relation of the whole transaction, so far as it had already gone; and to ask his advice whether he ought, in common discretion, to resume, or to relinquish, his pursuit of our heroine.

Book VI.

~

Chap. I.

When Miss Villiers rose in the morning, she found Mrs. Merrick in her dining-room waiting her coming, in order to attend herself, as she sometimes did, during breakfast.

The grave air of this good woman alarmed her; she enquired, with the utmost kindness of manner, if she was well.

"Very well, I thank you, madam, but"—

"But what, Mrs. Merrick? You generally meet with smiles."

"I am a little uneasy"—

"Is your uneasiness any thing I can remove?"

"Sure enough you can, my dear young lady, for it is entirely on your account."

After fifty apologies, and as many protestations that it was the first time in her life she ever thought her in the wrong, she took the liberty, which her long and faithful attachment to the family of Miss Villiers rendered justifiable, of remonstrating gently on the indiscreet party of the night before, and its probable ill consequences to her reputation, and of course to her happiness.

She placed the impropriety of this supper in so strong a light, that Maria, who had the utmost indulgence for her, in order to remove her anxiety, confessed to her, but under the strictest injunctions of secrecy, that she was in a very short time to be married to Lord Melvile.

She added, that Lord Melvile's motive for this seemingly ill-timed visit, was to consult her, without interruption, on the necessary settlements to be made on this interesting occasion; and that he chose the evening as the most certain time to find her without company.

She desired her to be under no apprehension of her displeasure; assured her she did not blame her, ignorant as she was of the only circumstance which could render her excusable, for thinking the party indiscreet.

She however told her, she expected, after such a proof of her unlimited confidence, that, whatever visits she might in future have occasion to receive from Lord Melvile, she should rest satisfied with the propriety of her conduct; which ever had been, and ever should be, regulated by the most punctilious rules of virtue and honour.

She proceeded to inform her, that she should in a post or two, which was really her intention, write to entreat Col. Dormer to come to town, in order to arrange the preliminaries of this marriage with Lord Claremont.

Mrs. Merrick, who thought there was no alliance to which her young lady had not a right to pretend; who knew her incapable of even the shadow of falsehood; and who had, from his beauty to which women are always partial, and his affability for which all the world have the same prepossession, a strong inclination to think highly of Lord Melvile; was almost out of her senses with pleasure, on receiving this unexpected intelligence.

She made Miss Villiers a thousand congratulatory curtsies, wished her joy almost as often, promised her the most inviolable secrecy, and hastened down to communicate this good news, having first exacted a solemn engagement that it should go no further, to her brother, a very honest tradesman in the neighbourhood, who happened to be then in the house.

She looked on this as no breach of confidence in respect to Miss Villiers; because, in the first place, it did not go out of the family; and because, in the second, she knew her brother to be an adept in the art of keeping secrets, having been, in his youth, for several years, the favourite domestic of one of the clerks in one of the most important of the public offices.

She was a woman of honour, and would not have betrayed her young lady for the world; but she knew the secret was as safe with her brother as with herself; for which supposition every reader, who is not unreasonable indeed, will certainly give her credit.

Chap. II.

The hours passed heavily on with our heroine the next three days.

She heard nothing of Lord Melvile; and would not venture to make a visit, lest he should unluckily call during her absence.

As the moments of expectation are not the pleasantest that can be conceived, she determined, as she was sitting at breakfast the fourth day, to go that evening to a rout, for which she had received a card three weeks before.

She resolved however not to play, because she had scarce money sufficient for one stake; but she could no longer support her own society; and some sort of dissipation was become absolutely necessary to relieve an anxiety rendered more exquisite by the natural warmth and impatience of her temper.

She was dressing for this purpose, when her French milliner, who had just been at Lady Blast's, where she had heard some circumstances not too favourable to our heroine, burst abruptly into the room, and, with an air and manner to which Miss Villiers had not been accustomed, demanded instant payment of her bill.

To pay her from the slender remains of her own finances was impossible; not to pay her was distraction.[1]

In this tumult of her mind, hurried away by honest pride and indignation, she took a step which that very pride would at any other moment have infallibly prevented.

She sat down and wrote a note to Lady Hardy, in which, after apologizing for trespassing on her friendship, of which she had already received so many striking proofs, she entreated her ladyship, till she could order a remittance from the country, to lend her an hundred pounds, for which she had an unexpected and immediate occasion.

She added, that, being perfectly acquainted with the nobleness of her ladyship's sentiments, she knew she was laying her under a distinguished obligation by making a request which gave her an opportunity of evincing the sincerity of her regard, and of those obliging offers of service so often repeated.

She observed further, that this request was the strongest mark she could give of her esteem for her ladyship's amiable virtues; and concluded by reminding her, that, amongst real friends, the greatest delicacy, in points of this nature, consisted in having no delicacy at all.

At the moment when Lady Hardy received this sentimental epistle, she was deliberating with herself whether to support Miss Villiers, and enter a caveat against Lady Blast's whole proceeding; or absolutely to give up her acquaintance, and acquiesce in the sentence of the venerable court of dowagers.

In other words, she was balancing in her own mind the arguments for and against our heroine's ever becoming Lady Melvile.

This letter removed every shadow of doubt, and operated like magic in making the unfavourable scale preponderate.

She called up Miss Villiers's new footman, who happened to be the bearer of the letter, and who, my reader may remember, had been recommended by herself.

"Pray, Harry, is your lady out of her senses!"

Harry bowed, and smiled.

"I should soon be in a fine way indeed, if I was to lend my money to every little adventurer"—

Harry looked grave—

"Do not be uneasy, Harry: I will get you a better place, or perhaps take you myself.

"In the mean time, you will extremely oblige me, if you will tell me all you know of this girl, by whom I have been shamefully taken-in."

A conversation ensued, in the course of which Harry related the anecdote of the supper, without subtracting the minutest circumstance.

He finished his narrative by informing her ladyship, that though he had no doubt of Miss Villiers's having been kept by Lord Melvile, yet he was inclined to believe the affair was entirely over, and that his lordship had very prudently left her to make her reflections on an adventure with which he had had so much reason to be displeased.

He added, that he apprehended his lordship was jealous of the strange gentleman, and very probably not without reason.

Just as Harry concluded his very accurate string of observations, Lady Blast was announced.

She came to demand a categorical answer to her letter containing Miss Villiers's sentence, and could not have arrived in a more fortunate moment.

Lady Hardy ordered Harry to stay: the history of our unfortunate heroine was recommenced, with which Lady Blast was so infinitely delighted, that she agreed to take Harry, who she observed appeared to be a very intelligent, honest, pretty, young fellow, into her service, as soon as he could get his *congé;* and to give him one third more wages than he had agreed for with Miss Villiers.

After a short consultation it was settled, that Harry should return, and say he had not found Lady Hardy at home.

CHAP. III.

The long absence of the servant left Miss Villiers without a doubt of having succeeded in her application to her *friend.*

Harry at length appeared, and informed her, that Lady Hardy was abroad, and was not expected home till midnight.

Though her confidence in her *friend* was not abated, yet her disappointment at this information was extreme.

She asked Harry peevishly why, if Lady Hardy was out, he had made so long a stay; he made an impertinent answer; she told him, with a haughty air, he was from that moment discharged her service; he returned the reply valiant, "That he did not care how soon:" the bell was rung for John, who was ordered to pay him the little wages due, and to discharge him.

This extraordinary scene did not add to the civility of the French milliner.

She renewed her solicitation in pretty lively terms, and Miss Villiers was reduced to the mortifying necessity of desiring her to call for her money the next morning; to which, with a good deal of murmuring, she consented.

The next morning? And how was the next morning to furnish her with the means of keeping this indiscreet promise?

Lady Hardy—a thousand things might happen—What thousand? Her uncle—but could she procure it from her uncle the next morning? Besides, whoever is acquainted with the human heart, and remembers how she wrung from him his reluctant consent to this journey, will know her uncle would be indeed her last resource.

She was however convinced she should get the money in time, though it was impossible to divine how.

A thought started; this rout—she had still twenty pounds remaining; she owed the milliner fifty; thirty was not much to win—she was determined to try—

This was a *possible* resource; she desired no more; her sanguine temper elevated it to a *certain* one.

She might even gain a much larger sum: she might be enabled to pay all she owed: she had seen people win a vast deal more at guinea quadrille,[2] at which she determined to engage.

She drest, and went to Mrs. Harwood's assembly.

The lady of the house, prepossessed by the malevolent misrepresentations of Lady Hardy and Lady Blast, the former of whom had just been apologizing for having ever introduced *this little adventurer* (so she stiled her), to her acquaintance, received her with a cold constrained civility, which a mind less ardent than hers would have seen in a moment.

Warm, unsuspecting, a little vain, and justly conscious of having a right to those unmeaning, yet agreeable, attentions which constitute the bond of mixed society, she had not an idea of their being omitted in her regard; the omission therefore must have been glaring indeed, if she had observed it.

Nor was Mrs. Harwood, who was a woman of great good-nature, capable of shocking any person who was her guest; and, though she determined, in what she supposed justice to herself, never to give Miss Villiers
another invitation, yet she humanely resolved to drop her acquaintance in
the quietest and most imperceptible manner possible.

As Maria passed through the apartments, she saw several ladies at
whose houses she had visited with Lady Hardy; one or two half returned her
curtsy; but the greater part looked full in her face, without betraying the
smallest consciousness of having ever seen her before.

She was astonished how to account for this general want of memory in
the ladies, when, turning her head, she observed Lady Hardy and Lady Blast
in close consultation, in a part of the room which she could not avoid passing by, in order to enter the next.

Lady Hardy held a paper in her hand, which she was reading in a low
voice to Lady Blast, and which seemed to afford infinite entertainment to
this amiable pair.

On approaching them, Miss Villiers, to her great astonishment, discovered the paper, which had so much amused them, to be her own letter to
Lady Hardy, requesting her to lend her an hundred pounds.

She now, for the first time, saw Lady Hardy in the light she merited;
and, trembling with surprize and resentment, was going to express her sense
of this infamous treatment with the spirit it deserved, when both ladies
turned full upon her, burst into a loud laugh, and, brushing rudely by her,
retired into the inner apartment.

This insolence, in which nothing but the most abandoned effrontery
could have supported them, was more than the lovely victim of their malevolence could bear.

She had, however, the courage to repress the almost starting tear, to
struggle with the rising passion which agitated her whole frame, and to
assume an appearance of tranquillity which ill-suited the tumultuous emotions of her heart.

She felt the insult strongly, but she felt it with dignity. She approached
Mrs. Harwood, and, with an air which was within an atom of haughtiness,
related the affront she had received, and from whom.

She added, that she had entered Mrs. Harwood's house, relying on that
protection from outrage which politeness and hospitality demanded, and to
which both her birth and character gave her a right; that this right had been

violated by two persons whose presence, after such behaviour, dishonoured every circle in which they appeared, and that she must that moment either give up her acquaintance or theirs.

Mrs. Harwood's heart was for our heroine; but her fears enrolled her in the contrary party.

She dreaded those envenomed tongues, from which no innocence was secure; and had the unpardonable weakness, instead of supporting her own honour, which was wounded by this shameful treatment of one who, as her guest, had a right to her protection, to tell Miss Villiers, though in the softest terms possible, that she was mistress of her own conduct, but not of hers.

Maria saw, and pitied, her pusillanimity; and, without making any answer, retired with an air of majestic disdain, which almost awed slander itself into silence.

She returned home, her heart swelling with honest indignation.

She sat down; she reflected on the unmerited insult she had received, and on its probable consequences; she saw her situation in its true colours.

She had expended the money she brought to town, she had incurred debts which she knew not how to pay.

Even the wretched hope of relieving the distress of the moment by play, a resource equally infamous and uncertain, was at an end.

She saw herself, she knew not why, driven from the society in which she had lived since her coming to town, and this in a manner the most humiliating that the keenest malice could have contrived.

The French milliner, who had prest her so rudely for money, was to call the next morning.

She was unable to satisfy her; she had every thing mortifying to expect from her resentment on being disappointed.

She had to suffer, what was much worse, the reproaches of her own heart, and the painful consciousness of having broken her word.

The tears, which she had hitherto restrained, now forced their way, and gave some relief to the agonizing sensations of her soul.

The tide of blended passions, by degrees, subsided; she saw the insult she had received, and the persons who had offered it, with the contempt they deserved.

Her pecuniary distress was of a more alarming nature; but even there, if she could gain a little time, she had still a variety of resources.

Her mind, recovering its natural tone, became every moment more tranquil and collected.

She ranged the whole expansive region of indulgent fancy for subjects of consolation; nor did she range that expansive region in vain.

The storm indeed was gathering round her, but she saw it unappalled.

She had one of those happy warm imaginations, which through the impendent darkening cloud can pierce the gloom, and discover the radiant blue sky behind.

Chap. IV.

Miss Villiers rose in the morning with no little heart-ach at the remembrance of her milliner's intended visit.

She had given her word to pay her; she found it impossible to keep it.

She saw no immediate possibility of fulfilling her promise, except by borrowing the money; but of whom?

Her *friend,* her only *friend* in town, had not only refused, but cruelly insulted her temporary distress.

She sat down to breakfast; the hour approached; her terrors began to return.

A rap at the door made her start almost from her seat.

Her heart sickened at the idea of seeing this dreaded visitant.

John came up, and delivered her a letter, which he told her was given him by a servant who said it required no answer.

She took it, trembling with the apprehension of other demands.

The writing of the superscription, and the seal, were equally unknown to her.

There is no describing her surprize at finding only a cover, without a single word, enclosing a bank-note for 100*l*.

Astonishment and joy rendered her motionless.

After a moment's pause, she fell on her knees to thank the Omnipotent Disposer of all for an event of which her feelings told her her imprudence had rendered her unworthy.

She vowed, in the fervid ardour of her gratitude, to merit, by her future conduct, this apparent interposition of Providence in her favour.

She resolved to dismiss her carriage, to retrench her expence, to pay instantly every demand she had incurred.

She almost resolved to return to the happy roof she had so precipitately deserted.

She would have quite resolved it, had not Lord Melvile's enchanting idea intervened.

It was, however, strange she had seen nothing of him the two or three past days: but a thousand causes unknown to her might have prevented his calling.

His father might be returned, might fill up all his time—She had every reason to depend on the sincerity of his attachment.

But a truce to her reflections—Madame Vipont came, was paid, and John dispatched to discharge all her other bills.

This pleasing task compleated, she turned her thoughts towards the unknown friend who had been the instrument of heaven in giving her this well-timed assistance—She could not form a conjecture—

Was it not possible Lady Hardy might have repented her unworthy behaviour, and have sent the money?

It must be so—she knew so few persons—and who else could have supposed she wanted such assistance?

Yet, when she recollected the unfeeling insolence of her behaviour, she found the supposition impossible.

She was bewildering herself in vain, when she received a card from Lord Claremont, desiring to know at what hour that evening he might have the pleasure of waiting on her.

Lord Claremont!—Her joy was now complete.

Every smiling vision of fancy returned.

The gloomy hour of adversity was past.

A brighter era had commenced with this happy dawn.

She was sorry Col. Dormer was not in town.

Her resolutions of dismissing her carriage, and retrenching her expence, were suspended.

She sent for the frizeur, and prepared for this important evening.

We will leave her for a moment to indulge her transports, and enquire what is become of Lord Melvile.

Chap. V.

On returning home on Tuesday night from his evening visit to Miss Villiers, Lord Melvile was informed his father was come to town, and had sent a message desiring to see him, to breakfast, at ten the next morning.

He had a strong inclination to have asked the servant whether Mademoiselle Dorignon was returned to town with Lord Claremont; but he felt the weakness of being interested in the question, and was ashamed to betray that weakness even to his servant.

He knew she was not returned to Grosvenor-street; the stillness of all around him sufficiently announced her absence: he was therefore not a little anxious to know how she was disposed of.

He however suspended his curiosity till the morning, when he attended Lord Claremont at the hour appointed.

Chap. VI.

After the breakfast was finished, and the servants had retired, Lord Claremont entered on the intended subject of this conference, the important business of Dorignon's abdication.

"You cannot conceive, my dear Melvile, how much I value myself on this negotiation; which, give me leave to say, required fifty times more dexterity than a treaty between two crowned heads.

"Having first made Dorignon the confidante of your intended marriage, and convinced her that she had nothing to expect in future from your attachment, I carried my point, by flattering her with the hope of marrying our West Indian.

"This hope I am not clear she will not be able to reduce to certainty; at least if she steadily pursues the plan I have taken the pains to trace out for her.

"He is, you well know, just arrived from one of the most uncivilized and barbarous of our West India Islands, and knows about as much of the world as a country school-boy of thirteen.

"I have regulated all Dorignon's future measures by the exactest scales of sound policy and knowledge of mankind.

"These proposed measures are as much calculated for her advantage as your safety, though the latter was undoubtedly my first principle of action.

"She is, by my intervention, secured in a very liberal allowance from this young man; and I have, unknown to him, presented her, in your name, with three hundred guineas for her *menus plaisers.*[3]

"They are to go abroad immediately; not to France, because there she is rather too well known.

"Not to Italy, because the Italian women are as amusing, and ten thousand times handsomer than herself.

"But they are to make the tour of the Northern courts, where the cards will be almost played into her hands.

"They set out for Vienna to-morrow; and if the women there are not found sufficiently *ennuieuse,* she may possibly proceed to St. Petersburg, in which case I look on her business as done.

"She desired to see you before she set out; but on this request I thought it necessary to put an absolute negative.

"By the way, I am not very discreet in mentioning this circumstance.

(Lord Melvile sighed.)

"I see, Melvile, I was right in my prohibition; and, to prevent all possibility of danger, I will not lose sight of you till this happy pair have left London.

"My chaise will be at the door in half an hour, and it shall carry us to pay a morning-visit to your intended bride, who is about twenty miles from town, at her father's villa in Surry."

"Your lordship will, I am sure, give me leave to dress."

"By no means: we will only call *en passant*,[4] as if airing accidentally that way, and make our visit of ceremony to-morrow.

"Besides, give me leave to observe, that your present *deshabille* is admirably fancied, and extremely becoming.

"Without any compliment, my dear Melvile, I know nobody who dresses so uniformly well."

CHAP. VII.

They set out, and reached Mrs. Harding's villa about two.

The ladies, that is to say, Mrs. Harding, and her daughter, the destined Lady Melvile, were in the dressing-room of the latter, who was at her harpsichord when her noble visitants arrived.

Lord Melvile entered the house with a reluctance which he was scarce able to conceal.

As he had heard nothing of his bride from Lord Claremont, but that she was rich, he had formed to himself an idea of her the most unpleasing that can be conceived.

His imagination had painted her in the most disgusting colours; and he had only reconciled himself to the marriage by considering the absolute necessity of this step to the emancipation of the family estate.

Full of the idea that the woman one marries for money can have nothing but money to recommend her; he had supposed her ugly, awkward, foolish, ill-bred, ill-dressed, uneducated; in short, a chemical compound of every species of imperfection.

If she had possessed any uncommon advantages, either personal or mental, Lord Claremont would naturally have mentioned (if he had not even exaggerated) these advantages.

Judge then of his astonishment at seeing, in a *deshabille* as elegantly fancied as his own, an extreme pretty little woman, perfectly well made; a brunette, but of the best style; unconstrained, *degagée,* with an air of the world, and a manner as completely French, as if she had never breathed beneath any sky but that of Versailles.

She addressed him with the most perfect ease, equally remote from English *mauvaise honte,* and unweildy Asiatic self-importance.[5]

Lord Melvile, from the information of the harpsichord, thought it necessary to ask her to sing, though he trembled at the idea of her compliance.

Ten minutes sooner, his expectations would have been circumscribed to,

"Love's a gentle, generous passion."[6]

They now rose as high as

"*Belle Iris.*"[7]

But he was agreeably surprized with one of Trajetta's[8] most affecting airs, sung, in a *voce di camera*[9] indeed, but with a taste and expression which would have satisfied the master himself, had he been present.

The family pressed their noble visitants to pass the remainder of the week at Harding-Place; to which, having no objection but what either of their valets de chambre, by going to town, could remove, they willingly consented.

Chap. VIII.

Miss Harding, who found her lover extremely to her taste, laid herself out to please, and she succeeded.

She was not long in discovering vanity to be Lord Melvile's predominant passion, and therefore on that side she made her attack.

She made this discovery with the greater facility, as it was the side on which she was herself most peculiarly vulnerable.

Without departing from what she owed to herself, she behaved to him with that insinuating, yet almost imperceptible attention, which supplies the place of every other species of merit, where every other species of merit is wanting.

This was however far from being the case in the present instance.

She had, both from the gifts of nature and those of education, an undoubted right to please.

She had at least her share both of mental and personal perfections.

She had an agreeable figure, an excellent understanding, a thousand striking fashionable accomplishments, and, above all, had sacrificed largely to the Graces.

But the resistless enchantment by which she proposed to bind Lord Melvile in silken fetters, was not the power of her own attractions, but the lively sense she should appear to have of his.

For her success in this attack on the heart of Lord Melvile, there were many very important reasons to be given, which we will particularize in the next Chapter.

CHAP. IX.

Setting aside the *agremens*[10] of his intended bride, she could not have found a more favourable interval in which to seduce his inclinations.

He had lost Dorignon, and was piqued at the equivocal conduct and supposed duplicity of the lovely Maria.

Miss Harding had besides every external advantage over her rivals which her father's almost princely fortune could bestow.

It was not a French opera-girl, a woman of abandoned character, supported by his infatuation; it was not a little unknown adventurer, in a hired lodging, who now solicited his attention; but the heiress of immense wealth, whose attachment must therefore necessarily be disinterested and sincere.

Her dress, her blaze of diamonds, her apartment, her attendants, all spoke rather an Asiatic queen than the daughter of an English private gentleman.

The house was noble, and furnished with all the splendour of Eastern magnificence.

The table was served in the most superb style, and covered with every costly delicacy of every land, and almost of every season; with a profusion of blended French and Oriental luxury.

Excellent music, amusing company, dancing, high play, the latter of which Lord Melvile passionately loved, made the hours pass away on rapid pinions.

But amongst all Miss Harding's auxiliaries in her conquest of Lord Melvile, none was more powerful in its effects than surprize.

Lord Claremont, who knew the effect of a *coup de main*,[11] had intentionally bounded his praises to the myriads Miss Harding was to bring with her to her husband, without hinting at her possessing one single attractive quality besides.

The event justified this precaution.

Had Lord Melvile been told she was a pretty woman, very accomplished, and that she sung like an angel, he would have found her a pretty woman, very accomplished, and who sung like an angel; but no more.

Contrasted with the unpleasing idea he had formed of her in consequence of his father's affected silence on the subject, she appeared to him almost a divinity.

His imagination was dazzled; he forgot Miss Villiers, or remembered her only to feel himself embarrassed by the recollection.

In short, this star of the East had, ere four days had fully elapsed, by flattering his self-love, and leading him through a round of the most animated amusements, convinced him of the absurdity of his projected arrangement with Miss Villiers, and determined him to put a stop to the treaty.

"Why keep, and at a heavy expence, a mistress who threatened, from her tiresome affectation of sentiment, to be as *ennuieuse* as a wife; when a wife was happily selected for him by a father he wished to oblige, who, besides bringing great riches into the family, promised, from her talents and *enjouement*,[12] to be as amusing as a mistress?

"Many a man of fashion had married the woman he had kept: why not strike out a different path, and keep the woman one marries?

"Keep one's wife! It would be droll—but it would be new—And is there a charm in human life equal to novelty?"

Thus reasoned Lord Melvile, as he was dressing on Saturday morning.

CHAP. X.

He communicated this idea to Lord Claremont, who came into the room just as the arduous business of the toilet was finished, and was beyond measure pleased with a plan which promised many family advantages.

Lord Melvile proceeded to inform his indulgent parent of his situation in respect to Miss Villiers, and of the offers he was proceeding to make her, when the extraordinary adventure of the stranger threw a damp on his beginning attachment.

He desired his lordship's opinion and assistance in respect to this lady, for whom he now felt not the least shadow of inclination, but who would have reason to think him a man without the least sense of honour or of gallantry, if he did not come to an explanation on a treaty which was in so advanced a state.

Lord Claremont kindly undertook the task of seeing our heroine, and of putting an absolute period to this languid and unmeaning negotiation.

CHAP. XI.

After a consultation in what manner to conduct this delicate affair, without wounding either humanity or *bienseance*,[13] it was settled that Lord Melvile should continue a few days longer at Harding-Place, where a masquerade[14] was fixed for the following Monday; and that Lord Claremont should go immediately to town, pay Miss Villiers a visit, and employ all his knowledge of the human heart, as well to discover her true character, as to lead her gently to the point of breaking off this idle connexion.

Lord Melvile begged his father to soften the blow, as well by some act of generosity like that he had shown to Dorignon, as by every soothing art in the power of man to employ.

He intreated his lordship to be particularly careful to avoid wounding the feelings of her heart, if he found reason to think her affection for him real.

Lord Claremont smiled rather sarcastically at his son's apprehensions on this head, and ordered his carriage to be at the door as soon as dinner should be ended.

He set off, pretending business of importance, got to town in the evening without being robbed,[15] and in the morning sent the card we have already recited to Miss Villiers.

CHAP. XII.

We should have observed in the last Chapter, that Lord Melvile, in the course of his narration, had mentioned, though very slightly, Sir Charles Watson's admiration of our heroine, from which a ray of light had darted on the mind of Lord Claremont, who was too proud of his success in respect to Dorignon, to think any design above the extent of his genius.

The idea of disposing advantageously of two ladies who had composed a temporary part of his family, was the most flattering possible to Lord Claremont; and as he entertained not the least doubt that Lord Melvile's connexion with Miss Villiers had been of the same intimate kind as that with Dorignon (though Lord Melvile had assured him of the contrary), he resolved on seeing her Lady Watson, and in the mean time on supporting her in the situation, whatever that should be, in which his son, as he supposed, had already placed her.

As he had heard the story very imperfectly, and under the disadvantage of continual interruptions from the officious attention of Mr. Harding, these conjectures were very natural.

Under the full impression of these conjectures, he prepared for his visit, and regulated his plan accordingly.

Book VII.

~

Chap. I.

Miss Villiers expected Lord Claremont's visit with an impatience which will easily be imagined; but an impatience mixed with the most alarming apprehensions.

He might not see her with the same eyes as his son; he might, on finding the disproportion of fortune so very great, think the attachment imprudent, and insist on a sacrifice, which, however painful to love, filial duty might render indispensable.

Chap. II.

At eight, on Sunday evening, February the twenty-sixth (the reader must have been very inattentive if he has not observed the precision of our chronology, a point on which we pique ourselves as much as Virgil on the geography of his immortal poem),[1] Lord Claremont entered Miss Villiers's apartment, and by the easy politeness of his address, for he was one of the best-bred men in the world, dispelled in five minutes all the apprehensions to which she had given way before his appearance.

His lordship was not only one of the best-bred, but one of the handsomest men in town; and though considerably past fifty, might have passed for about thirty-eight.

He had beyond most men, the happy art of rendering himself agreeable to others, by putting them in good humour with themselves.

He practiced this art with so much success in his first half hour's conversation with Miss Villiers, that she found herself inclined to have as implicit a confidence in him, as she could have had in Col. Dormer had he been present.

When, by a series of the most delicate and well-directed flattery, he had brought her mind to the very state he wished, he proceeded to communicate, but by the gentlest gradations, the motives of his visit, and his ideas in respect to her future conduct.

"Will you, madam, pardon the liberty I take, when I tell you, you are the most lovely woman I ever beheld?

"You have every thing to expect from such a profusion of charms, but you do not appear to know the use of them; and want a friend to conduct you through the devious path of life.

"In me behold that friend; command my utmost services, and open your whole heart to me without reserve.

"Depend on my cares to place you in the situation to which your beauty gives you the best possible right to pretend; but first tell me, with that amiable sincerity which is so visibly painted on your countenance, what is really the nature of your present connexion with Lord Melvile."

The vivid crimson on the cheek of Maria, who was equally charmed and embarrassed by a conversation which seemed to lead to all she wished; and the faltering of her voice when she attempted, but in vain, to make a reply, confirmed his lordship beyond the possibility of a doubt in his very probable conjecture in respect to their present intercourse.

He therefore proceeded on that supposition, and, willing to spare her confusion, continued his harange without waiting for an answer.

After telling her he was sorry so tender an intercourse should be so soon interrupted, he informed her, that his son's intention had been to have made a settlement on her for life, and to have continued her the mistress of his heart, though family considerations obliged him to give his hand to another.

He begged her to be assured of the sincerity of Lord Melvile's attachment, and of the extreme difficulty he had found in convincing him of the imprudence of the step into which his passion for her had almost seduced him.

He added, that as Lord Melvile's marriage with Miss Harding, which was to take place in a few days, would render the continuance of their connexion highly improper, it was become absolutely necessary to put an end to it, whatever regret such a sacrifice might cause Lord Melvile.

That, thus circumstanced, and compelled by the arguments of an indulgent father, to relinquish the plan of life he had promised himself such happiness in pursuing, Lord Melvile had employed himself, as the person dearest to him, to convey to her his most passionate adieux, and to assure her that no time should ever obliterate the remembrance of her past condescension.

He stopped a moment, but observing she seemed unable to reply, and imagining the assiduity of a new lover the most effectual consolation for the neglect of an old one, he proceeded to inform her of the conquest she had made of Sir Charles Watson.

He assured her, as his opinion, that this young man, who knew much less of the world than Lord Melvile, might even be brought in time, if she played her cards well, to change the rosy fetters of illicit Love, for the more durable and more respectable ones of Hymen.

"I will to-morrow," said his lordship, "give a supper, of which you shall be the heroine, and invite Sir Charles to be of the party.

"In the mean time," added he, taking out a pocket-book, and offering her a banknote, "Lord Melvile entreats you, madam, as a grateful acknowledgment of that amiable partiality he must for the future unwillingly decline, to accept this note for five hundred pounds, with which I have the honour to present you in his name."

CHAP. III.

From the commencement of Lord Claremont's harangue to the moment of its very unexpected conclusion, Miss Villiers had kept the profoundest silence.

Deceived by its beginning, pleasure had embarrassed her the first ten minutes; astonishment had next taken its turn, and had been succeeded by a degree of indignation which had almost suspended all her mental faculties.

Her excess of resentment and surprize, from the instant when Lord Claremont mentioned his son's intended marriage, had rendered her incapable of expressing what she felt at a discourse so very humiliating.

Petrified by the disappointment of all her dearest hopes, this offer, so alarming to her pride, and so totally destructive of every idea that Lord Melvile loved her with honour, first aroused her to a perfect sense of her situation.

Though wounded to the soul, and torn by contending passions, she had the fortitude to command all the tumultuous feelings of her breast.

Her mind, supported by its own native consciousness of worth, rose in proportion to the insult received.

She had acquired one very important advantage from this extraordinary conversation, and she felt it the moment her powers of reasoning returned, the advantage of being clearly informed as to the nature of Lord Melvile's designs.

She could now be no longer the presumptuous dupe of her own easy credulity, or of Lord Melvile's equivocal addresses.

Lord Claremont's degrading offer, like the sudden rush of the tempestuous North wind, had dissipated the too flattering fabrick of hope, the air-built fabrick raised by delusive imagination.

Adieu! the pleasing vision of expectation! Adieu! fortune! distinction! title!

Adieu! what she valued infinitely more, the tender union of consenting hearts, of those hearts she had fondly fancied made for each other!

She had the mortification to find, this *most amiable of men*, this *all-accomplished* Lord Melvile, this Lord Melvile, whose soul was *an emanation of the divinity*, a perfect resemblance of the *first good, first perfect*, and *first fair*, had never regarded her in any more honourable light than that of a kept-mistress.

Chap. IV.

To Lord Claremont's offer of the bank-note Miss Villiers had made no other answer than a repulsive, and not less graceful, wave of her hand, and a smile of ineffable disdain; but that smile expressed more strongly than language could have done the laudable resentment which filled her whole soul.

Prepossessed as Lord Claremont was with the idea of her dishonourable connexion with his son, he was yet awed by the air of dignity which she assumed.

He hesitated, and was at a loss in what manner to proceed, when, having recollected herself, she addressed him in the following terms:

"I am too sincere, my lord, to dissemble; nor would dissimulation avail with a man of your lordship's discernment and knowledge of the world.

"Your lordship has awakened me from a pleasing dream to a lively sense of my own childish infatuation.

"Both Lord Melvile and myself have been mistaken: I, in imagining him a man of honour; he, in supposing me a woman devoted to infamy.

"I am above disguise, my lord; I will not deny that I have loved Lord Melvile; or rather, that I have loved the beautiful idol of my own creation, the ideal, the all-perfect Lord Melvile, who no longer exists but in the traces of my deluded imagination.

"I am punished; my self-love perhaps merited this punishment, therefore I submit to it without complaining, and am thankful I am undeceived so soon.

"I would say something in my own vindication. I am incoherent, my lord, but it is perhaps impossible to be otherwise at this moment.

"I do not condemn Lord Melvile; every man has his own characteristic way of thinking.

"I am unknown to you, my lord, which is your only excuse for what I have just heard; but from this moment learn to respect a woman whose family is not inferior to your own, whose virtues do not disgrace her birth, and whose error in this instance has been owing only to her youth, her inexperience of the depravity of mankind, her frank her open unsuspecting temper, her too great esteem of Lord Melvile; and, in some degree, perhaps, to a vanity which is pardonable at her season of life.

"Perhaps I am, however, still more culpable, perhaps Lord Melvile's rank was one of his attractions; perhaps my heart, filled as it was with tenderness for an object which appeared to me most amiable, yet adverted in some degree to those external advantages which ought to have been below my attention, and that I looked forward with too much pleasure to a situation to which my fortune gave me less right to aspire in this age of unexampled venality, than those who are in every other respect infinitely below me.

"I know not the lady whom your lordship has mentioned as the intended bride of Lord Melvile; but perhaps fortune is the only advantage she has over the descendant, and that not very remote, of one of the noblest houses in the kingdom.

"Do not mistake these tears, my lord; they are not those of weakness, but of generous indignation.

"Your lordship must necessarily observe the present agitation of my mind, and the painful effort I make to behave as becomes me; and therefore have, I am convinced, too much politeness to prolong a visit which cannot but be extremely embarrassing to us both."

Lord Claremont regarded her with a mixture of surprize and admiration.

Ill as he thought of human-kind, he almost believed her a woman of honour.

At all events, however, he could not deny her the praise of being at least a woman of spirit.

He could not determine whether she played a part or not; but if she did, he allowed her the merit of playing it admirably.

He felt, as strongly as Miss Villiers, the propriety of shortening the visit; and, after attempting an apology, which he had better have let alone as it only served to encrease their mutual embarrassment, he retired, and left our unfortunate heroine to her reflections.

CHAP. V.

To her reflections? Alas! what reflections?

She threw herself, exhausted, and almost breathless, into a chair; the tears trickled down her face, which she covered with both her hands, as if ashamed of her weakness, though without spectators.

Not the injured royal Constance felt more strongly the Dauphin's perfidious alliance—

"Gone to be married? gone to swear a truce?"[2]

Impossible! Lord Claremont had deceived her, in order to break off the attachment.

These arts were common amongst avaricious fathers.

She had read of them in an hundred novels, and at least half a dozen true histories.[3]

How should she know whether her conjecture was founded in truth?

She owed it to Lord Melvile, as well as herself, to come to an eclaircissement.

Suppose she should write to him!

Write to a man who had treated her with such indignity?

But how was she certain it was Lord Melvile from whom she had received this indignity?

If her suspicions were true, he was not only innocent, but equally injured with herself.

They must be true; Lord Melvile's soul was the genuine seat of honour.

She sat down—she began—she burnt the letter—she wrote a second—she threw away the pen—all her resentment revived at the remembrance of Lord Claremont's last insult.

After a moment's reflection she determined, at all events, to write; justice to Lord Melvile made this step an absolute duty.

The most abandoned criminal had a right to be heard.

She, however, thought it prudent to defer the execution of this design till her mind should be a little less agitated.

The succession of her ideas was astonishingly rapid.

She considered the whole transaction in every point of view; and every moment felt more strongly the impossibility of Lord Melvile's being a party in the indelicate behaviour of his father.

From thinking it *possible* Lord Melvile might still be the amiable being she had ever believed him, she proceeded to suppose if *probable;* from thence the transition to its being *certain* was amazingly easy.

Behold the naturally progressive action of a sanguine temper!

Her mind became, by degrees, more calm.

A ray of hope darted across the *palpable obscure*[4] of the preceding half hour.

Lord Melvile's idea once more presented itself in all its charms: she saw the smile of truth and candour on his lips.

We will leave her to renew her acquaintance with the gay phantom which had already misled her, and do ourselves the honour to pay a visit to Lady Blast.

CHAP. VI.

This most dove-like of all possible dowagers had taken Harry into her service the moment he quitted that of Miss Villiers.

Amongst her other perfections, Lady Blast was a pretty good scribbler, and had more than once enriched the ———— Magazine with little anecdotes of her most intimate female friends; anecdotes which wanted no recommendation except the very useless one of being true.

She had interrogated Harry with the precision of an inquisitor, and had discovered enough to form an admirable *tete-a-tete* history of Lord M-lv-le and Miss V-ll—rs.

Harry had accidentally mentioned Mrs. Merrick's affectionate attachment to our heroine, and that she had sometimes called her by the tender appellation of *the dear child.*

The dear child, must undoubtedly have been Harry's mistake; she must, to a certainty, have said, *my* dear child.

Yes, *the* must have been an interpolation of Harry's: nothing was so easy as such a mistake.

The genuine original text must, undoubtedly, have been *my*.

The meaning of this very endearing expression was obvious; Mrs. Merrick was, to an absolute certainty, her mother.

This discovery was happy; the brilliant invention of Lady Blast supplied the rest.

CHAP. VII.

Her ladyship's manuscript, replete with gall, in its journey from her library to the press, had fallen into the hands of the compositor to a scandalous magazine, who, besides his being a man of so much feeling as to detest his present employment (an employment by which, however, he supported a wife and seven children), was a particular friend of Mrs. Merrick's brother, had often visited Mrs. Merrick, and had more than once seen our heroine as she passed the door of Mrs. Merrick's sitting parlour to her carriage.

The names of Mrs. M-rr-ck and Miss V-ll—rs had struck him on his beginning to set the press.

As he proceeded, he found the scene of this infamous romance to be Berners-street.

The similarity of names and places was too great to be accidental.

His heart now became interested; he left his work unfinished, put the manuscript into his pocket, and hastened to find his friend.

A moment's digression if you please, gentle reader, on the present fashionable manufacture of printed calumny.

CHAP. VIII.

Amongst the evils of the present hour, there is not one which more loudly demands redress, or which is more difficult to be redrest, than the licentious malignity of that press, the liberty of which is at once the glory and the strength of our constitution.[5]

Beauty, youth, genius, all which can distinguish one human being from another, are the destined mark, the helpless prey, of the literary slanderer.

He counteracts the bounty of the benignant Creator, and turns the choicest blessings of heaven into curses.

His venal pen, tempted by a gain more shameful than that which pays the midnight robber, sacrifices the peace of families, the honour, the tranquillity, nay sometimes the lives, of the most virtuous individuals, on the merciless altar of Envy.

Yes, indignant reader, you feel the atrocity of his crime: you justly execrate the man who scatters arrows and death, and says, "Is it not in sport?"

The murderer of reputation merits the severest punishment which human laws, framed for human happiness, can inflict.

He merits to be driven from society, the sweets of which he tinges with the deadliest poison; to be driven from human converse to herd with congenial monsters, with the merciless inhabitants of the howling wilderness.

The just object of universal abhorrence, what punishment does not his crime deserve!

The pangs of poverty, dishonour, exile—death, if you please—I will not plead his cause; death is perhaps too mild an expiation of his offence.

But let us pause a moment—You—What do not you deserve?—You, who read his unshallowed works with approbation?

You, who tempt his distress to forge the savage tale?

You, who unsolicited by hard necessity, his dreadful plea, cruelly wound the fame of your unsuspecting neighbour, to gratify a malignant temper, or the idle curiosity of a moment?

Do you not—unfeeling as you are—by encouraging such detestable publications, wantonly plant yourself the envenomed dagger in the bosom of innocence?

It is in your power alone to restrain the growing evil, to turn the envenomed dart from the worthy breast.

Cease to read, and the evil dies of itself: cease to purchase, and the venal calumniator will drop his useless pen.

Think, whilst the cruel smile yet mantles on your cheek, that your own heart may be the next that is wrung by the malignant tale.

The amiable friend of your choice—the sister endeared to you by the tender ties of blood—the blooming daughter you educated with such anxious care—

Yourself—may be the next devoted victim.

Reflect one moment, and you will execrate the barbarous pleasure you have felt on reading these slanderous chronicles of falsehood.

You wish to be amused; I pardon, I commend your wish; but you may be amused without wounding the better feelings of your soul.

Believe me, the human mind is curious, not malignant.

It delights in well-painted pictures of life and manners, but does not demand that they shall be all drawn in shade.

The lovely form of virtue; of virtue, crowned by prosperity, or nobly struggling with the tide of adverse fortune, will amuse, will interest, will charm, beyond the blackest tints, wrought by the baleful hand of the literary assassin.[6]

But to our story, which has been perhaps too long interrupted.

Chap. IX.

Our compositor had a wife and seven children, dependent on his labours for bread.

His heart had always revolted against his present employment, but there were reasons for continuing in it which had hitherto stifled its generous murmurs.

We have said, he had a wife and seven children dependent on him for bread.

He could not, perhaps, hope to be so well paid for attending a press more worthily employed.

If he declined this illiberal engagement, another, less scrupulous, would certainly accept it.

He had not till this moment seen in full light the pernicious tendency of this species of publication.

The injury might, for aught he knew, be, with the personages, merely ideal.

Lord H—— and Lady M—— were beings in the moon, nor did he know that such characters actually existed; they were as much out of the circle of his knowledge as if inhabitants of Japan.

This was the first instance of his knowing that any of the parties traduced had real existence.

From this moment he resolved to quit his present employment.

His children should not, he determined, eat the bread which was moistened by the tears of calumniated virtue.

He gave notice to the person who employed him, and whom he met accidentally on the stairs, to provide himself with another compositor.

His heart grew lighter as he spoke.

The pleasurable swell of self-approbation expanded his honest bosom.

The benevolent Father of all must certainly (thus he reasoned) see with more than indulgence a resolution founded on the best feelings of the human heart.

To Providence therefore directing his industry, he resolved to trust for his future support.

To Providence we will leave him for a moment, and return to Berners-street.

CHAP. X.

We left our heroine struggling, against conviction, to believe Lord Melvile faithful to engagements which he had never entertained the remotest idea of forming.

Engagements, which, to do his lordship justice, had their existence only in her credulity, her pardonable vanity, her sanguine temper, and absolute ignorance of the world.

He had intended to *seduce,* but had no design to *deceive* her.

On the contrary, he had offered her *a settlement* in terms, which, being sufficiently intelligible to himself, he concluded were so to her.

She was, however, determined to believe, and therefore did believe, his marriage a fiction invented by an interested father, and for interested ends.

This was not a very improbable conjecture; but it has been well observed by somebody, that probability is not always on the side of truth.[7]

She rose on Monday, after a sleepless night, half resolved to write Lord Melvile a narrative of his father's visit and conversation, and to demand an eclaircissement on a point in which both his happiness and honour were so deeply interested.

That quick sensibility to the *beautiful,* the *becoming,* in the intercourse of life; that spontaneous feeling of

"A grace, a manner, a decorum,"[8]

in morals; to which women owe half their virtue, alone prevented her taking so humiliating a step.

CHAP. XI.

There was another subject on which it was necessary for her to think; another care which obtruded itself even through all her anxiety in respect to Lord Melvile; nay, which that very anxiety contributed greatly to heighten.

She had entered into a style of life not to be supported at a trifling expence.

She had not five pounds in the world, nor did she know where to get a supply.

She had tried her *friend* Lady Hardy, and we have seen the mortifying result of the experiment.

She had but one friend to whom it became her to apply, Col. Dormer, her respectable uncle; and how should she assume courage to tell him of her extravagance?

How acquaint him, that, a dupe to hope, misled by the glittering of a meteor, she had expended the revenue of years in little more than a month's absence from Belfont?

Her literary hopes were at an end.

Alas! was not her every hope as ill founded?

Lord Claremont's story, it was at least *possible,* might be true.

She shuddered at taking a view of her situation.

She could not expect another hundred pounds to drop from the clouds: John had, by her orders, paid it all away, though it was Sunday when she received it.

By the way, to whom could she have been thus obliged?

The doubt must have struck my reader, as well as the lovely Maria.

Chap. XII.

As we are not writing a fairy tale, but the true history of a young lady in Old England; a country where these little benevolent beings have long left off their delightful midnight gambols, and do not even condescend to drop a sixpence in the shoe of Marian;[9] it may be necessary to account for this very well-timed, though anonymous, act of friendship.

Chap. XIII.

Lady Hardy and Lady Blast, whom we left whispering in a corner, at Mrs. Harwood's assembly, were tittering over our heroine's letter to the former, requesting her to lend her an hundred pounds till she could receive a remittance from the country; when Mr. Hammond, whose visit to Mrs. Harwood that evening was merely accidental, happened to approach the benevolent pair.

As he was nearly related to Lady Blast, he took the liberty of asking the cause of their exuberant mirth, when Lady Hardy very politely gave him the letter to read.

Both the name and the writing were too familiar to him to be mistaken.

He very composedly put the letter in his pocket, and left the room without speaking a syllable.

The ladies called after him, but to no manner of purpose.

He crossed the street to Mrs. Merrick's, and received from her a very circumstantial and very satisfactory account of the birth, fortune, connexions, virtues, hopes, and romantic expectations, of Miss Villiers; expectations of which he knew the fallacy, being perfectly acquainted with Lord Claremont's negotiation with Mr. Harding.

After enjoining Mrs. Merrick's secrecy on the subject of this conversation, he retired to his lodgings, took a bank note of an hundred pounds out of his bureau, sealed it up in a blank cover; and, in the morning, sent it to Miss Villiers by a servant on whom he could depend, in the manner we have already recited.

But his philanthropy did not stop here.

He saw her on the borders of a precipice, and determined to withdraw her from it, in spite of herself.

He saw the utmost delicacy must be preserved in the attempt.

He was a poet, therefore his ideas were rapid.

He formed his plan in a moment, and ordered his chaise to the door, to put it in execution.

Book VIII.

~

Chap. I.

If Mr. Hammond's wheels had been as rapid as his ideas, he would have reached Belfont (for thither he bent his course) with the velocity of a spirit.

He arrived at this abode of tranquillity about twelve on Monday morning, and found Col. Dormer hanging with undissembled rapture over an expanding rose-bud in his Lilliputian[1] green-house.

Mr. Hammond could not have met with a more favourable occasion of being eloquent, and even poetical, than the present.

He knew all of which Lady Blast was capable.

He had, by accident from a female friend, heard all the slanderous effusions of the pair of dowagers, in respect to our amiable heroine.

His fears for her reputation were much stronger than those he felt in respect to her fortune, though he thought both in the most imminent danger.

He might have similized in the garden for an hour, without going a step out of his way.

He might have observed to Col. Dormer, that, whilst his green-house engaged his attention, a fairer rose than any which bloomed there, was menaced with a blight from the empoisoned breath of Envy.

He might have said—

In short, he might have said a thousand pretty things, if saying pretty things had been the purpose of his journey.

This, however, not being the case, and being determined not to enter abruptly on the subject nearest his heart, the dangerous situation of Miss Villiers, he for once went out of his character, and made use of an innocent artifice to avoid alarming Col. Dormer too soon.

After having apologized politely for what appeared an intrusion, he reminded Col. Dormer, who had totally forgot him, of their having been fellow students and friends at Oxford; and, without entering on his real motive for this visit, told him he could not pass the door of an old acquaintance, without stopping to enquire after his health.

He added, that he had an additional motive for calling, which was, to tell him he had seen his amiable niece, Miss Villiers, a few days before, in town, and had left her in good health and spirits.

There are no people so happy in meeting unexpectedly with their friends, and especially the friends of their youth, as those who, in advanced age, pass their time retired in the country.

In this situation, the arrival, even of a common visitant, is of consequence, as it relieves the too regular uniformity of occupation, which is the only drawback on the tranquil delights of retirement.

The arrival of a *friend,* in such a situation, is an event, a little era, worthy of special note in the chronological table of secluded life.

Col. Dormer's garden was to him a source of inconceivable pleasure— But—always the garden!

Besides—more than half the real value of every enjoyment depends on the social idea of its being communicated.

There is no such thing as solitary happiness.

The vernal family of Col. Dormer acquired new charms in his eyes in proportion as they became the admiration of others.

Mr. Hammond was a new admirer, whose praises enhanced the beauties of every flowret which engaged his attention.

He was also a new companion to fill up the void in the society of Belfont, occasioned by the absence of Maria.

Louisa's conversation would have been sufficient to Col. Dormer's happiness, had he not been also habituated to that of her sister.

We feel severely the privation of every pleasure to which we have been long accustomed.

The lovely prattler!—

The creative eye of fancy presented her tripping, with Louisa, delighted by his side.

That lovely prattler!

With what impatience did he not expect her return to Belfont!

CHAP. II.

After a tour round the garden, a particular visit to every favourite daughter of the spring, and a little retrospective chat on the subject of old college adventures; Col. Dormer, having first obtained Mr. Hammond's promise of spending a few days at Belfont, presented him to the bright Louisa, who appeared to him only less charming than her sister.

For that sister the good old man felt an enthusiastic partiality, which, had he been younger, would have amounted to a passion.

He regarded Louisa with admiration; she was, he acknowledged, lovely—But Maria—

Louisa had the finest blue eyes in the world, but he hated blue eyes.

Maria's were eyes indeed—eyes informed by the radiant blaze of genius—

The vivid glow of her complexion—the animated changes of her countenance as her ideas varied—the enchantment of her smile—

In short, he was ready to exclaim, in the words of the Spectator,

"Louisa is beautiful, but Maria, thou art beauty!"[2]

They passed a chearful evening, and retired early to bed, in favour of Mr. Hammond's fatigue.

He slept little during the first part of the night; he revolved in his mind the circumstance which occasioned his journey.

He found a thousand difficulties in respect to the manner in which he should enter on the subject of Miss Villiers's situation.

He might have said, with more propriety, her *indiscretion,* but he would not even allow that she was indiscreet.

He called her profusion the ebullition of a noble mind; and found merit even in that heedless inattention to forms which threatened such dreadful consequences.

He at last determined, as he intended staying two or three days, to trust to the chapter of accidents,[3] and only be on the watch to find a favourable moment.

He could not, even in this short intercourse, have missed Col. Dormer's prevailing passion; and rightly judged that a mild vernal shower, or the blowing of a new auricula, might have the best effect possible on the mind of his friend.

The morning being uncommonly fine, the carriages were ordered to the door at eleven.

Col. Dormer proposed to give Mr. Hammond the pleasure of seeing Burghley,[4] the celebrated seat of the still more celebrated statesman[5] whose name it bears, from whence Belfont was distant only a few miles.

To Burghley therefore they proceeded.

As a lover of the imitative arts, Mr. Hammond was charmed with seeing the noble works of the divine masters with which this magnificent seat is ornamented and enriched.

But he felt (as a patriot worthy of the name) a much sublimer pleasure in calling to remembrance the public virtues of the great, the wise, the uncorrupt, minister, who raised the glory of his country to its utmost summit.

He regarded his portrait with reverential delight.

He fancied he saw his venerable shade in every apartment through which he was conducted.

Our party returned to Belfont, but not alone.

They met in the avenue, within a few paces of the house, Mr. Montague, the rural philosopher of whom we have spoken before, as lord of the manor of Belfont.

His was coming on a visit to the benevolent master of this superb mansion, who was however, at this time, absent in London.

His son, the object that had reconciled Louisa to shades and solitude, and whom our little family supposed to be attending his studies at Cambridge, was with him.

They were both on horseback, and both stopped on seeing Col. Dormer's carriage.

Mr. Montague the younger had been ill of a fever at college, and had been sent home (where he arrived the evening before) for change of air, by his physicians.

His illness had left a paleness which only rendered his countenance, if possible, more interesting than ever.

Mr. Hammond was struck with a face so full of expression, and was going to ask his name, when he approached the chaise in which the good old man was with the lovely Louisa.

On seeing the object of her tenderest affection in a manner thus unhoped and unexpected, the cheek of Louisa became suffused with the liveliest crimson; her heart beat thick, her voice faltered, and her repeated attempts to speak terminated in broken and inarticulate accents.

By a movement, not only involuntary, but unknown at the time to herself, she, with a trembling hand, let down the glass of the carriage at Mr. Montague's approach.

He addressed her with an emotion which, though perhaps favourable to his beauty, was far from being so to his elocution.

The confusion, the agitation, the pleasure visible in the countenances of both, were too perceptible to escape Mr. Hammond's observation.

Their looks were sufficiently intelligible to stand in no need of an historian to inform him of the situation of their hearts.

He now thought Louisa as handsome as her sister.

She had lost that air of still-life which had at first sight extremely displeased him.

Her blue eyes were become lovely by being impassioned.

In short she appeared to him another being; so much does beauty depend on animation.

She was no longer a faultless statue, but an enchanting woman; an object, not merely of admiration, but of passion.

Mr. Montague left his son by the side of Miss Villiers's chaise, and, giving his horse to a servant, returned to Belfont in that of Col. Dormer.

The party separated at Mr. Montague's door, who invited himself, and his family, consisting of this son, and a very amiable daughter, to spend the afternoon at Col. Dormer's.

CHAP. III.

When we last set out for London, we left Mr. Montague the younger at Col. Dormer's gate, where he arrived in the intention of explaining himself in the clearest terms to Louisa on the subject of his passion.

This resolution we have observed had been a little precipitated by the report that a man of great fortune had made proposals to Col. Dormer for his niece; which report, however, happened not to be true.

As minute details of conversation between lovers are much more interesting to the parties concerned than to anybody else, we shall wave particulars, and only say, that Mr. Montague was not dissatisfied with the interview; and that during the three weeks of his stay at Belfont, for he went to college a week sooner than he intended, he had brought her to promise never to marry any other man, though she persisted in refusing to enter into any positive engagement with him, unless with his father's most perfect approbation.

He went to Cambridge satisfied in some degree with this promise, and determined to write the state of his heart to his father.

He was, however, prevented by a fit of illness, brought on by his fears that Mr. Montague, indulgent as he was, would not approve an alliance in which interest had so little share.

He had forgot that this excellent father was a philosopher in the most extensive sense of the word; and that, setting his philosophy aside, his very prejudices would in this instance be in his favour.

In short, he was not, though he ought to have been, exempt from the baneful error of young people, in supposing it possible they can have any friend half as much interested in their happiness as a parent.

He wrote, however, to his sister, who had always been the confidante of his passion, and told her his determination to ask his father's permission to marry Miss Villiers, as soon as he should return to Belfont.

On hearing of his illness, alarmed for his life, Miss Montague disclosed the secret to her father, who had ordered his carriage to be ready in the morning, in the intention of going himself to fetch him from Cambridge, when he arrived in a post-chaise at the door.

Mr. Montague, who thought happiness the first object of every rational being, and knew it did not depend on wealth, was perfectly satisfied with the choice his son had made; but as marriage is a step there is no retrieving, he was anxious to be clearly informed as to the inclinations of the young lady, before he took any measure preparatory to a union, to which, supposing their attachment mutual, he had not the shadow of an objection.

The ride of this morning had, accidentally, saved him much trouble on this subject.

He had observed the countenance of Miss Villiers, on his son's approach, with the most scrutinizing eye, and had not a doubt remaining.

In the full conviction that the future felicity of both depended on their union, he had taken his place in Col. Dormer's chaise, and had asked his consent to present his son to Miss Villiers in the afternoon, as a candidate for the honour of her hand.

There was but one point in which these two excellent men had disagreed.

Col. Dormer was for deferring the marriage two or three years longer, and Mr. Montague for concluding it immediately.

When the former had exhausted all his arguments, which Mr. Montague heard with more patience than he was accustomed to show when contradicted, he made the following reply:

"I cannot, my good friend, account for your arguing so unphilosophically, on any principle except that of your supposing a little assumed reluctance becomes you, as standing in the place of the young lady.

"But let me entreat you to lay aside your coyness for a moment, and talk like a reasonable being.

"My son's happiness depends on his being united with Miss Villiers; and let me, with the pardonable pride of a parent, add, that the qualities of his heart promise that the happiness consequent on this union will be reciprocal.

"You and I, by keeping in the formal beaten track, may postpone the era of their felicity a few years longer.

"But reflect a moment, and answer me one plain question; do you think it possible to be happy too soon?

"The poet justly complains, that

"Man never *is*, but always *to be*, blest."[6]

"I am afraid this is too generally our own fault.

"We are preparing for happiness when we might be enjoying it.

"Human life is too short, and too uncertain, to have its best hours wasted in expectation.

"You talk of his staying at college till he has taken a degree.

"I have not the least objection to his keeping the necessary residence till that time, which is not very distant: but I see no reason to delay his marriage on that account, as he is not a candidate for a fellowship.

"As to foreign travel, I am in this respect a little singular; but I am not ashamed of being singularly in the right.

"I do not wish him to wear out his heart, poison his principles, and ruin his constitution, by despicable connexions with French opera girls, or Italian courtezans.

"Still less do I wish him to run the effeminate circle of *frivolité* and *ton* at Paris; or to pore over rusty coins, and study *vertù* at Rome.[7]

"A young antiquarian is every way a solecism.

"If a young man must have pursuits, as he certainly must, let them be the pursuits of his season of life.

"I can forgive even an irregular passion for animated beauty; but the man who at twenty-two,

"Sighs for an Otho, and neglects his bride,"[8]

should be disinherited if a son of mine.

"But to our business; I am the happiest man on earth in the choice my son has made; and in being convinced Miss Villiers honours him with her esteem.

"The favour of such a woman might make an emperor proud.

"I have long hoped their childish affection for each other would ripen into love; and had I never observed their mutual tenderness before, their meeting just now would have flashed conviction on my mind.

"Determined to guard my son against the misery of selling himself to keep the family estate together, I have always had this moment in view.

"My estate is three thousand pounds a year, of which I have laid by half ever since I was married; that I might become rich enough to make my children happy, without retrenching my own expences.

"I have purchased Charles a thousand pounds a year, with a pretty house, about six miles off; and have ten thousand pounds to give my daughter whenever she chuses to marry; and all this without lessening my paternal fortune a shilling."

As Mr. Montague pronounced the last sentence, the chaise stopped at his door.

Col. Dormer set him down, and entered his own house with an air of satisfaction which did not escape Louisa.

He was gay beyond his usual custom; his eye spoke the most perfect content whenever it met that of his amiable niece.

CHAP. IV.

Mr. Hammond, who observed this without absolutely knowing the cause, could not find in his heart to damp the joy of his friend by speaking to him on so painful a subject as that of Maria's indiscretion.

A day or two had elapsed in visits to and from the Montagues.

The most important articles of the marriage treaty were settled; Mr. Hammond had arranged, in idea, his intended conversation with Col. Dormer, and was waiting the latter's return from the manor-house, where he was in consultation with Mr. Montague, when he received, by the post, from Mrs. Merrick, the malevolent history of Maria, which had been brought to her by the honest compositor of whom we have spoken in the last book.

Our heroine, in this infamous picture, was drawn in the darkest colours that falsehood and envy in conjunction could furnish.

She was described, and with some appearance of plausibility, as an adventurer, and of the most abandoned kind.

As the illegitimate daughter of Mrs. Merrick, by a certain foreign dancer, whom we are authorized to say Mrs. Merrick never beheld.

As having received from this ideal father an education which distinguished her from her equals, and a degree of art and address which enabled her to undertake, and to support, the difficult *rôle* of a woman of birth and condition.

As having been educated by her supposed parents expressly for the purposes of prostitution.

As having been sold at seventeen to Mr. Hammond, who had taken an apartment at Mrs. Merrick's for that very purpose; and as having been supported by him in an expensive style of life, in order to draw in some young man of fashion to marry her.

As having failed in her plan in respect to Lord Melvile, and as having condescended to live with this nobleman on other terms, when she found her hope of seducing him into a matrimonial engagement abortive.

As having been left by him on the approach of his intended marriage, and being now on sale to the highest bidder.

The reader will judge of Mr. Hammond's feelings on reading this diabolical scroll, but no words can paint his astonishment at finding himself one of the heroes of the tale.

If he had wanted a proof of its falsehood, could one have been produced equally decisive with this?

He was now doubly obliged to stand forth her champion.

How should he act on so extraordinary an occasion?

Should he communicate this vile fable to Col. Dormer?

He knew his warmth of temper and quick sense of honour, and therefore dreaded the consequences of trusting him with a secret of this kind, in which he was so nearly interested.

He knew the world, and the delicate nature of female honour.

The press must be stopped at all events.

He trembled at the idea of what might happen in his absence.

He regarded the manuscript with more attention.

The hand-writing was disguised, but he instantly knew it to be that of Lady Blast.

Afraid of trusting so dark a transaction to an amanuensis, this good lady (who had made the penny-post[9] her vehicle of conveyance) had transcribed this benevolent offspring of her brain for the press herself.

This circumstance was extremely fortunate for our heroine.

Her ladyship hated, but she also feared, Mr. Hammond.

It was not probable she had sent the printer a second copy of her libel, as such a step might have led to a discovery of the author.

The first was happily in Mr. Hammond's own possession.

The most important point was to see Lady Blast as soon as possible.

In such a situation not an instant was to be lost.

It was not necessary to embarrass Col. Dormer with this disagreeable affair.

His mind was more pleasingly occupied by the approaching marriage of Louisa.

It would be inhuman to disturb the felicity of his friend.

Allons, donc! [10] The carriage was immediately ordered.

Col. Dormer returned from his early visit, and was astonished to find Mr. Hammond's chaise at his gate.

The good old man apologized for this unexpected flight.

Some business, which he had only that moment recollected, rendered it impossible for him to continue an instant longer one of the happy group at Belfont.

Chap. V.

Mr. Hammond's wheels never stopped till he reached the door of Lady Blast.

He defied, and he escaped, all the dangers of Enfield chace, [11] and arrived about eleven at night at the house of this respectable dowager, which he found full of company.

He sent for her down to her dining-parlour, and, without the least preface, looking her earnestly in the face,

"Do you know this paper, Madam?"

If she could have turned paler, she would at the sight. She hesitated—"That paper, cousin"—

"I disclaim all relationship, Madam, till you have atoned for this infamous action.

"I will not expose you to your visitants, but let me see you at my lodgings early to-morrow morning: I hope, for your sake, I am the only person who knows of this affair."

His looks, his authoritative tone, and her own consciousness of guilt, appalled her.

She told him with hesitation, she would see him in the morning, and returned trembling to her company.

Mr. Hammond went from thence to Mrs. Merrick's, where he learned from a servant, Mrs. Merrick being out, that Miss Villiers had been gone three days into the country.

"Into the country? She was not at Belfont."

He was bewildered; but as he was also extremely fatigued, he thought it best to go home, and give the night to repose.

His mind was still that of a knight-errant, but his body was not quite so able to keep pace with its flights as it had been at twenty-two.

Chap. VI.

The morning after Mr. Hammond had set out for Belfont, Miss Villiers, though she knew not half her danger, had risen in a state of mind which Lady Blast herself would almost have pitied.

She saw the precipice on the borders of which she stood, though she saw it not in all its horrors.

She knew not Lady Blast's inventive genius, nor did she know herself the object of her malice.

She saw disappointment, she saw distress, before her; but she had not the remotest apprehension of infamy.

She knew not the blow now levelled at her fame.

She knew not that the stroke, if given, would probably be fatal; that the wounds of calumny are never perfectly healed.

The human mind, impelled by its own restless nature, fond of the marvellous, and ever seeking food for that curiosity which carries us to so much good and so much evil, imbibes with eagerness the animated tale of slander, because animated.

To investigate its truth, to withdraw the veil which covers a well-invented falsehood, requires a cool dispassionate exertion of the understanding, a patience of enquiry, to which few, not personally interested, will submit.

It is an effort, and from all effort the mind of man naturally flies.

Infatuated girl! Why did she leave her household gods?

Those household gods are alone the certain guardians of female honour.

We have said, her quick sensibility of the *becoming,* had prevented her writing, *on Monday,* to Lord Melvile.

That sensibility gave way, *on Tuesday,* to the august idea of justice.

Lord Melvile had a *right* to be heard in his own defence.

After resolving, doubting, re-resolving, an hundred times, she sat down, and wrote him a letter full of confidence and sentiment.

"What inconsistency!" It is true, but the human heart *is* inconsistent.

She owned her tenderness; a tenderness justified, and even rendered meritorious, by his virtues; by virtues which it would be profaneness even to doubt.

She recounted, but with as much softening as the case would admit, the supposed artifices of Lord Claremont to break this union of two enamoured hearts; of two hearts so evidently *formed for each other.*

She proceeded, like a miss educated in shades, to promise him everlasting love.

Could she do less?—He was so superior to all his sex!—"To her the whole universe contained no other being."[12]

In short, she ran on in the high romance style the length of two quarto pages, and then dispatched John to his lordship's house, with orders to deliver it to himself, if at home, and to wait his answer.

Her chariot, which she had determined *indeed* to keep only that *little week* (a week could not make much difference in the expence), drove up to the door about a quarter of an hour after John set off; and in five minutes was obliged to give way to another, which Miss Villiers took for granted was that of Lord Melvile.

Interested as she was in the question, she had not courage to satisfy herself by going to the window.

The rustling of silks on the stairs first informed her she was mistaken in her conjecture.

The door opened, and she saw—not Lord Melvile, but Mrs. Herbert, whom she supposed to be still in France.

Mrs. Herbert! What unexpected happiness!

The friend of her heart at the moment when a friend was most necessary.

She was breathless with joy—

"My dear Miss Villiers, need I say how charmed I am to find you in town?"

"My dear madam—no words—"

"I was afraid you had company, as I saw a chariot at your door."

Maria blushed—

"By the way, my dear, you will pardon the disgression?—May I ask whose chariot it is? It is by much the prettiest I have seen in England."

She hesitated—

"It is—it is mine, madam."

"Yours, my dear? Do I understand you? Are you then married?"

"Not yet—But I am so happy to see you"—

At this moment John entered, and informed Miss Villiers, that having asked for Lord Melvile, he was informed his lordship was gone into the country, to the seat of his intended father-in-law, Mr. Harding, and would not be in town till after his marriage.

His marriage!—Her misery was then certain—she sunk motionless into a chair.

As Miss Villiers had too little art to hide her feelings, and Mrs. Herbert too much knowledge of the world to mistake them, the latter was soon *au fait*[13] as to the interest her friend took in all that related to Lord Melvile.

She however spared her confusion, told her she looked pale, that she saw the town did not agree with her, and insisted on taking her for three or four days to the villa of her mother-in-law, Lady Sophia Herbert, about twenty miles from town.

"I will send off one of my servants this moment to apprize Lady Sophia of our intended visit, and if you please, my dear, we will be with her at dinner to-morrow: this day I insist on your spending with me: we will be denied,[14] and chat over all our Rutland adventures."

Our heroine was too unhappy at home, and too weary of her own society, not to be delighted with the proposal.

She endeavoured to hide the emotion she could not absolutely restrain; and Mrs. Herbert, who saw her distress, and wished to give her time to recover from the shock, pretended to have visits to pay, and left her till dinner to herself.

We have said Miss Villiers had a mind, which, though full of sensibility, was naturally carried to see every thing on the brightest side.

Mrs. Herbert's absence was, as she imagined it would be, a relief to her friend.

She sat down, she read the letter John had brought back; she dropped a tear of regret—she dropped a second.

She wept the loss of the *most charming of mankind;* she grieved such a letter, for it was admirably written, should be thrown away.

No ray of hope remained as to the first source of her grief; as to the second, she determined to insert this letter in her next novel.

"Her next novel?" Is she not then cured of the disease of writing?

Alas! my friend, it is plain you have never been an author.

One rational motive of consolation however remained.

Her folly in writing that letter was only known to herself.

It had not reached the hand for which it was destined.

It had not swelled the triumph of the intended Lady Melvile.

She also felt that certainty of evil is more supportable than doubt.

These reflections were interrupted by her frizeur.

A fresh subject of consolation now offered.

She approached the glass—

O Vanity! benevolent goddess! How much are human miseries alleviated by thy celestial influence!

Chap. VII.

Our fair heroine, drest with the utmost taste, and with an air of *ton* which surprized Mrs. Herbert, arrived a little after four at the house of that lady.

They dined; Miss Villiers wished to unbosom herself to her friend, but wanted courage.

Her presence, however, restor'd some part of her tranquillity.

They talked of Belfont, of Col. Dormer, of her sister: her heart seemed lightened of half its load.

Mrs. Herbert made her smile by drawing ridiculous pictures of some of her country acquaintance.

They were drinking their coffee in Mrs. Herbert's dressing-room when a servant threw open the door.

"Blockhead! Did I not give orders to be denied?"

"It is Col. Herbert, madam."

"My brother? You will excuse me, my dear Miss Villiers; I am never denied to him."

Maria rose, and turning her head, saw enter the room the very man who had broken in on her *tete à tete* with Lord Melvile.

He was even in the same dress; it was impossible she could be mistaken.

She blushed—she looked down—

Mrs. Herbert introduced her brother; he addressed Maria without shewing any consciousness of having ever seen her before.

His eyes had, however, betrayed him.

Maria had remarked a glance of mixed enquiry and surprize, from which he recovered in a moment, but which convinced her he had not forgot the adventure.

She felt his delicacy, and was charmed with it; but it humbled her infinitely in her own eyes.

Was there a moment of her life for which she had occasion to blush?

In what a light must she have appeared to the brother of her friend!

What must he think of her when he felt it necessary to dissemble that he had seen her before!

She was superior to every evil but loss of honour.

Was hers suspected? And for whom? For a man who had left her for another—who had not even deigned to bid her farewell.

Would to heaven she had never seen Lord Melvile!

Her reverie was interrupted by Col. Herbert, who acquainted his sister he came ambassador from Lady Sophia to invite her to spend a few weeks with her in Surry.

"And I, my dear brother, have this morning sent William to acquaint Lady Sophia of my intention to pass some days with her, and to have the pleasure of introducing this young lady."

"What say you, Miss Villiers? will you do the maddest thing in the world, despite the danger of travelling in the dark, and set out for Surry this moment?"

Col. Herbert looked at his sister: he had been surprized at finding with her a person whose character appeared to him something beyond equivocal.

He was much more so to find she intended to introduce her to his mother.

He must be mistaken: she could not be the person whom he had surprized at midnight *tete à tete* with Lord Melvile.

It was necessary to clear his suspicions before the visit to Lady Sophia was undertaken; yet he would have died rather than have hinted those suspicions to Mrs. Herbert.

He called her into another room on pretence of business, and after speaking in raptures of the beauty of her visiter, asked, but in a careless manner, as if a mere accidental question, who she was.

Mrs. Herbert, who observed the emotion which he endeavoured to hide, and who attributed it all to the charms of Miss Villiers, smiled at his affectation of unconcern, and assured him her friend was as amiable as she was lovely, and had but one fault in the world, which was, that her fortune was inadequate to her birth.

That she was a woman of perfect honour; but with all the fire, and she was sorry to say, all the indiscretion of the very opposite character.

That, as a proof of this, she had found her in town, on her return from France, in the most improper situation imaginable, alone, in a lodging, and passing her time in *a certain set.*

"A *set,* my dear brother, which I need not tell you is the very worst of all possible society, especially for a young woman, whose reputation is equally endangered by their malice and their example.

"A *set,* who are wholly engrossed by play, intrigue, and scandal; and so particularly devoted to the first, that they see the approach of the genial spring with horror.

"For them no vernal shower descends, no roses bloom; they prefer December to May, and execrate the smiling Zephyrs for blowing away their cards.

"In order to restore the bright polish of her fame, which must have been a little injured by this indiscreet connexion, I am going to introduce her to the shrine of honour; that is, in plain terms, I intend to put her for a few weeks under Lady Sophia's protection.

"My acquaintance with her began last summer in Rutland, where I found her in the bosom of domestic happiness, with her uncle, one of the most respectable characters I know.

"A man of the finest understanding, and politest manners; and who, I believe, never did a foolish thing but when he suffered Miss Villiers to come to town unprotected.

"In short, it is amazing to me how a man of Col. Dormer's turn of mind could suffer his niece—"

"Col. Dormer! Let me understand you, sister: did you say Miss Villiers was the niece of Col. Dormer?"

"I did."

"Is it possible you can be in earnest? You have no idea, my dear sister, how happy you have made me.

"I began my military life a cadet of seven years old in Col. Dormer's regiment: he is the man on earth to whom I am most obliged."

Mrs. Herbert smiled—

They returned to Maria, who began to be alarmed at their absence.

Col. Herbert, whose doubts were all dispelled by the conversation which had just passed, approached Miss Villiers, his eyes sparkling with pleasure, and made a thousand enquiries after the health of his friend.

Mrs. Herbert's chariot, and her brother's horses, came to the door; they set off, though it was almost dark, and reached Lady Sophia's little villa exactly at ten o'clock.

CHAP. VIII.

If Virtue—gentle, indulgent, feminine Virtue, had chosen to descend on earth in a human form, she would have assumed that of Lady Sophia Herbert.

With a figure still elegant, and a face which wanted only the bloom of youth to be beautiful, she had an air which spoke her birth to have been the most distinguished: an air which would have been commanding, had not its impression been softened by the smile of undissembled goodness.

Her countenance spoke, in the most expressive language, that calm sunshine of the soul which is the happy monopoly of virtue.

She was perfectly well-bred, without the remotest tincture of affectation.

She had mixed in the *world*; but her inclination, and the mediocrity of her fortune, had preserved her from mixing in the *ton*.

Left a widow extremely young, she had devoted her whole time to the care of educating Col. Herbert, her only child, and pointing out his road to glory, by showing him the paths marked out by his illustrious ancestors.

He had returned her cares by meriting them, and by a filial affection which bordered on enthusiasm.

Mr. Herbert's estate had been inherited by his eldest son, born of another mother, the husband of Miss Villiers's friend.

On his death, without children, what remained of the family fortune had descended to Col. Herbert.

He received it a good deal impaired by his brother's profuseness, and by Mrs. Herbert's jointure.[15]

He had, however, remaining about seven hundred pounds a year, which he divided with his mother, whose situation was before by no means suitable to her birth, but which this addition made perfectly easy.

She had remonstrated, but to no purpose; he rightly observed, that he was a single man, and that whilst he continued so, a handsome lodging, and a hired chariot, were all the exteriors for which he had occasion, and that his pride was much more interested in her ladyship's appearance than his own.

CHAP. IX.

A word or two, gentle reader, in respect to this young man; after which we will leave the party at Lady Sophia's to get acquainted, and see what is become of Mr. Hammond.

Col. Herbert had entered into the army, as we have observed, a perfect child, where he had acquired all the frankness and generosity of the military character; to which, by the cares of his mother, he had added a competent share of learning, and a particular taste for polite literature.

He had travelled, not in the modern style, under his own guidance, at nineteen, with some needy dependent French adventurer as an apology for a tutor, but with a nobleman, his near relation, who had been ambassador at one of the first courts in Europe.

He had therefore literally seen courts, and had conversed, not with little Abbés,[16] Parisian *Gens de Loix,*[17] or the despicable beings that in France assume the name of *Philosophers,*[18] but with the first, the best, the most accomplished, persons in every country through which he accompanied Lord L——.

Too poor to be flattered, too well-born to descend to flatter others, he had acquired dignity of mind without vanity or pride, and ease and attention without servility.

He had fine sense, which his natural fire, and proper self-confidence, produced on all occasions to the best advantage.

He was open, brave, generous, sincere, well-bred; and, being in perfect good-humour with himself, was extremely inclined to be so with others.

He loved women, but he also esteemed them, because he had been accustomed to the society of the most estimable, and had besides seen the female character in its most beautiful light at home.

His person was rather pleasing than what is generally called handsome.

He was of the middle stature, well-made, easy, genteel, and had the air and deportment of a man of fashion.

His education, and his military life, had given him great perfection in those exercises which improve the figure, and are becoming a soldier and a gentleman.

His complexion was brown, and rendered browner by his profession; he had very fine chesnut hair, and the most expressive dark eyes in the world.

Let us leave our friends to amuse themselves by little tours about the neighbouring country; to read, chat, sing, dance, play at quadrille, and be happy, whilst we return a moment to town.

CHAP. X.

After a comfortable night's sleep, Mr. Hammond rose, in good spirits, to receive Lady Blast's visit.

She came, she apologized, she almost blushed.

He menaced, she trembled, she acceded to the conditions of forgiveness he proposed, which were, to burn her delectable manuscript, and give the honest compositor an hundred pounds as a small reward for having saved her the infamy of publishing so shameful a libel.

Our heroine's fame being thus rescued from the danger which threatened it, Mr. Hammond pleaded business to shorten Lady Blast's visit, and went to Mrs. Merrick's; where, finding the good woman at home, he learned that Miss Villiers was at Lady Sophia Herbert's in Surry, where she was to stay a fortnight longer.

His heart glowed with pleasure; half his work was done to his hands; he was the intimate friend and near relation of Lady Sophia, knew her virtues, the estimation in which they stood, and the importance of the visit to Miss Villiers.

He enquired into the state of her finances, and, venturing to act as her parent for the time being, paid the few debts she had remaining, discharged her lodging and her chariot, wrote to Col. Dormer that she was in the country on a visit to the most respectable woman in the world, where he intended to join the party, and, attended by Miss Villiers's faithful old John, who had been left behind, set out for Lady Sophia's villa.

CHAP. XI.

There are some people who have the happy art of gaining, not only your friendship, but your confidence, in a moment.

Col. Herbert was one of these.

Warm, sincere, open, undisguised himself; it was almost impossible to have disguise with him.

He had made it a point to gain the esteem and confidence of Miss Villiers, and had succeeded.

After passing five or six delightful days at Greenwood, in that sweet social intercourse of congenial minds which wants a name, she had taken courage, as they were walking in the garden together, whilst the two ladies were paying a visit of form, to mention the evening in Berner's-street.

"I am ashamed, Colonel," said she, with some hesitation, "to own I have seen you before, and feel most sensibly your delicacy in not appearing to recollect a circumstance so little to my honour.

"My indiscretion did not merit this delicacy; and yet I feel that I could not bear my folly should be known to any person less candid than yourself.

"I should even be shocked if it was known to Mrs. Herbert, though I love her with the warmest affection.

"As I must appear to you at present in a very unfavourable light, and as I have the most ardent desire of convincing you I am not unworthy your esteem, I will beg you to hear me with patience whilst I explain to you every little particular in respect to my acquaintance with Lord Melvile, whom I blush to own I *did* love, and whom perhaps I do not yet think of with the indifference I ought."

She proceeded to relate her little history, and to draw a faithful picture of her heart, with a sincerity in which Col. Herbert found a thousand charms.

She even owned that the splendor of Lady H's equipage had first misled her, and that ambition had had too large a share in her partiality for Lord Melvile; though she insisted, and with a vehemence which Col. Herbert did not dislike, that she really *had* loved him.

He knew that a woman seldom owns a passion till it ceases to exist.

He began to love her, and thought Lord Melvile far from a dangerous rival, even had not his situation in respect to Miss Harding been what it was.

He, who was himself a man of fire, believed it impossible a man of *ton* should inspire a lasting affection: sensibility alone is the food of sensibility.

He had been struck *en passant* with Miss Villiers's person the first moment he saw her, but thought no more of her till they met at Mrs. Herbert's.

When he found her not only a woman of honour, but the niece of his friend, her charms appeared with redoubled lustre.

From that evening he determined to gain, at least, her friendship.

Her friendship! How are we misled by words without meaning?

It was her love to which he aspired, and which he resolved to gain.

Charming in London, at Greenwood he found her divine.

Having with him no designs, no pretensions, no views either dictated by ambition or love, she was with him perfectly at ease; and only exerted that general desire of pleasing, which a young and beautiful woman naturally feels with an amiable man who shews her particular attention.

The thorn of anxiety, which her visionary schemes had planted in her bosom, and which had always given a constraint to her manner in her conversations with Lord Melvile, was withdrawn, and had left her all herself.

She was now natural, artless, gay, vivacious, undesigning.

In short, she was the Maria of Belfont, not of Berner's-street.

The ingenuity of the confession she had just been making had touched Col. Herbert in the most lively manner.

It was not her beauty, her genius, her various accomplishments, which had riveted his chains, but her noble sincerity, and the feelings of her heart.

She expressed sentiments for Lord Melvile, of which he died to be himself the object.

A momentary silence had taken place, and both seemed immersed in thought, when they were aroused by the sound of carriages.

As the road was directly under the low wall on the top of which they were leaning, Miss Villiers immediately knew Lord Melvile, who was in a splendid chariot with—Lady Melvile—for their hands had been joined about an hour.

The train of attendant coaches, and the white favours[19] in the hats of the servants, made it unnecessary for her to ask any questions.

A glow of mingled disdain, expiring love, and wounded vanity, suffused her cheek.

We need not say in what manner Col. Herbert felt this event.

It is however necessary to account for the new-married pair's having passed Lady Sophia's wall.

The seat of Mr. Harding, though we did not find this of consequence enough to mention sooner, was only two miles distant from the villa of Lady Sophia.

As the families did not visit, this had escaped Miss Villiers's knowledge.

Lady Sophia kept little company, and was extremely delicate in the choice of it: meer money was by no means a sufficient passport to the happiness of her acquaintance.

She had a particular objection to admitting Mr. Harding into her co-terie, which was that *his* father had been a menial servant to *hers*.

But to our business.

Our heroine was embarrassed, and Col. Herbert a little at a loss how to resume the conversation, when they were relieved by the arrival of the ladies and Mr. Hammond, who had accidentally met at the gate.

Mr. Hammond at Greenwood? Mr. Hammond a friend of this family? What a pleasing surprize to the lovely Maria!

She blushed however at the idea of his being the confidant of her authorship.

She hoped he had too much honour to betray her.

He approached her with all the gallantry of sixty-five, proclaimed his passion before the whole company; and observed, after St. Evremond, that there was not the least impropriety in an old man's loving, though there might be in his expecting to be beloved, to which happiness he assured her he made not the smallest pretension.[20]

After a turn round the garden, Lady Sophia proposed adjourning to a party at loo in the drawing-room.

Whilst the cards were preparing, Mr. Hammond regarded Maria with looks of the strongest compassion.

"I cannot suffer her to return to town. I must withdraw her from the precipice, but without letting her see the hand which saves her.

"The utmost delicacy is requisite on this occasion: a mind like hers will bear no reproof but its own."

These were his reflections; and they produced a proposal of making a tour of a week, in which he was to be master of the revels, with unlimited power to amuse them in whatever manner he thought proper.

Miss Villiers, who, not having money to settle her affairs, was unable to quit London intirely, who dreaded returning to it, who wished to avoid even the possibility of meeting Lord Melvile, and who was too happy in her present society to think without reluctance of changing it, accepted the proposal with transport.

It was at least throwing reflection at a week's distance, which is an amazing point gained.

Whilst Lady Sophia and Mrs. Herbert were settling the necessary preparations for this little party, Miss Villiers and the Col. set down to picquet.[21]

Miss Villiers had never observed him so attentively before; the fire of his eyes, the spirit of his whole countenance, formed such a contrast with the maukish, unmeaning, uninformed, macaroni faces about town, as could not fail to strike very forcibly a woman of her turn of mind.

He was certainly not so handsome as Lord Melvile—O! not a thousandth part so handsome—

And yet she knew not how—but he was more interesting—had more soul—

There was an animation—something so speaking in his every look—not an atom of Lord Melvile's *sang froid.*

In short, he was a very amiable man, and though a woman would be unpardonable who should *love* twice, yet there was certainly no impropriety in having a friendship for a man of such distinguished merit.

There was something so charming in his attention to his mother—he was so perfectly well-bred to women—so much more than well-bred, so much in earnest, so *empressé,*[22] to oblige them—

But what was all this to her?—Lord Melvile was false, but his falsehood would be a very inadequate apology for hers.

Yes, he was indeed false, but he was still as dear to her as ever.

"Adored object of my tenderness, whilst this heart beats, it shall beat for thee."

Col. Herbert interrupted this sentimental reverie by producing point, quint, and quatorze,[23] which finished the game almost as soon as it was begun.

The ladies and Mr. Hammond returned; the play became general; loo took the place of picquet: supper was announced, Pam retired; they chatted away an extremely pleasant evening, and set out at nine the next day; Lady Sophia and Mr. Hammond in her ladyship's post-chaise; and Col. Herbert, with Miss Villiers and his sister, in that of Mr. Hammond.

CHAP. XII.

The plan of our travellers was to have no plan at all, which we take to be the most rational and eligible that human invention can suggest.

They went every day exactly as far as they chose, without giving attention either to hours or mile-stones; flew like the wind, or passed leisurely to observe the face of the country, just as inclination pointed out.

They mounted every hill that promised an agreeable prospect,[24] whether it lay in or out of the direct road; stopped at a twelve-penny hop,[25] at a strolling play,[26] at a wake,[27] at a village-wedding; and partook of twenty more little innocent amusements which we have not time to specify.

They saw all the fine houses on the road which contained any thing worth observation; but, as we think seeing fine houses the dullest of all things which assume the name of pleasure, we beg to be excused descending to particulars.

The sixth day of their tour arrived; the proposed week was almost at an end.

Lady Sophia first observed it was time to think of returning to town.

Miss Villiers's heart sunk at the proposal: return to town! return to anxiety, to solitude, to distress!

She had been so happy! They were become so much one family! She adored Lady Sophia; perhaps she might never see her again.

A sudden damp pervaded every bosom: they lamented that the hours of happiness should ever have an end; that friends so well suited to each other should ever part.

A sigh of regret escaped Maria; Col. Herbert observed it, and pressed her hand by an involuntary impulse.

The dreaded order was given; the horses' heads were turned towards London, from whence they were now distant eighty miles.

They travelled later this evening than they had ever done before, in order to reach an inn which Mr. Hammond strongly recommended, and which was kept by one of his servants, for whom he had a great affection.

In vain the host of the inn they left exhausted all the common-place rhetoric usual on these occasions; assured them the roads were bad, being cross the country; that there were highwaymen abroad; that it threatened a storm.

Mr. Hammond was obstinate, the ladies compliant, and the chaises moved forward.

After they had gone about ten miles in a very indifferent road, the night came on almost imperceptibly.

To render its shades more gloomy, a thick cloud obscured the whole horizon.

They were now at the entrance of an extensive common: the postilions stopped, declared themselves utterly unacquainted with the road, and unable to proceed farther without a guide, which it was now impossible to procure.

It was happy for them that Col. Herbert had been accustomed to *reconnoitre:* [28] he quitted the chaise, mounted his servant's horse, and directing the postilions to stop till his return, undertook to be their *avant coureur.* [29]

The storm now broke at once upon them; the big tempest rose, the winds whistled round and shook the trees to their lowest roots, the rain descended in torrents, the thunder rolled, the streaming lightnings ran along the ground, and produced a luminous glare more terrific than darkness itself.

Col. Herbert had been gone from them half an hour; an interval of which my reader will imagine all the horrors.

What a situation for women! For women delicately bred, and unused

"To bide the pelting of the pityless storm."[30]

Their fears were more than doubled by Col. Herbert's long absence, and by their anxiety on his account.

They called to him, but no sound returned, except that of their own voices, reverberated by the echo.

It is easy to image the feelings of a mother on such an occasion; nor were those of Mrs. Herbert and Miss Villiers much less keen.

Mr. Hammond said every thing he could to encourage them, but to no purpose: their apprehensions were raised to the highest pitch, all contributed to make them pant for an asylum, when Col. Herbert returned, and informed them, that, dark as it was, he had discovered the track of wheels, and had heard, though faintly, the barking of village dogs.

With what transport they received this intelligence none but those who have been in a similar situation can conceive.

They now hoped to regain the haunts of men.

At all events Col. Herbert was safe.

The storm lost half its terrors from this consideration.

They advanced, though slowly and with caution, in the track Col. Herbert pointed out, and in about an hour had the happiness to hear a clock strike; and to see, through a coppice of trees, a glimmering light at a little distance.

Directed by the light, they turned the corner of the coppice, and passed a row of cottages, at the end of which, a little detached from the road, on a gently-rising ground, they saw a house from whence the light which had directed them proceeded.

They rang at the bell, two servants came with lights, a lady and a gentleman followed them to the gate, and on getting out of the chaise Miss Villiers found herself in the arms of her sister.

"Maria!"

"Louisa!"

They could say no more: astonishment and joy rendered them breathless.

Col. Dormer, though not less happy to see her, was less agitated, and enough master of himself to do the honours of his house.

He was charmed to see Lady Sophia, with whom he had been acquainted in her married state, though he had not seen her since she had been a widow.

What surprized Maria most was, to find Mr. Hammond so well acquainted in the family.

Our travelers entered the hospitable walls of Belfont, and, instead of being intruders on strangers, as they expected, had the delight of finding themselves at home.

CHAP. XIII.

It is unnecessary to paint the joyous evening at Belfont; but it may not be amiss to observe, that Mr. Hammond was in such spirits after supper, that he fairly owned the meeting of this group of friends to have been, not accidental, but a surprize of his contriving; and that he had communicated the scheme, by letter, to Col. Dormer, who therefore had expected and prepared for them, but without betraying the secret, even to Louisa, who was as much astonished at the meeting as her sister.

"I protest, however," said he, "that I did not act in concert with the storm, though I found it a very useful auxiliary.

"I was under particular obligations to the thunder, because, being unseasonable, and therefore unexpected, it had ten times the more effect.

"I must give the ladies credit for their courage; they faced with heroism a war of elements, which would have terrified a *macaroni* into hysterics.

"Confess, ladies, did you ever see so charming an object as the light in this parlour window?"

The hours passed on so rapidly, that it was four in the morning before even the female part of the company thought of retiring.

Mr. Hammond, who was a *bon vivant,* because it had been the *ton* in his youth, insisted on one bottle of claret more to the health of the ladies who had just left them.

His share of this bottle elevated Col. Herbert, who was before a little *in alt*,[31] to the pitch of declaring his passion for Miss Villiers to her uncle, and protesting that, though he was too poor at present to marry her himself, he would run any other man through the body who should dare to think of her.

He was the best-humoured creature that can be imagined, sung *beviamo tutti tre*,[32] danced an allemande[33] with Mr. Hammond, drank the king's health, and the ladies, on his knees, threw the glasses over his head, and committed a thousand indecorums, not one of which had the least analogy with the present style of elegant society.

Not but that he was one of the soberest men in the world, but—after a storm—to the health of one's prince, or one's mistress—I forgive him with all my heart.

It was with great difficulty Mr. Hammond prevailed on him to retire to his chamber, where, instead of going to bed, he kept the good old man two hours to hear him protest five hundred times over, and in nearly the same words, that Cleopatra[34] and Helen of Greece[35] were dowdies compared to the divine Maria Villiers.

Morpheus[36] at last took compassion on Mr. Hammond, and inclined our young soldier to let him retire to his apartment.

The leaden god kept possession of the whole company till eleven the next day, when on assembling in the breakfast parlour, they met Mr. Montague with his son and daughter, who, having heard of Maria's arrival, with her friends, came to invite them to a little ball the next day at the manor-house.

The invitation was accepted, and the Montagues consented to spend the day at Col. Dormer's.

Col. Herbert, after making a thousand apologies to Col. Dormer for having kept him up the night before, took him into the garden; and having, as in duty bound, paid his devoirs to the reigning Sultana of his green-house, a hyacinth of distinguished beauty, very *soberly* asked his permission to address his lovely niece.

"Your claret, my dear sir, has done a great deal for me, by precipitating my confession.

"I love Miss Villiers, and my reason and my heart are equally touched. Besides regarding her as the most lovely of women, I find myself unhappy at the idea of losing her society.

"If I had a throne, I would offer it to her; I have only a cottage, and I esteem her enough to believe, that, if I am so happy as to be agreeable to her, the difference between one and the other is not essential.

"My paternal fortune is small; and I divide it with my mother, whose little income before was really insufficient to support her with decency.

"I have only to offer, the glorious hopes of a soldier; a soldier well-born, well-allied, and fond of his profession, which he has not disgraced.

"If Miss Villiers will condescend to share those hopes, and, in the mean time, to conform to my present situation, I shall be the happiest man on earth.

"My mother is at this moment pleading my cause with Miss Villiers; may I ask you to add your persuasions?"

"Here she comes herself, my dear Charles, and I leave you to settle the point with her.

"You will say more for yourself in five minutes, than Lady Sophia and I should say in ten years.

"I have only to observe, that gain my niece's consent, and you are sure of mine at any time."

There is no eloquence so successful as the language of an impassioned heart: before this conversation ended, Miss Villiers was convinced of two truths very important to female happiness, that it is possible to love twice, and to be happy without either a coach and six or a title.

Miss Villiers left him not devoid of hope, and hastened to dress with her sister, her own apartment being given up to Lady Sophia.

During this interval the two sisters entered into mutual confidence on all which had happened to them during this absence; and Maria had the pleasure to find the amiable Louisa was in a few days to be united to a man she had always loved.

She then related her history, and dwelt particularly on her first interview with Col. Herbert.

"If I should marry him," said she, "it would be the most extraordinary commencement of a matrimonial engagement that ever happened.

"I have been very indiscreet indeed, Louisa, but the inconveniences I have found from that indiscretion will make me a pattern of circumspection for the future."

On relating the circumstance of the hundred pounds which had dropped from the clouds, Louisa's suspicions fell very rightly on Mr. Hammond.

The whole constellation of friends, the Montagues included, were drinking their coffee after dinner, when Col. Dormer's servant, whom he had sent on business to Stamford, returned, and brought him his letters from the post.

The first he opened was from his tulip-merchant at the Hague, with advice of his having purchased him a polyanthus,[37] which he assured him would grace the garden of an emperor.

Joy lighted up his whole countenance on reading the second; he gave it to Mr. Hammond, who, by his desire, read aloud as follows:

"MY LORD, Naples, Jan. 15, 1775.

It is my duty to inform your lordship, that my old lord, your honoured kinsman, the Earl of Clairville, died this morning, and has left your lordship the family estate, with sixty thousand pounds in the stocks.

It is expressed in the will that my lord left the estate and money to your lordship, both that it might not be divided from the title, which is your lordship's by inheritance, and to make you amends for his having treated you harshly in his life-time.

I hope to have the honour of being continued in your lordship's service, and am,

My Lord,
With respect,
Your Lordship's dutiful Servant,
WILLIAM JOHNSON.

P.S. I have directed the letter in your lordship's old name, for fear of mistakes at the post-office."

The relationship was so distant, and the late Lord Clairville's treatment of the present so unworthy, that grief could not be supposed to have any share in the feelings of the latter.

Congratulations are points taken for granted, had not every person present been, what however they were, personally interested in the change of Col. Dormer's situation.

"I have always," said he, addressing his nieces, "expected this event, but would not communicate my hopes to you, lest they should end in disappointment. I may now be allowed to build castles in the air; it depends greatly on you, my dear girls, to realize them.

"I have more money than I know how to make use of myself: I therefore present each of you with twenty thousand pounds, and leave it to yourselves to bestow it as you please.

"I wish you (though in this I leave you perfectly free) to fix in this neighbourhood, because no accession of fortune would make me amends for the loss of your society.

"Louisa has already made a choice which leaves me nothing to wish in respect to her.

"Maria, are you determined on celibacy?"

Her eyes were involuntarily turned on Col. Herbert; she perceived it, looked down, and blushed.

"I understand you, and am happy: I will spare your confusion, my dear Maria, and give you to my cadet.

"And now for my airy project; it is to form a neighbourhood of persons endeared to each other by the most tender ties.

"My duty to my prince and my country will oblige me to reside part of the year in London: I will take a house there sufficiently large for us all, where every one shall be at home, and without the shadow of restraint.

"For our best, our rural, house, as Lord Clairville, who lived abroad, and hated his native country, long since sold the family seat of his and my ancestors, I have a house and little domain in view for myself, not two miles distant, at the top of yon hill, on the other side the rivulet which divides the two counties.*

"Col. Herbert and Maria, being soldiers, and therefore citizens of the world, shall, if, as I hope, it is agreeable to them, make mine their country-house.

"There, perhaps, Mr. Hammond, to whom Maria has obligations of which she is at present ignorant, will join our sylvan party, and be literally

"Our guide, philosopher, and friend."[38]

"And there," said the good old man, "your lordship shall build us a theatre; and Miss Villiers and I will, in defiance of managers, write tragedies, and play them ourselves."

Maria blushed, and Lord Clairville proceeded.

"We will build a little, plant a great deal, and above all, garden to infinity.

"Perhaps Lady Sophia will dispose of her villa in Surry, and honour Belfont by making it her future residence.

---

*Of Rutland and Northampton.

"You will love this country, madam; it is still

"A land unspoil'd by barbarous wealth,"[39]

and inhabited by our old race of English gentlemen.

"I will write directly to my lawyer, and my correspondent at the Hague: the marriage settlements shall be drawn, and the polyanthus imported.

"I will indulge an innocent folly, if it is a folly, which gives offence to no one, and extremely gratifies myself.

"And now who will say that Fortune, though in herself contemptible, does not sometimes contribute to happiness?

"She has enabled me to spend the evening of my life in the society of all those most dear to me, to give my amiable Louisa and Maria to the two men on earth who, in my opinion, most deserve them, and to have a collection of vegetative beauty which shall be the wonder and the envy of the universe."

THE END.

Notes to the Novel

~

Preface

1. Brooke chooses her company well. Samuel Richardson (1689-1761) was the author of *Pamela* (1741), *Clarissa* (1747-48), and *Sir Charles Grandison* (1753-54). Richardson's first novel was a sensational success and made novel writing respectable. Samuel Johnson (1709-84), a friend and important literary influence on Brooke, had written *Rasselas* (1759), an Oriental tale. Henry McKenzie (1745-1831), the best known of the writers of the sentimental novel, was author of *The Man of Feeling* (1771) and *Julia de Roubigné* (1777). *The Vicar of Wakefield* (1766) by Oliver Goldsmith (1730?-74) has comic, sentimental, and moral elements.

2. *The Rambler* was one of Samuel Johnson's periodicals and his first published prose work (published semi-weekly from 20 March 1750 to 14 March 1752); it was also the periodical Brooke cited as her model for her own, entitled *The Old Maid.* This particular number was written by Samuel Richardson and advised "appropriate behavior" during courtship and marriage.

3. Anna Louise Élie de Beaumont, *Lettres du marquis de Roselle* (London and Paris, 1764); translated into English and published as *The History of the Marquis de Roselle, in a Series of Letters* (London: Becket and DeHondt, 1765).

4. John Pinkerton, ed., *Select Scottish Ballads,* 2 vols. (London: J. Nichols, 1783). Pinkerton admitted to writing some of these "ancient" Scottish manuscripts himself.

5. Slightly altered from James Thomson, "Spring" [1728], l. 1152.

Book I.

1. Rutland is the smallest shire in east-central England, nestled between Leicestershire and Lincolnshire.

2. A squire was a principal landowner in a small country district. The eighteenth century stereotypically characterized squires as men who hunted, drank, and indulged in coarse "country" pastimes.

3. On the north bank of the Trent River, Nottinghamshire contains some of the grandest country estates in England.

4. Philip Dormer Stanhope, fourth earl of Chesterfield (1694-1773), to whose *Letters . . . to His Son* Brooke refers several times. In a letter dated 9 March 1748, Chesterfield encourages his son to "sacrifice to the Graces," which instill proper notions of conduct, specifically "good sense and breeding," necessary for the development of a gentleman. *Letters . . . to His Son,* 2 vols. (1774; London: New Temple Press, 1912), 1:184-87.

5. Aglaia, Thalia, and Euphrosyne are often referred to as the Graces. Daughters of Zeus, others were Auxo and Kale. Givers of beauty, grace, and charm, all of the Graces encourage music, poetry, dance, and the other arts, pursuits associated with the development of a genteel character.

6. This indicates that £3,000 is the amount of money left for the daughters after the father's property and estate were liquidated to pay his debts.

7. Intelligence; dignity.

8. Quiet tenderness; gentleness.

9. Maria's dark complexion and, in the following line, her Greek nose signal sensuality and passion.

10. Conventional poetic language for a gentle breeze. In classical mythology Zephyr is the west wind, son of Aeolus and Aurora and lover of Flora.

11. In the second half of the eighteenth century, Berners Street was a part of Marylebone's artistic colony, London's earliest Latin quarter (*London Encyclopedia*).

12. Alert. "Qui-vive?" is the sentry's "Who goes there?"

13. A female gorgon with snakes for hair; in mythology, the mere sight of Medusa turned a person to stone.

14. Brooke and Mary Ann Yates became managers in 1773 at the King's Theatre in the Haymarket, known as the Opera House.

15. Ranelagh was a fashionable gathering spot for masquerades, garden walks, concerts, and fireworks. Frances Burney condemns it in her novels, and Tobias Smollett notes its opulence in *Humphry Clinker.*

16. The Pantheon was designed by James Wyatt as the "winter Ranelagh." It had one large main room, where popular masquerades were held, with smaller rooms for card playing, tea, and supper.

17. Dull.

18. Waived; brushed aside.

19. A small crown, denoting rank below the monarch; here, the family crown of a duke.

20. A hired, light carriage seating two to four people and pulled by two, four, or six horses. The driver rode one of the horses.

21. That is, without bothering to close the shades.

22. One of several satiric references to popular novel devices. This one conflates elements of Richardson's *Pamela* and *Clarissa.*

23. Natural laziness and contentment.

24. Brilliance; magnificence.

25. The Bell Inn, located in Stilton. The town was situated along the main postal route from London to York in the 1750s. Stilton is famous for a rich, waxy cheese with blue-green mold. Howard Robinson, *The British Post Office: A History*

(Princeton: Princeton Univ. Press, 1948), 104; Adrian Room, *Dictionary of Place-Names in the British Isles* (London: Bloomsbury, 1988).

26. A market town north of London in Bedfordshire, southeast of Bedford and southwest of Cambridge.

27. The last king of Babylon, who built the hanging gardens, one of the Seven Wonders of the Ancient World. The reference here records his unconventional behavior, which earned him the reputation for madness (Daniel 4:25). His name was actually Nabonidus (555-539 B.C.); the author of the biblical passage mistakes his name.

28. An evening party or reception fashionable during the eighteenth century.

29. Similar in size to a business card today, often only including a person's name and left as evidence of an attempted social call. People often wrote notes on them, as Lady Hardy has in this case, and sent them by a servant to friends.

30. Alexander Pope (1688-1744), "Epistle to Arbuthnot" (1734), l. 128. This line emphasizes what Maria feels is her natural poetic talent. Pope dominated English poetry from the publication of his *Essay on Criticism* in 1711 and of a miscellany of poems in 1712 until his death.

31. An oblong leather case or bag that opens like a book, with hinges in the middle of the back; used for carrying clothing and other necessities when traveling.

32. David Garrick (1717-1779), an actor lionized for his portraits of leading Shakespearean tragic characters and praised for his comic roles, began acting in 1740. In 1742, he signed a contract with Drury Lane theatre, became part owner in 1747, and acted all but one season there until he retired in 1776. Garrick often acted as many as eighteen different roles in one season; he also wrote original plays, prologues, epilogues, and numerous adaptations of other plays.

33. Casting himself. Garrick added only one new role (Sir Anthony Branville in a revival of Frances Sheridan's comedy *The Discovery*) to his repertoire during the ten years before his final season.

34. Because each theatre had stable companies, playwrights usually wrote parts to match the strengths of the particular actors and actresses.

35. The two patent (royally licensed) theatres in London—Drury Lane and Covent Garden—were in stiff competition with each other.

36. That is, she intends to send her play to the company with the best, most suitable actors.

37. A scene of combat or contest (Alexander Pope, *Homer's Odyssey*, 8.107-10).

38. A mountain in central Greece sacred to Apollo and the Muses; a reference to excellent literature.

39. Economy.

Book II.

1. The knave of clubs.

2. Gambling; commonly believed to be an addictive vice.

3. This paraphrases Thomas Hobbes's description of natural human conduct, which therefore requires both self-control and external government.

4. A sorceress in Greek mythology and the lead character in Richard Glover's eighteenth-century tragedy (1761) by the same name. The only performance of *Medea* in the 1774-75 season was a benefit for Mary Ann Yates on 20 March 1775 at Drury Lane; Yates played the lead.

5. The lead character in the opera *Montezuma* by Antonio Maria Gasparo Sacchini, performed at King's Theater (1775), which Maria later attends.

6. Fashionable society, the only world worth belonging to; literally, "beautiful world."

7. Widow; the root of the word associates it with "to leave behind."

8. A card game played by a varying number of players. In gold loo, winnings were paid in gold coins, not in paper script, which had fluctuating value and could be hard to collect.

9. The last meal of the day; its eighteenth-century usage often implies entertaining. "Dinner" was the main meal, usually eaten around the middle of the day.

10. A joint stock company, which was both an economic and a military organization, chartered by Queen Elizabeth I in 1600 and given a monopoly on trade with the entire Eastern Hemisphere. Between 1748 and 1760, the East-India Company won victories over the French and Dutch and therefore governed large parts of India. In 1774 Parliament assumed joint control of the company in order to share its profits and prevent its most egregious exploitative practices.

11. Above "a certain set"; the truly elite, fashionable people.

12. Literally, nobility, but implying lofty manners, perhaps class pretentiousness.

13. A woman of doubtful reputation or questionable chastity. Edward Thompson's poem *The Demi-rep* (2nd ed., 1766) attacked the decadent life of London's leisure class and included lengthy sections on card playing and gossiping and reputation-killing older women.

14. Past middle age; "on the wane."

15. Bashfulness.

16. Latin for "in her own person," as herself.

17. Flower bed.

18. A sensitive plant has a high degree of irritability (its leaves close up when touched), while a frost plant can survive even when ice crystals shoot out from its roots.

19. A card game played by four people with 40 cards (the 8's, 9's, and 10's are discarded). Edmond Hoyle, *Hoyle's Games Improved* (London, 1775), 92-114. As in gold loo, stakes had to be paid in gold.

20. Arthur's Chocolate House, a popular gathering place.

21. This echoes the narrator's comment about Lady Bellaston in Henry Fielding's novel *Tom Jones* (1749), book XV, chapter IX. Fielding (1707-1754) influenced many women writers through both *Tom Jones* and *Amelia* (1751); he was also arguably the most innovative dramatist of the day.

22. Literally, systems of taxing, but used here to refer to ways of acquiring money to pay expenses.

23. Daughter of Zeus and Hera and wife of Heracles. As the cupbearer of the gods, Hebe appears in scenes of Olympian domesticity and is associated with adolescence and youthful beauty.

24. Venus, the mother of Eros (Cupid), was celebrated for her many amorous adventures and pranks.

25. Apollo was the Greek god of the sun and of poetry, music, and healing. The Belvedere Apollo was the model of perfect masculine beauty, used in medical textbooks from the Renaissance forward. It was an ancient marble statue, believed to be a Roman copy of a bronze votive statue set up in Delphi in 279 B.C.

26. Charming; winning; making its way into the heart.

27. That is, he had allied himself with the "Opposition," those who challenged the ministry in power, after being equally prominent in the government before his party fell.

28. *Hamlet* 1.5.108. Hamlet's words after the ghost of his father reveals that he was murdered by his brother, Hamlet's uncle.

29. Statira in Nathaniel Lee's *The Rival Queens* (1677), 1.1.48.

30. Harmony of disposition; shared attitudes.

31. John Dryden, *All for Love* (1678), 2.1.284. A downy pinion is literally a wing of a young bird; it is used here metaphorically to characterize the youthful excitement of love.

32. See introduction, pp. xxiii-xxiv.

33. Pindar (518-438 B.C.) was a Greek lyric poet whose odes influenced English poetry in the mid-seventeenth century and again in the mid-eighteenth; Pindar's odes were noted for musicality, thematic digressions, personal comment, and free expression of feelings.

34. Town crier.

35. Brooke, like Henry Fielding and many mid-century novelists, styles herself a "historian," a recorder of truth and observer of human nature and events.

36. Built and developed between 1720 and 1734 and inhabited by nobility and other people of distinction.

37. Eagerness to please.

38. The model of perfect feminine beauty; the Venus de' Medici, a marble statue with both hands held modestly before her body, was brought to Florence by Cosimo de' Medici III in the late seventeenth century and, like the Belvedere Apollo, was used as a medical text illustration. This reference tells us that Lord Melvile had done the fashionable thing, gone on the Grand Tour of Europe.

39. Alexander Pope, *Essay on Man* (1733-34), 4.254.

40. "I don't know what"; that indefinable something.

41. Twickenham was Alexander Pope's country home on the banks of the Thames.

42. Alexander Pope, "Epistle to a Lady" (1735), ll. 50-52. "Calypso," who is named at the beginning of the quoted verse, is cunning and seductive; earlier lines capture her contradictory power: "Aw'd without Virtue, without Beauty charmed; / Her Tongue bewitch'd as odly [sic] as her Eyes."

43. Mercenary soldiers.

44. An exclusive street in Paris on which was found the entrance to Molière's theatre in the right wing of the Palais Royal. H.C. Chatfield-Taylor, *Molière: A Biography* (New York: Duffield, 1906), 96.

45. My Lord English.

46. And these guests.

47. Cute little Jane; the suffix "ton" was a diminutive, a way of making a pet name.

48. Politeness; civility.

49. Make plain her desires.

50. A gold French coin worth twenty francs, short for *louis d'or*.

51. Trickery; deception.

52. Provocative whims; small caprices.

53. But so playful, so amusing, so lively!

54. Tedious; boring; causing ennui or weariness.

55. It's not important; never mind.

56. Disordered; to live a disordered life.

57. Discharge; dismissal.

58. Beloved father.

59. Playfulness, provocative whims, and little vivacities.

Book III.

1. The person holding seignorial rights, that is, feudal rights to fees from tenants and the right to hold a manorial court, one of the types of legal courts of England. Manors were districts or large landed estates given by rulers in early medieval times along with special privileges.

2. Still a leading private boys' school, Eton College was founded by Henry VI and, during the eighteenth century, maintained about seventy students. Scholars were selected annually from Eton to attend King's College, Cambridge University.

3. Founded by Henry VIII in 1546, Trinity is the largest college at Cambridge, and Mr. Montague's attendance there reflects the classical education that his father encourages.

4. The Macaroni was a club for fashionable young men. It began as a society of enthusiasts for Italian culture and became a group dedicated to flouting traditional virtues, including English patriotism. In the public mind the "*macaroni* race" was associated with excess, folly, and foppery. Paul Langford, *A Polite and Commercial People* (Oxford: Clarendon, 1989).

5. A sport in which a marksman shoots at birds. George Markland, *Pteryplegia; or, The Art of Shooting-Flying* (London, 1727).

6. The quarter-staff is a six- to eight-foot long pole with an iron tip, used for fighting and exercising.

7. Great, mighty hunters; "like Nimrod, a mighty hunter before Yahweh" (Genesis 10:8-9) became a common saying.

8. Alexander Pope, "Epistle to Burlington" (1731), l. 108; part of Pope's description of Timon's Villa in which he satirizes pride, excess, and lack of common sense. Brooke juxtaposes this image of weak, modern men with the reference to hardy Nimrods.

9. Quintus Horatius Flaccus (65-8 B.C.). Horace was educated at Rome and Athens and is admired for his *Epodes, Satires, Odes,* and *Epistles,* including *Ars Poetica.* Horatian satires became one of the models for eighteenth-century poets, including Alexander Pope.

10. Francesco Petrarca (1304-1374). An Italian scholar and poet whose highly polished love poetry was much imitated in England.

11. Today often called the bass viol; a large stringed instrument held between the knees, with the range of a cello. This was the instrument of choice for cultivated gentlemen; the painter Thomas Gainsborough (1727-1788) often played it and included it in his paintings of men. Brooke thus assigns Montague an instrument with class, gender, and cultural significance.

12. The river that flows through Cambridge University.

13. The local name of the Thames River, which serves as metonymy for Oxford University.

14. Built by the French king Louis XIII as a hunting lodge, and located about twelve miles southwest of Paris, Versailles was made the primary palace residence of the French monarchy by Louis XIV.

15. A small street or alley; also a small reception.

16. The wife of the president of a tribunal, or court. Brooke is implying that this type of woman was the hostess at a salon, a gathering place for political and literary talk.

17. A hair stylist; literally, one who curls hair.

18. That is, her hair was "curled like an angel."

19. An eighteenth-century term for a psychological ailment akin to melancholia and marked by depression, excessive dejection, and anger.

20. Venanzio Rauzzini (1746-1810), an Italian soprano and castrato singer, composer, and harpsichordist. He made his London début on 8 November 1774 in the opera *Armida* at King's Theatre and played the lead in Sacchini's opera *Montezuma,* which opened 7 February 1775, the opera to which Brooke refers here.

21. Antonio Maria Gasparo Sacchini (1730-1786), an Italian composer of chamber music, oratorios, and nearly fifty operas. Sacchini came to London in 1772, and, until he fled England in 1781 under the threat of imprisonment, many of his operas were performed at King's, including *Montezuma.*

22. Giovanna Baccelli, an Italian dancer popular in England from 1774 to 1801, known for her expressive style of dancing and for her support of a controversial reform allowing shorter skirts on dancers' costumes to permit freer movement. Baccelli danced in the new ballet *La Fete de Flora,* and the grand ballet *Les Mexicains,* after *Montezuma* at this particular performance.

23. Citizen of Bologna, the Italian city that was a center for learning. Italians were reported to be great lovers.

24. Henry Johnson was the boxkeeper, assistant treasurer at King's in 1777-78. Lady Hardy has no "interest with" him, meaning she might not get good seats—or seats at all.

25. Literally, last resource. The narrator is satirizing Lady Hardy's attitude toward her card-partner's death.

26. A keyboard instrument resembling a grand piano and popular from the sixteenth through the eighteenth centuries. Like the *viol de gamba* it had gender (here feminine), class (aristocratic), and cultural significance.

27. Simonin Vallouy (Vallouis), popular dancer, active at King's from 1769 to 1777, who danced with his wife and Baccelli in the grand ballet *Les Mexicains* after the performance of *Montezuma*.

28. Sight.

29. A passage up the center of the pit of theatres in which fops and dandies congregated in order to be seen and admired.

30. Italian for good taste.

31. Flowing hair.

32. Mr. Fierville was a dancer at King's during Brooke's and Yates's tenure as managers. He married his partner, Anne Heinel. After Fierville contracted smallpox, Heinel had the marriage annulled under the authority of Popish Laws, since they had not been married by a Roman Catholic priest. Heinel then married another famous dancer, Gaëton Appoline Balthazar Vestris, known as "le dieu de la danse" ("the god of the dance").

33. Literally, "map of the countryside." Charles is asking Lord Melvile for "the lay of the land," whatever he can be told about Maria to allow him to impress or charm her.

34. In good company; said sarcastically.

35. "Head of the house," supervisor of the butlers and other servants.

36. Incompletely dressed or dressed in a careless or negligent manner. It was fashionable to receive guests this way throughout the century and often had arrogant or sexual nuances.

37. A cup of hot chocolate, then a fashionable drink.

38. A young man of striking good looks, after the Greek myth about the beautiful youth loved by Venus and Proserpina.

39. A pose struck deliberately.

40. An Englishman who returned from India with a large fortune acquired there. Nabob was usually a derogatory term.

41. Established in 1772 as an architecturally innovative area.

42. An English inhabitant of the West Indies. Many returned to England very wealthy and sought high social and political positions.

43. Charles II was king of England from 1660 to 1685; he had fled England during the civil war and was restored to the throne by vote of Parliament. Charles was inconsistent because he attempted to placate the Dissenters (see note 44, below), of whom Brooke, as a loyal supporter of the Church of England, disapproves, even as he privately ridiculed them and their beliefs ("prejudices" in Brooke's pejorative terms).

44. Nonconformists; Protestants who did not belong to the Church of England or take communion there.

45. Although not a definite identification, there is intriguing evidence that this is Charles James Fox, M.P. Fox was a notorious gambler who won and lost thousands of pounds. He later operated a faro bank, and Brooke was accused of publicly parodying his exploits.

46. Italian for conversation.

47. Lively; witty.

BOOK IV.

1. £52.5.

2. David Garrick, who bought half interest in Drury Lane Theatre from James Lacy in 1747 for £8,000, was responsible for hiring new talent and overseeing production; Lacy handled the finances.

3. A fashionable paper, supported through advertising, which reflected the opinions of the "leisured class." Its first issue was published 2 November 1772, and Henry Bate served as the paper's editor until 1780. John Wheble, a Fleet Street bookseller, was its first publisher. Among *The Morning Post*'s twelve original proprietors were John Bell, an especially entrepreneurial bookseller; James Christie, the founder of Christie's; the Rev. "Dr." Trussler, the inventor of book clubs; Richard Tattersall, the founder of Tattersall's; and Joseph Richardson, a minor playwright who helped manage Drury Lane. Wilfrid Hindle, *The Morning Post, 1772-1937: Portrait of a News paper* (London: George Routledge and Sons, 1937; Westport, Conn.: Greenwood Press, 1974), 5.

4. Myrtle wreaths crowned the victors of early Olympic games; Maria here dreams of "winning" Melvile. Because the laurel was sacred to Apollo, god of poetry, music, and the arts, and was also awarded for victory and merit, she dreams of being honored for her tragedy. The poppy has been the symbol of death and sleep since classical times and, although there are many varieties of poppies, including many bright garden flowers, "poppy" often refers to opium, which is derived from the plant.

5. *Braganza*, a critically acclaimed play by Robert Jephson (1736-1803), which premiered at Drury Lane on 17 February 1775 and ran for nineteen performances in its first season.

6. Managers throughout the century were reluctant to take new pieces because sets and costumes were expensive and, compared to reviving tried-and-true plays, posed a financial risk.

7. The person in charge of a theatre's business and ticket sales.

8. Mary Ann Yates (1728-1787) played the Duchess in *Braganza;* she was also a close personal friend of Brooke and co-managed the King's Theatre with her. See Brooke's "Authentic Memoirs of Mrs. Yates," *Gentleman's Magazine* (July 1787).

9. Playwrights throughout the century complain about their audiences' habit of talking freely and loudly among themselves during performances.

10. The name of the Duchess in *Braganza;* specifically, Mary Ann Yates (see note 8 above).

11. John Milton, *Paradise Lost* (1667), 8.488-89; part of Adam's description of Eve.

12. Vigorous; energetic; strong.

13. Strong; vigorous; forceful.

14. The part of the "traitor," Valesquez, was played by William Smith (1730-1819), who worked exclusively at Covent Garden for twenty years and performed the best roles in tragedy and high comedy. Smith was an audience favorite, and Garrick had added him to the Drury Lane Company in September 1774.

15. Raffaello Sanzio (1483-1520), painter and architect of the Italian High Renaissance whose work is known for its fluidity of form and depiction of idealized human grandeur.

16. "Molière [Jean Baptiste Poquelin, 1622-1673], as we are told by Monsieur Boileau [in *Critical Reflections on Longinus, Works* (1711-12), ii.89], used to read to his House-keeper, as she sat with him at her Work by the Chimney-Corner; and could foretell the Success of his Play in the Theatre, from the Reception it met at his Fire-Side: For he tells us the Audience always followed the Old Woman, and never failed to laugh in the same Place." Joseph Addison, *The Spectator,* no.70, 21 May 1711.

17. Excessive; exaggerated; overdone.

18. The chorus's initial invocation of artistic invention in Shakespeare's *Henry V.*

19. An error for *savoir vivre:* breeding, knowledge of how to behave.

20. A drinking song, obviously not appropriate for a woman.

21. Daughter of Helios, the sun god, a powerful sorceress who seduced Odysseus and turned his men into swine.

22. Grantham is in Lincolnshire, in the center of England's eastern coast. It was considered a very prosperous market town, and its inhabitants were generally wealthy.

23. A mistress or concubine of a Turkish sultan.

24. An aged, wise counsellor of youth in Homer's *Iliad.*

25. Jean-Jacques Rousseau (1712-1778), Voltaire (François-Marie Arout) (1694-1778), Charles-Louis Montesquieu (1689-1755), and Étienne Bonnet de Condillac (1715-1780), whose writings on human nature and society were revisionary. Rousseau's major work on social theory, *The Social Contract,* and on education, *Émile,* contributed to the French Revolution and to Romanticism. Voltaire spoke out against established religious and political institutions while proposing his own philosophical and moral schemes; *Candide* (1758), a satire on philosophical optimism, is perhaps his best known work. Montesquieu's *Spirit of the Laws* (1750) presented a new theory of government, advocating, among other things, a separation of powers, which influenced the creators of the Constitution of the United States. Condillac's "Essay on the Origin of Human Knowledge" (1746) advocated and advanced John Locke's ideas regarding the formation of human knowledge and became the basis for the French philosophical movement Idéologie, which was taught in French schools for fifty years. Brooke does not approve of their skeptical bent, which she sees as threatening to religion.

26. In both cases, ritual molding was practiced.

27. Self-love; vanity.

28. Discarded; out of fashion.

29. Free-thinkers.

30. Lower classes; riffraff.

31. Refusing to submit reason and conscience to any authority in matters of religious belief. A group of people, including the Deists, declared themselves free-thinkers in the early eighteenth century. Church of England members who respected doctrine thought this was shameful.

32. The lovely damsel! Ah, what shall I do?

33. Christoph Willibald Gluck, *Orfeo ed Euridice* (Vienna, 5 October 1762), 4.1. "What shall I do without Euridice?"

34. Displaying easy confidence, casual.

35. Maria fantasizes about giving her dowry to Louisa because she herself will be so rich once she marries Lord Melvile. That he is preparing to marry out of economic necessity makes this idea ironic.

36. The largest of the royal parks (covering more than 340 acres) and one of the places fashionable people went to be seen. By the 1770s, it had become notorious for duels (*London Encyclopedia*). It was never as fashionable as the Mall and St. James's Park, and Brooke is signalling that Maria has learned from "a certain set" rather than from the *ton*.

37. Whole effect.

38. Whist is a card game played by four players, with the two sitting opposite as partners. A renounce occurs when a player fails to follow suit when he or she is able to or when a player who cannot follow suit wins the trick by playing the only card of a suit he or she has. Edmond Hoyle, *Hoyle's Games Improved* (London, 1775), 113.

39. Classical prophetesses and doomsayers who gathered from various parts of the world.

40. The pot or the amount of stakes and fines of the players in a card game. Edmond Hoyle, *Hoyle's Games Improved* (London, 1775), 111.

41. A tribunal court in the Ottoman Empire.

42. Chancery, the court having jurisdiction over equity cases. It was informed by common law precepts but grounded in conscience and principles of "natural" justice. Chancery was the court most people chose in which to initiate legal actions because it differed from the courts of Common Pleas, King's Bench, or assizes in that the plaintiff did not have to purchase a royal writ, a legal document (a command, a precept, or an order issued by a court in the name of the sovereign).

BOOK V.

1. A set of household articles; things required to maintain an establishment completely.

2. But, to return to our subject.

3. Not identified.

4. It was quite expensive to own or hire a coach; an annual income of at least £1,000 was necessary to maintain a coach. Betty Rizzo, *Companions without Vows* (Athens: Univ. of Georgia Press, 1994), 34.

5. Johann Christian Bach (1735-1782) began producing operas at King's in 1763, and beginning in 1764 he and Karl F. Abel, a band member at King's, began giving subscription concert series at Spring Gardens, Almack's, and Carlisle House. These concert series were popular and fashionable events and continued until a year before Bach's death.

6. Composure; literally, cold blood.

7. Hannah More (1745-1833), one of the most prominent and respected writers of her generation, inaugurated the *Cheap Repository Tracts,* which were Sunday school readings of moral stories, poems, sermons, and prayers. She was a great admirer of Garrick, and her poems "Ode to Dragon" and "Sensibility" paid public tribute to him. The "Ballad of Bleeding Rock" (1775) was a sentimental tale of the death of a nymph deserted by her lover.

8. A morning assembly held by a person of distinction, often a reception of visitors held shortly after arising from bed.

9. Force of comedy.

10. In the last scene of *Braganza,* the traitor, Valesquez, is murdered, the Duchess is saved, Braganza is empowered, and happy times return to Portugal.

11. Adapt; managers often hired playwrights to adapt old or foreign plays for an English audience or their particular company of actors and actresses.

12. Refined, delicate, or poignant wit exhibited in discourse or literary composition.

13. Since Willoughby Lacy might have made commitments without Garrick's knowledge, the uncertainty here about whether or not Maria's play will be accepted the next season could be genuine, but that Garrick would have agreed to let Lacy's decisions override his own, especially since Garrick was acting manager, is unlikely.

14. Covent Garden, managed by John Rich, was the only other patent house (royally licensed theatre). Maria fantasizes about not accepting payment.

15. Horace, *Ars Poetica* (ll. 386-89), advises keeping a manuscript nine years before publishing; see Alexander Pope, "Epistle to Arbuthnot," ll. 40-41.

16. Three kinds of theatres flourished during Elizabeth's reign: court, elite, and popular, or, as they were formerly called, "court, public, and private," respectively. The Phoenix and Blackfriars are examples of "elite" theatres and drew an audience of court, gentry, and substantial merchants. The Globe, the venerable open-air theatre on Bankside, attracted the most heterogeneous crowd in the city. James I brought the theatres under the control of the crown, and some companies were consolidated. Even so, in addition to court performances, London supported seven vigorous theatres, some elite and some popular, until 1638, when the theatres were closed because of the civil war. Brooke is reminding her readers of how much better the theatres were supported before the war. Stephen Orgel suggests some of the problems with the term "private theatre" in *The Illusion of Power* (Berkeley: Univ. of California Press, 1975), 6 n.3.

17. Knowledge of acting; specifically, how to move audiences and get desired responses.

18. Mary Ann Yates.

19. Almack's Assembly Rooms, a fashionable gathering spot during the middle of the eighteenth century. The guest lists were strictly controlled by four ladies, and all the gentleman had to wear knee britches and white ties (*London Encyclopedia*).

20. Without hopes of financial or other material gain.

21. Kent is considered one of the most delightful places in Great Britain, with an abundance of oysters, fruit, cattle, corn, cherries, hops, excellent timber, and beautiful gardens.

22. Literally, French for blank card; having full authority and unrestricted power to have one's way.

23. Contracts that set the terms and arrangements for settling property on a person. It commonly meant "marriage settlements," and Maria, therefore, does not exaggerate the possible implications of Melvile's speech.

24. Settled; contracted, as a firm engagement.

BOOK VI.

1. Frenzy; extreme emotional distress.

2. A high stakes game of quadrille; the set bet was a guinea or £1.05.

3. Small pleasures; money a man spends on his mistress.

4. In passing.

5. The British often mistook the ceremonial, restrained conduct of the Chinese and Indians for haughty reserve. He might expect this type of behavior to have developed in the English living long abroad.

6. Unidentified.

7. Unidentified.

8. Tommaso Michele Francesco Savario Trajetta (often spelled Traette; 1727-1779), composer. Several of his operas (*Germondo, I Capricci del Sesso,* and *Telemaco*) were performed at King's Opera House while Brooke was managing.

9. Literally, "voice of the chamber," meaning modulating the voice for the size of the room.

10. Charms.

11. Surprise attack.

12. Power of giving pleasure.

13. Propriety; decorum.

14. An evening party at which the revelers wear costumes and hide their own identities carefully while guessing others. Masquerades were reputed to be good places for illicit meetings.

15. Londoners believed themselves in the midst of a crime wave, and indeed many travelers were robbed by footpads and highwaymen at night.

BOOK VII.

1. In the *Aeneid,* Virgil's meaning depends in part on his mapping the mythic world of the Trojan War onto the real geography of the Mediterranean known in his day. Hence, he is careful to provide detailed, explicit geographic markers throughout his poems, as at 1:109-110. (Mary Kuntz).

2. From Constance's troubled response in Shakespeare's *King John III* (3.1.1) when she learns from Salisbury that the Dauphin, Lewis, is to be married.

3. This is the author's satiric commentary aimed at popular courtship novels, some of which were called "true histories" on the title page. The female characters in these works were regularly depicted as believing that novels and the events in them accurately reflected life. Charlotte Lennox's heroine Arabella in *The Female Quixote* (1752) is the most famous example.

4. Milton, *Paradise Lost* (1674), 2.406; refers to Hell.

5. Freedom of the press continued to be a serious and embattled issue in Great Britain; here Brooke notes the slanderous nature of the press but takes a stand for liberty. See introduction, p. xii-xv.

6. This description echoes much of Samuel Johnson's *Idler* no. 30 of 11 November 1758, on the corruption of newswriters. (Isobel Grundy)

7. A theme of Henry Fielding's *Tom Jones* and discussed there explicitly several times, as in chapter 1 of book 8.

8. Not identified.

9. Marian, a generic name for a country girl; according to an old legend, fairies rewarded a good housewife by leaving a sixpence in her shoe. Bishop Richard Corbett, "Faeryes Farewell: Or God-A-Mercy Will" (1647); Phyllis McGinley, *Sixpence in Her Shoe* (New York: Macmillan, 1960), 1.

BOOK VIII.

1. Tiny. Book I of *Gulliver's Travels* by Jonathan Swift is set on Lilliput, the island of miniature people.

2. From the *Spectator* (1 March 1711-6 December 1712), which was reprinted and sold as bound sets many times throughout the century and influenced *The Old Maid.* Richard Steele (1672-1729), in no. 144 (Wednesday, 15 August 1711), defines "beauty" in women as inner goodness and virtue, dignity of behavior, and pleasing physical appearance: "Others are Beautiful, but Eucratia thou art Beauty!"

3. Put his faith in a favorable opportunity.

4. A "great house" in Lincolnshire built by William Cecil, Lord Burghley (see note 5, below); visiting such estates had become a tourist industry. Here and later, Brooke compliments her friend, Lady Elizabeth Cecil, the current owner of Burghley; the second edition makes the praise more explicit.

5. William Cecil (1520-1598), first baron Burghley, served as secretary of state for King Henry VIII and principal advisor and Lord High Treasurer to Queen Eliza-

beth I. Under Elizabeth, England defeated the Spanish Armada and through the wool trade became a commercial powerhouse—thus the country was at "its utmost summit."

6. Alexander Pope, *An Essay on Man* (1733-34), 1.96.

7. The modern meaning is knowledge and love of the fine arts, but Roman *vertù* was the ideal moral conduct of a citizen.

8. Alexander Pope, "To Mr. Addison, Occasioned by his Dialogues on Medals" (1720), l. 44. The coins of Otho are the rarest in a popular series of the twelve Caesars, and Mr. Montague is developing his ideas about antiquarian collecting and the appropriate priorities for young men.

9. The postal system, established c. 1680 for London, which would deliver letters and parcels within a ten-mile radius for a penny each.

10. Surely not!

11. An ancient royal hunting forest long notorious for its dangers, as the title of publications such as this show: *Bloody newes from Enfield; being a true but sad relation of the bloody fight and dangerous engagement between eightscore countrey-men with pikes, halberds, forks, and swords, and a party of foot souldiers with their arms on Monday last near the said Enfield Chase. . . .* (London: George Horton, 1659).

12. Unidentified.

13. Completely aware; knowledgeable about.

14. The servant should say that she is not at home.

15. The provision of land or income for a widow, usually negotiated in a marriage settlement. Susan Staves, *Married Women's Separate Property in England, 1660-1833* (Cambridge: Harvard Univ. Press, 1990), 95.

16. Churchmen.

17. Lawyers.

18. Literally "philosophers," but here a sarcastic reference to those who set themselves up as sages and, Brooke may feel, elevate philosophy and its speculative methods over religion. "Contests" between philosophy and religion were common in novels of the period; see book IV, note 22, above.

19. A ribbon, rosette, or ornamental knot of ribbons worn at a ceremony such as a wedding or christening as evidence of goodwill or celebration.

20. M. de St. Evremond (often spelled Evremont, 1613-1703), a French author who wrote moral, critical, and philosophical essays on a variety of subjects, ranging from a characterization of the Roman people to critiques of Italian opera. Two of his essays, "Of Retirement" (*The Works of M. de St. Evremont* {London: Awnsham and John Churchill, 1700}, 2:69-78) and "That Devotion is the Greatest of our Loves" (*The Posthumous Works of M. de St. Evremont* {London: Jeffery Wale, 1705}, 3:176-80) express these sentiments regarding old men.

21. A card game played by two people; the low cards from 2 through 6 are excluded and points are scored on various groups or combinations of cards and on tricks.

22. Eager.

23. Points are gained by tricks and are used to score the game; a quint is a sequence of five cards in one suit; a quatorze is four of a kind. Edmond Hoyle, *Hoyle's*

Games Improved (London, 1775), 64-65.

24. The view of a landscape that forms a scene or beautiful picture. One test of architectural excellence was to see if views from windows framed prospects.

25. Slang for an informal dance or dancing party.

26. Play performed by an itinerant company of actors and actresses.

27. A parish festival held annually in honor of a patron saint, often one associated with the town's history.

28. English spelling of *reconnaître,* to survey or scout, in common military usage even today.

29. A forerunner; a horseman riding ahead of a traveling group to make arrangements.

30. Shakespeare, *King Lear,* 3.4.29.

31. Literally, in the heaven.

32. "Let's the three of us drink!" This is perhaps a colloquial reference to a drinking song.

33. A lively eighteenth-century country dance in three-quarter time.

34. The queen of Egypt, mistress to Julius Caesar and Mark Antony in turn. Legendary for her beauty and seductiveness, she is the subject of many tragedies.

35. Helen, wife of Menelaus, eloped with Paris and thus brought about the destruction of Troy. Often called Helen of Troy, she is an epitome of beauty, the subject of lines such as Christopher Marlowe's "Was this the face that launched a thousand ships?"

36. The god of dreams, one of the sons of sleep. Morpheus sends visions of human forms while his brothers Ikelos and Phantasos send dreams of beasts and inanimate objects. Ovid, *Metamorphoses,* II.633 ff.

37. Primroses with clusters of variously colored flowers.

38. Alexander Pope, *The First Epistle of the First Book of Horace* (1738), I.I.177: "Is this my Guide, Philosopher, and Friend?" and his *Essay on Man* (1733-34), 4.390: "Thou wert my Guide, Philosopher, and Friend?" That in these lines Pope addressed Henry St. John Bolingbroke, a politically controversial statesman whose political and social idealism Pope admired and whose friendship he valued, is irrelevant here.

39. Unidentified.

Revisions Made in the Second Edition

~

The following notes indicate changes made by Brooke in the second edition of *The Excursion*. The numbers refer to the page and line in the present edition. The closing bracket separates the wording of the original edition from that of the second edition. Statements in boldface represent editorial commentary.

Volume I
Book IV, Chapter VII

61.4-5: as much convinced as] still more convinced than
61.5: the manager] any manager
61.6: merit,] merit; or to use her own expression, such a *sweet pretty* tragedy,
61.8-10: **This paragraph deleted.**
61.11-12: Whatever knowledge . . . of the theatre.] Maria could not be mistaken; whatever knowledge she wanted, she had a perfect knowledge, she was certain, of the world. A little error into which people are very apt to fall at the age of eighteen; especially if, like her, they have studied that world amidst rural solitude, in the reflecting mirror of a library.

Volume II
Book V, Chapter IV

79.15 snow:] snow; a frost plant in the beautiful garden of Nature, which glitters in the sunbeam, yet, impervious to its enlivening rays, can scarcely be said to vegitate.
79.15-16 or, . . . country-women:] **New paragraph:** Or, to express my idea in the animated expression of one of my fair country-women:

Book V, Chapters V-VIII

Brooke extensively revises these chapters in the second edition. For Chapter 5 of the first edition, she substitutes the following text:

"What reason can there be in nature for these hard hearts?" says the great painter of human life and manners.

That youth, in the gay spring of life, should be hurried into those destructive excesses which originate in that ungoverned warmth of temper which is equally the source of vicious pursuits, and of the sublimest exertions of philanthropy and beneficence, is natural, and therefore pleads some indulgence; but that the unfeeling selfishness, usually the characteristic of age, should pervade the bosom where the warmest emotions may be supposed to reign, is a paradox for which it is difficult to account.

Let the *vegetable* of society, the man whom no passion but vanity inspires, content himself with being a blank in the creation; let him glide unperceived through existence, useless to others, and a burden to himself, as if born meerly to *consume the fruits of the earth,* and contempt alone shall be his portion.

But if he attempts to pass the bounds his heart prescribes, to engage in those inhuman pursuits which even the torrent of passion cannot excuse; if he dares to meditate the seduction of innocence, he becomes an object of horror as well as of derision, and merits to be driven from the chearful haunts of men.

But a truce with reflection: a moment, gentle reader, let us step to Lady Blast's.

Brooke adds a new Chapter 6, in which the first six paragraphs expand upon the second paragraph of Chapter 5 in the first edition:

We left this amiable matron at her bureau, dispatching cards of invitation to a select party of her *peers,* the respectable censors of female honour, to sit in council the next morning on the little events which we have related respecting Miss Villiers.

Ten dowagers obeyed her summons and hurried to the scene of deliberation: the merits of the cause were fully investigated; and after debates which might have done honour to the senatorial abilities of A—— and B—— themselves, debates whence ministers and patriots might have culled the fairest flowers of elocution, Miss Villiers was found guilty of being young, lovely, unknown, and indiscreet.

Lady Blast pronounced a truly Ciceronian harangue on the necessity of maintaining order in the female commonwealth; of repressing the pride of youth, and insolence of beauty.

She assured the court, where her veracity was unsuspected, that she had not only herself been an eye-witness of Lord Melvile's stopping the night before at the door of our heroine, but that she was morally certain his lordship's stay there had exceeded three hours, though in reality he had not staid as many minutes.

On such authentic information, doubt was lost in conviction: every bosom beat with the rage of offended decorum, the transport of unexpected discovery, every countenance was drest in undissembled smiles, and the withered roses almost bloomed anew.

The unhappy Maria was declared by her indiscretion to have forfeited all title to be one of *the world;* and was, in consequence, adjudged to be degraded from the place she at present occupied in the immaculate coterie into which Lady Hardy had so kindly introduced her.

The final two paragraphs of Chapter 6 appear in the first edition as the final two paragraphs of Chapter 5, with only one change:

79.30: The dreadful sentence of banishment] The votes having been collected, the dreadful sentence of banishment

From this point all chapters in Book V are renumbered, so that Chapter 6 in the first edition becomes Chapter 7 in the second and so forth.

Book V, Chapter VI (Chapter VII in second edition)

80.4: Absorbed in her fairy dream,] Unconscious of the dread sentence just pronounced, absorbed in fairy dreams

80.8: gay fantoms of happiness] gay phantoms of imaginary happiness

80.9: in her imagination] in her animated fancy

80.10: **New sentence inserted at end of third paragraph:** She reflected, she reasoned, she was convinced of the fallacy of Col. Dormer's censures in respect to the world; she had happily experienced their fallibility. **The rest of the chapter is deleted.**

The following text for Chapters 8 and 9 in the second edition replaces the text for Chapters 7 and 8 in the first:

Chapter VIII

Lost in reflection, she had not observed a rap at the door. She started from her reverie, on John's announcing Mr. Hammond.

A new source of pleasurable expectation opened on her mind; he could only come to bring her an account of her tragedy.

The lively red on her cheek went and returned as Mr. Hammond drew near; sanguine as she was, a little mixture of doubt intruded, nor had she courage to look up, and seek the information she might have found on the countenance of the amiable old man, where the traces of disappointment were too strongly painted to have been mistaken.

"It is with pain, madam," said he, "I find myself compelled to give you a less favourable account of my negotiation than I had hoped.

"When I told you I had interest sufficient to get your tragedy read, I overrated my own importance.

"I have seen and conversed with the manager; there is, it seems, an etiquette in respect to the reception of theatrical pieces, of which I was not aware, and which, however plausible, is unpropitious to true genius, and little calculated for the impatient *muse of fire.*

"This etiquette precludes even the perusal of an offered play, till a certain limited time before the season in which, if approved, it may, in rotation, be accepted.

"The manager pleaded prior engagements for two seasons to come; but offered, from friendship to me, to read this tragedy some little time before its due course of appearance at the dramatic tribunal.

"That is, young lady, he promised, if you would send it him, in the summer of one thousand seven hundred and seventy six, he would read it with attention, and give you his sincere opinion as to its fitness or unfitness for representation."

Maria, whose active mind had over leaped the narrow bounds, not only of probability, but of possibility itself, stood aghast at the latter part of Mr. Hammond's harangue.

She had expected, with the impetuosity of her time of life, and perfect inexperience of the world, to hear it was going into immediate rehearsal, had anticipated the soft music of uninterrupted applause, had imaged fame extending the verdant bay over her head, and had even regarded the profits as a bank on which she might have depended in the course of a few revolving weeks; nay, on which she might almost have drawn at sight.

Judge then of her surprise. The summer of *one thousand seven hundred and seventy-six?* He might as well have proposed a summer in the succeeding century. Why had he not said, the summer of *eighteen hundred?* 'Twas not to be borne—An interval of near twenty tedious months?—But no matter—'Twas very well—She paused—She recovered her powers of recollection.

Pride in a moment came to her rescue, and enabled her to bear this unexpected stroke with a spirit that did her honor.

She repressed the tear which was ready to start, the tear of blended resentment and distress.

She calmed her mind by determining to make no further application to the theatres till she should glitter in the gay circles as Lady Melvile; when she would let the manager know *whose* play he had not condescended to read.

She might perhaps *then* make a present of it to the other theatre, or give the profits to some public charity, a circumstance which could not but extremely accelerate its reception.

Elated with these ideas, the ideas of a romantic girl, she thanked Mr. Hammond with the best grace in the world, for the trouble he had so kindly taken in the hope of serving her, and replaced the unfortunate tragedy in her bureau, with an air of tranquillity, which effectually deceived him.

Mr. Hammond was now convinced of what he had before, from her apparent anxiety, a little doubted, that fame was the primary object she had in view, and that no inconvenience would arise from her waiting a more favourable moment.

Perfectly at ease in this interesting point, Mr. Hammond proceeded to give her his opinion on the general subject of writing for the theatre.

He endeavoured, by arguments which all her politeness scarce restrained her from interrupting, to dissuade her from a pursuit in which her whole soul was irresistibly engaged; a pursuit in which he asserted with the earnestness of a partiality the natural consequences of so many accumulated attractions, that her sex, her delicacy of mind, her rectitude of heart, her honest pride, and even her genius, were strongly against her success.

"Genius," said he, "my dear madam, is at once proud and diffident of itself: the Muses are a bashful train, and rather avoid than court observation; they advance with an unassured air, and retreat at the first glance of indifference.

"I therefore take the liberty of a friend, to advise you, either to think no more of the stage, or to keep your piece, not nine years, as Horace advises his poet, but till more liberal maxims than have yet been known to exist shall take place in the important empire of the theatre; an empire on the faithful administration of which depends, not only national taste, but in some degree even national virtue.

"Instead, however, of stopping to examine what theatrical managers *are,* let us proceed to consider what they *should be* if they would wish to fulfill the noble task to which it is their duty to attend; the task of again raising the English stage to an equality with the justly boasted ones of Greece and Rome.

"As men, not distinguished from the mass of mankind, we will allow them to be subject to the same passions, the same prejudices, the same errors; errors, however, too often fatal to literature.

"This situation is a difficult, a perilous one: misguided by adulation, the constant attendant, the bane of those entrusted with power of any kind; and swayed, like others, by that selfish principle (faulty only in its extreme) which superior minds are alone capable of rising above; their views will, too probably, be confined to the little circle of cold official statements, when they should be expansive as air, and unlimited as the copes of heaven.

"Pardon, young lady, the ardor of a man impassioned with the subject before him. The influence of the theatre, on both public and private virtue, makes it an object of the highest importance to the state, of which a director ought to consider himself as the favoured substitute: 'tis his, by the most disinterested culture of dramatic genius, to give fresh vigor to the rising shoots of poesy; to extend the reign of uncorrupted taste, of polished elegance, of heroic virtue, and that purity of manners of which happiness is the inevitable consequence."

On a favorite subject the garrulous old man would have expatiated much longer, had he not observed an air of impatience in Miss Villiers, who was not inclined to attend to reasoning on a subject where both her passions and her interest were so much concerned.

He therefore took his leave, though with reluctance, and promised to call on

---

*This part of the present work originally contained a few pages of pleasantry, perhaps too sarcastical, on the subject of theatrical direction, at the expence of a late admirable actor, who is now no more.

Those pleasantries, though justifiable at the time, and from the cause, when a sudden impulse of well founded anger gave its deepening shades to the pencil of the writer, would be unpardonably illiberal, when this incomparable performer has long ceased to be an object of the resentment, and is only that of the most lively regret.

Possessed of that sublimity of genius, to which judgment is not always a companion, at once daring and correct, he copied nature with the same accuracy of drawing, the same glow of colours, as characterized his divine master, on whose inimitable writings his performance was the truest comment.

If it were possible to limit the powers of the human mind, or say where its efforts shall stand still; it might be asserted that he not only threw new lights on the beautiful science of acting, but reached the summit of theatrical perfection.

The author of this work, with a sensibility of admiration which will be credited by all who are acquainted with her enthusiasm for real genius of every kind, joins the public voice in her again in a few days; a ceremony with which she could, without difficulty, have dispensed.*

Book V, Chapter IX

Grateful as Miss Villiers really was for Mr. Hammond's friendly, though unsuccessful interposition, with respect to the tragedy, she saw him leave the room with a pleasure she was unable to dissemble.

Her pride, that consciousness of superior talents which modesty itself is not always able to repress, had supported her whilst he was present; but on his returning she felt the advantage of being at liberty to shed the tear, and breathe the complaint of mingled anger and disappointment, which she had with so much difficulty hitherto suspended.

Yet, to be candid, she observed the manager might not be so much to blame; he had only pursued a regular system of business, which, half informed as he was, he could have no reason for interrupting in favor of her tragedy.

On one point her resolution was fixed, never again to employ an ambassador of sixty.

She did not find that Mr. Hammond, this icy, this unimpassioned, advocate had entered into any particulars respecting the play, its subject, its tendency, or execution.

He had not even mentioned its being "the production of a woman." (He might, though that did not occur to her, have added, of a young, an amiable woman, of respectable family, and unblemished reputation.)

He had not told the manager, what the natural ardor of protection, of *offered* protection, should have placed in the strongest point of view, that in his opinion (for that opinion he had declared) it had interest, poetry, pathos; and, what was of the greatest possible importance, that the character of the heroine was exquisitely adapted to display in full light the brilliant powers of the actress who filled the principal female characters at his theatre.

The circumstances he had thus injudiciously omitted to mention, appeared to her of infinitely more importance to her success than the solicitation of fifty peevish misanthropes like himself.

They would naturally have had great weight with a man of genius, who as such could not fail of being a man of refin'd gallantry, and a zealous partizan of female excellence."

She had hinted all this to Mr. Hammond the first time he had attended her on this business; but a sarcastical smile of disapprobation had prevented her entering further into the subject.

---

lamenting a loss, of which posterity, not having witnessed his astonishing dramatic powers, will be unable to form an adequate idea.

Retracing his various perfections on the faithful tablet of memory, she is happy in adding her little branch of laurel to the verdant wreath which is the unenvied mead of *departed* excellence; that wreath which candor will allow to have been fairly won, and exult in twining round his brow.

Book V, Chapter IX

88.1: Sanguine] Sanguine and romantic

89.35: She talked—good gods! how she talked!] She talked like ten thousand angels.

89.37: She praised] She praised, though with hesitation, his dress;

90.1: He was in all so superior to other men!] **deleted**

90.22: appear pleased] appear charmed

90.27: that chearful ease] that elation of the heart

91.4-5: by her smiles of undissembled affection (for she really loved him)] **deleted**

Book VI, Chapter IV

101.26: 100*l*] one hundred pounds

Book VII, Chapter V

115.24: Suppose she should write to him!] Suppose she should write to him?

Book VIII, Chapter II

125.31: celebrated seat] celebrated seat, in another age,

125.33: they proceeded.] they proceeded; once the abode of that political wisdom which determines the fate of the nations; now sacred to the fine arts, to the muses, to taste, to the milder virtues of private life.

125.34: the imitative arts,] the creative science of imitation,

126.1: much sublimer] still sublimer

126.7: Our party returned] After some hours pleasingly spent in viewing the wonders of art with which this noble palace abounds, our party returned

126.7: but not] but returned not

Book VIII, Chapter III

130.6: My estate] My income

130.7: since I was married;] since I married,

130.8: retrenching my own expenses.] impairing my estate.

Book VIII, Chapter VI

136.13: How] how

Book VIII, Chapter VII

139.5: friend.] friend Col. Dormer.

Book VIII, Chapter XI

142.33: affection: sensibility alone is the food of sensibility.] affection; sensibility alone, he was convinced, could be the food of sensibility.

144.26: week] fortnight

144.33: week's] fortnight's

145.17: Yes, he was indeed false, but he was still as dear to her as ever.] "He was indeed false, but he *ought*, notwithstanding, to be as dear to her as ever."

145.18-19: "Adored object of my tenderness, whilst this heart beats, it shall beat for thee."] "A woman of delicacy is by no means absolved from her obligation to be constant by any change of conduct in the object of her tenderness."

"No certainly; she *ought* to love him for ever."

Book VIII, Chapter XII

145-146: **Paragraphs three and four are altered:** They saw every fine house within the sphere of their observation, mounted every hill that promised an agreeable prospect, whether it lay in or out of the direct road; stopped at a twelve-penny hop, at a strolling play, at a wake, at a village-wedding; and partook of twenty more little innocent amusements which we have not time to specify.

146.5: sixth] thirteenth

146.22: left] were going to leave

Book VIII, Chapter XIII

149.8: and the ladies] and that of the ladies

149.27: the day] the present day

149.37: society.] society, in which, independent of her beauty, I have found a thousand charms.

153.1-3: "You will love this country, madam; it is still

"A land unspoil'd by barbarous wealth," / and inhabited by our old race of English gentlemen.] "You will love this country madam; it is still 'a land unspoil'd by barbarous wealth,' and inhabited by our old race of English gentlemen."

153.5: polyanthus] Polyanthus

153.8: now who] now, my friends, who

153.13: vegetative] vegetable

SELECTED BIBLIOGRAPHY

~

EDITIONS OF *THE EXCURSION*

The Excursion. 2 vols. London: T. Cadell, 1777. The first edition. This edition has been microfilmed for the *Eighteenth-Century Short Title Catalogue* collection.

The Excursion. 2 vols. Dublin: Price, Whitestone, Corcoran, R. Cross, Sleater [and eighteen others in Dublin], 1777.

The Excursion, 2d ed., 2 vols. London: T. Cadell, 1785.

SELECTED FURTHER READING

Primary Works

Brooke, Frances. *The History of Lady Julia Mandeville.* 2 vols. London: R. & J. Dodsley, 1763.

———— [Mary Singleton, pseud.]. *The Old Maid.* 15 Nov. 1755-4 July 1756. London: A. Millar.

————. *The History of Emily Montague.* 4 vols. London: J. Dodsley, 1769. Facsimile, New York: Garland, 1974.

————. *Rosina: A Comic Opera.* London: T. Cadell, 1783.

Burney, Frances. *Evelina; or, A Young Lady's Entrance into the World.* 3 vols. London: T. Lowndes, 1778; and ed. Margaret Doody, New York: Penguin, 1994.

Duncombe, John. *The Feminead; or The Female Genius.* London, 1757, lines 268-77. Reprint, Augustan Reprint Society no. 207, London: Cooper, 1954.

Fielding, Henry. *Amelia.* London: A. Millar, 1751; and ed. David Blewett, New York: Penguin, 1987.

Griffith, Elizabeth. *The History of Lady Barton, A Novel, In Letters.* 3 vols. London: T. Davies & T. Cadell, 1771.

Haywood, Eliza. *History of Miss Betsy Thoughtless.* London: Gardner, 1751; and ed. Dale Spender, New York: Pandora, 1986.

Lennox, Charlotte. *The Female Quixote; or, The Adventures of Arabella.* 2 vols.London: A. Millar, 1752; and ed. Margaret Dalziel, New York: Oxford Univ. Press, 1989.

McKenzie, Henry. *Julia de Roubigné: A Tale. In a Series of Letters.* 2 vols. London: W. Strahan & T. Cadell, 1777; and ed. Patricia Köster and Jean Coates Cleary, New York: Oxford Univ. Press, 1995.

Scott, Sarah. *A Description of Millenium Hall, and the County Adjacent.* London: J. Newberry, 1762; and ed. Jane Spencer, London: Virago, 1986.

Sheridan, Frances. *Memoirs of Miss Sidney Bidulph, Extracted from Her Own Journal.* 3 vols. London: R. & J. Dodsley, 1761; and ed. Sue Townsend, New York: Pandora, 1987.

Sheridan, Richard Brinsley. *School for Scandal.* Dublin: Ewling, [1778].

Smollett, Tobias. *The Expedition of Humphry Clinker.* 3 vols. London: W. Johnston & B. Collins, 1771; and ed. Thomas R. Preston, Athens: Univ. of Georgia Press, 1990.

Secondary Works

Armstrong, Nancy. *Desire and Domestic Fiction.* Oxford: Oxford Univ. Press, 1987.

Ballaster, Ros. *Seductive Forms: Women's Amatory Fiction from 1684 to 1740.* Oxford: Clarendon, 1992.

Benedict, Barbara. "The Margins of Sentiment: Nature, Letter, and Law in Frances Brooke's Epistolary Novels." *Ariel: A Review of International English Literature* 23.3 (1992): 7-25.

Berland, Kevin. "Frances Brooke and David Garrick." *Studies in Eighteenth-Century Culture* 20 (1990): 217-30.

McMullen, Lorrain. "Double Image: Frances Brooke's Women Characters." *World Literature Written in English* 21 (1982): 356-63.

———. "Frances Brooke's Early Fiction." *Canadian Literature* 86 (1980): 31-40.

———. "Frances Brooke's *Old Maid:* New Ideas in Entertaining Form." *Studies on Voltaire and the Eighteenth Century* 264 (1989): 669-70.

———. *An Odd Attempt in a Woman: The Literary Life of Frances Brooke.* Vancouver: Univ. of British Columbia Press, 1983.

Moers, Ellen. *Literary Women.* New York: Oxford Univ. Press, 1985.

Needham, Gwendolyn. "Mrs. Frances Brooke: Dramatic Critic." *Theatre Notebook* 15 (1961): 47-55.

Rogers, Katharine M. "Sensibility and Feminism: The Novels of Frances Brooke." *Genre* 11 (1978): 159-71.

Sellwood, Jane. "'A Little Acid is Absolutely Necessary': Narrative as Coquette in Frances Brooke's *The History of Emily Montague.*" *Canadian Literature* 136 (1993): 60-79.

Spector, Robert. *English Periodicals and the Climate of Opinion during the Seven Years' War.* The Hague: Mouton, 1966.

Spencer, Jane. *The Rise of the Woman Novelist: From Aphra Behn to Jane Austen.* New York: Blackwell, 1986.

Teague, Frances. "Frances Brooke's Imagined Epistles." *Studies on Voltaire and the Eighteenth Century* 304 (1992): 711-12.

Todd, Janet. *The Sign of Angellica: Women, Writing, and Fiction, 1660-1800.* New York: Columbia Univ. Press, 1989.